ACCLAIM FOR H.T. NIGHT:

"H.T. Night is a riveting storyteller, capturing the essence of the vampire genre."
—**April M. Reign**, author of *Beyond Today* and *Dividing Destiny*

"*The Werewolf Whisperer* is a wonderful story that incorporates friendship and love with a lot of great vampire action."
—**Summer Lee**, author of *Angel Heart* and *Beach Angel*

"A hip and timely vampire novel filled with real characters and some of the coolest vampires since *The Lost Boys*! You're going to love Night's completely original take on the supernatural."
—**J.R. Rain**, author of *Moon Dance* and *The Body Departed*

"*Bad Blood* is fast, hilarious and sexy. Rain, Nicholson and Night just might have created the coolest vampire since Kiefer Sutherland. The Mount Shasta setting is dreamy. The cult is deliciously creepy. And Spider is as sexy as they come. I was pressing the ereader's 'forward' button so fast that I broke it. Let's hope we hear more from Spider."
—**H.P. Mallory**, bestselling author of *Fire Burn and Cauldron Bubble* and *To Kill A Warlock*

WITCH TO CHOOSE

OTHER BOOKS BY H.T. NIGHT

VAMPIRE LOVE STORY

Vampire Love Story

The Werewolf Whisperer

Forever and Always

Vampires vs. Werewolves

One Love

Divine Blood

Sons of Josiah

Love Conquers All: Part One

Love Conquers All: Part Two

HEART OF A WITCH SERIES

Witch to Choose

A Witch's Magic

DEADLY DREAMS

Controlled Chaos

Massacre Revealed

WITCH

TO CHOOSE

////

H.T. NIGHT

Published by
Crop Circle Books
212 Third Crater, Moon

Printed in the United States of America.

First Edition

ISBN: 978-1-312-74690-9

Dedication

I dedicate this book to my Facebook fan site. A nice place to have friends.

Acknowledgments

Special thanks to Eve Paludan, A.J. Silver, Rhonda Plumhoff, Leslie Whitaker, Sara Wales, J.R. Rain, Margaret Cervenka, April M. Reign, P.J. Day and Liz Jones for all their help.

Chapter One

I stepped out of my modest, three bedroom home on Fullerton's west side. I locked the front door, and before hurrying to the driveway, I turned around and made sure every light was off before I left. Electricity bills in California were outrageous, and last month's bill was no exception.

I took a moment to gaze up at the smog-blurred stars. Where I lived, smog alerts weren't uncommon. Fullerton's rolling hills trapped the brown muck as if it were some holding pen, before slowly drifting out by the late afternoon toward Riverside. It has been getting better though, and I could actually see through the haze tonight and spot half a constellation or two.

I loved the night air; so mysterious, so alluring, but sometimes dry...like tonight, where I would be wishing upon a smog-blurred star for a whole new beginning.

Hopefully, for something beautiful and meaningful.

I took a much deserved moment and allowed myself to breathe. The past two years have been extremely trying, to say the least. My parents passed away, and the guy I was supposedly madly in love with turned out to be a sex addict. Apparently, he had been with hundreds of women while we dated, including my two best friends.

1

Saying that my trust in men and friends had been rather bleak would be putting it mildly.

I had been alone the last few months, growing so much with isolation, that I have craved human contact once again. And on this dry night, I decided to take a chance.

It was Saturday night and I arranged a date with a man named Robert. It was way past time that I got out of my shell and ventured out into the dating wilderness once again, and he seemed safe enough, at least at first glance.

I stepped onto my driveway and pressed my garage door opener that I carried in a small black purse, which happened to match my outfit quite splendidly tonight, if I might add. A modest, back dress that oozed elegance and wonder, and miraculously, it also seemed to take a couple pounds off too.

I normally go to the garage through my back porch, but on this night, I needed to take a moment alone and actually listen to the night, without a patio cover blocking my view. I needed to see the sky, in full, before I left, so I could listen to my heart and understand what it might have been telling me.

Again, a lot has happened over the past two years. My parents dying one month from each other, with two different life-ending illnesses, was not only life-altering, but completely devastating for their only child to go through.

After my parents had passed, they willed me the house and everything else they owned.

So there I was, staring at my car in the garage, packed with all my parents' stuff that I just couldn't let go of, and with the hazy, star-pocked sky above my head, realizing that I was all alone in this big giant world trying to make it on my own.

I thought a night out was well deserved. How could it not? I deserved the opportunity to repel loneliness before it tried to completely consume me.

I opened the car door and stepped into my light blue Mazda. I snapped on my seatbelt, looked in the rearview mirror and checked to see if I had lipstick on my teeth. *Nope.* Nice and clean.

The fact that my date was a full time writer had given me a

slight paranoia that he would be overly examining me on the date.

I was laughing at myself for going through with this date. We were going to… of all places for a first date…Knott's Berry Farm in Buena Park, California.

My makeup and hair looked as put together as it could get. My long, reddish-brown hair had a nice, layered cut and was at a sexy length, like Julia Roberts in *Pretty Woman.* Fine, maybe not quite to that level of amazement, but it sure looked better than my Goth days back in high school.

So I had retired the Goth-do, and the makeup; well, let's just say the makeup had been toned down to *emo* level. I had to, for conformity…a paycheck. But I did make sure my wardrobe stayed the same. Alright, not entirely, I've been spotted wearing pastels on casual Friday.

I'd turned thirty last month. *Thirty…yikes.* I remembered my parents watching a TV show called *Thirtysomething.* I used to think thirty was real old, because they looked so much older than me. Looking back now, I swear all the characters looked forty, *or maybe they were forty and tried playing thirty*, or maybe I was just fooling myself. Either way, I was their age now. Life continued to roll on.

Maybe I should put on more lipstick. My lips did look a bit dry. I opened my little black purse, found my cherry red lipstick, and applied it. I looked at my face in the mirror; a face that was familiar, but not the face of my youth.

Through the years, many had said I owned a deep soul with many secrets. It's true, I'd always felt in the past that I used to show people on the outside what was actually a contradiction on the inside.

During high school, one could say I was definitely a Danzig and Sex Pistols girl, but since college, you could say I enjoyed an eclectic style of music. Where Air Supply, Eminem and Phantom of the Opera were all on the same playlist.

Not all changes had been about style, taste, and finding my true self. As I'd gotten older, two things had gotten bigger: my boobs and my butt.

Maybe it was because my waistline had gotten a tad bigger.

Luckily, I was curvy in the right places. At least that's what I'd been told by the weird old man who sometimes stood in front of the Quickie Mart. He was sure to tell me something sexually disgusting at least two to three times a week. It got to where I actually missed the days when he wasn't there. He usually gave me a good laugh on my coffee runs on my way to work at the marketing job I'd had for the last six years.

I hadn't dated much, or at all, these days. However, there was a little hot streak in my twenties when I was dating men right up there with the best of them. Those days were long gone though, so I decided to sign up with three dating websites. All of them had promised me a perfect match or a soul mate, and what have I received so far? Empty promises and a bouncing PayPal account.

But I remained determined. These days, if you didn't Internet date, you didn't really date. It was a miracle if two people could meet in public and find anything in common but physical attraction. I couldn't remember the last time I'd met a guy in a public place and was asked out by him, not even at a bar.

Even though Robert and I had only emailed and talked on the phone a couple of times, I had a feeling we were as good a match as any. He'd only uploaded a couple of pictures on his dating profile, both didn't look half bad for 39, and I knew that whenever a guy uploaded one or two pictures, it usually meant he was a bit insecure, vulnerable—you know, *not a dick*. I didn't mind though, it took some of the pressure off me. I'd be begging for trouble if he were completely out of my league. Just a tad bit was okay.

Had an alpha-stud ever asked me out on a real date? I guess the answer to that is 'yes' and 'no.' I'd had some great-looking drunk guys want to take me home and sleep with me. I have self-respect, though, or perhaps it had more to do with the fact that I didn't trust guys who drove an El Camino. Anyway, there was this one guy. A gym rat named Donovan, and quite possibly, the most gorgeous man I'd ever seen—at least in person he was.

Everything about his physique was perfect. And that face, *Oh Lawdy*, a face that looked as if it were ripped straight from the steamiest romance cover of all time.

Whenever I'd hit the elliptical machine, I'd hear the occasional gossip about Donovan from a different girl each week. Nothing scandalous. Just assumptions. Conjecture. *Bullshit*, basically. Like was he gay? How much money did he make? Was he hot in the bedroom?

Gay or straight, he was the hottest guy I knew. He'd bust his behind three times a day at the gym because his occupation demanded it.

One day, we bumped into each other and he handed me his business card. He was leaving the gym dressed very sharp in a gray suit. I was very impressed.

The business card read,

Donovan Parker, personal trainer, certified masseuse, model.

I wasn't surprised. It was three common occupations for hot guys, where you're tipped on looks, not skills. I didn't know why that guy has made such an impression on me, but some guys do that. I was probably just horny.

Someone like Donovan didn't seem real to me. He was a walking underwear ad.

Tonight, I was going out with Robert. Definitely not an underwear model. I didn't need any of that. I just was hoping for a nice guy and good conversation.

After a short but hypnotically thought-filled drive, I'd finally arrived at Knott's. Most of the parking lots were filled to capacity, so I parked in the farthest one a block away from the amusement park. As I walked the sidewalk, I pulled out my phone and checked Robert's profile one last time. Definitely handsome. Sandy-brown hair, blue eyes, probably chubby, as neither picture showed his entire body. And he hated being called Bob, according to his *about me* section.

I had been no better. I hadn't taken a picture below my boob line in years. Luckily for me, my best assets still remained unchanged, but still made me worried I'd attract the wrong type of guy. No cleavage, just a burst of femininity through a moderately tight sweater.

There was one thing that concerned me about Robert, though.

He'd mentioned he'd recently grown a beard, but had trimmed it down. It wasn't that I thought beards were potential turn-offs, it was just that beards tended to make my face itchy when being kissed.

In the end, though, it was just a beard. I just hoped, when it was all said and done, Robert brought with him some compatible chemistry... or better yet, *magic*.

I didn't know if it was the poetry I had written in high school, or the fact that I had never missed a romantic comedy or a Nicholas Sparks movie in the last ten years—*I know, kill me*. I still believed in the biggest cliché of all: love at first sight. I didn't believe it happened to everyone, but I believed it happened to folks often enough that there had to be a reason why such a cheesy and idealistic phrase was invented in the first place.

We'd planned to meet at the front gate of Knott's Berry Farm by the trees and benches, which buttered me up with nostalgia. It made me feel 15 again, for better or worse.

On the dating site, he had also checked the box that stated his income was over $250,000. I'm by no means a gold digger. Truthfully, I had no idea he had checked the highest income bracket on the website until after I had agreed to date. While hunting for *Mr. Good Enough,* I just wanted a guy who had a reliable car and a steady full time job. I was done with guys who stayed at home and didn't work—you know, full time Call of Duty players. This was probably one of the main reasons why I hadn't been dating as much; it seriously felt like an epidemic out there; men holding off adolescence for as long as humanly possible.

But tonight, I was going to put all those fears aside and have a good time...if Robert wasn't in fact attempting to pull the wool over everyone's eyes of course.

I scurried by the remaining shops, absorbed by the dim lighting because I decided to wear my black blouse and black satin skirt. I was Irish, so I had pretty, white, pale skin. I thought that was why I always compensated by wearing black all the time. *That, and it's a slimming color.*

I made my way toward the park entrance. I continued passing by some more eclectic souvenir shops and dessert stores. I never quite understood the theme that was going on with this park...there was no theme.

As I approached the main entrance, I held my breath and snuck around the corner of the last store to scan the benches in front of the trees.

I recognized him. He definitely resembled his profile pic. Five feet, ten inches tall. He seemed well put together, but with a bit of a pot belly. Light-blonde hair, with surprisingly gorgeous blue eyes that seemed to reflect the flood lights.

He spotted me, then began walking toward me. "Sahara?" he asked.

"Robert?" I responded like a dork.

"That's me," he said and smiled.

Nice voice. Deep and sexy, like how he sounded over the phone.

"I'm Sahara," I said.

"You look stunning," Robert said with giant, sweet smile. "Your profile didn't do you justice. I already bought our tickets," Robert said in an extremely friendly voice. "We can go in now if you like."

I looked at Robert and he was very pleasant. Didn't get a weird guy vibe from him at all. Not that he seemed that type, anyway.

Robert had a kind demeanor. So far, every time he or I had spoken, he had looked me in the eyes with a gentle and guarded type of confidence. Not overt.

We both received one another with a mildly awkward, albeit positive, first impression. A decent enough start, I thought. If something special was going to happen, tonight was as good as night as ever. But first, I had to let the date run its course. "Let's head on inside," I said.

Robert walked over to me. A disparity of five inches, at least. He definitely was taller when up close.

"I guess I'll do that awkward hug at the beginning thing." Robert laughed.

He sure gave me a quick, friendly hug.

It wasn't that awkward. I thought it was sweet.

Chapter Two

We entered the park, and we decided to get something to snack on while we casually planned our night. It would also give us a chance to get to know each other.

I liked how Robert maintained eye contact with those smiling eyes of his. He definitely knew how to make a girl feel safe on a first date. Most men's eyes usually darted around and scanned furiously. He seemed to recognize that women were taking a giant leap of faith when meeting a guy for the first time in a strange place. Making a woman feel safe and comfortable right out of the gate was a huge plus in my book.

We walked up to a snack stand. I was so bad as I had indulged with some funnel cake and Robert, who was a bit more cautious, and carefully licked away at a plain vanilla ice cream cone. I had anticipated a few drips of ice cream making their way through his thick goatee, but he was a pro; he knew just how to dip it in his mouth. He definitely had a way with that tongue of his. *Not that way*...it was just enough skillful maneuvering to be commendable.

"So, have you had their funnel cake before?" Robert asked.

"No, first time," I said.

"Let me know how it tastes."

I stared straight right through his blue, piercing eyes. We weren't talking about anything important, as it was just small talk regarding carnival food, but I started to feel a level of intensity there—or maybe it was the sudden sugar rush. No, in fact, I sensed his radiant spirit and it somehow began to find its way to me. Could it have been the natural chemistry that I hadn't felt in quite some time? Was it a rush of insulin sparked by sugary, imitation vanilla and strawberry syrup, or the actual budding chemistry of friendship or romance?

Okay, I had to slow down and prepare myself for him to say something that was a deal-breaker like, "*I love your dress. I have one just like it at home.*" Or, "*You know, you're the first girl I've been on a date with in 10 years.*"

Nope. Neither of those things surfaced.

He just smiled at me as if he knew a secret about me. It was very alluring. His confidence was building. It was as if someone released the air out of him and he was finally himself.

As soon as I felt the tension lift, he seemed familiar to me. "I feel like we've met before?" I said.

"No, no we haven't. Funny though, I get that a lot."

"You do?" I asked.

"It's like every high school had a big, muscular, blond guy."

"Muscular?"

"Oh, most of this love you see before you is 100-percent, muscle-bound beef."

"Are you real strong?" I asked, thinking I was playing along with some form of sarcasm on his part.

"What does that mean?"

"It means what I asked," I said, slowly realizing he might've actually been serious and compensating by his statement.

"Well, if you mean, am I strong like if I can fight, I'd say I really don't know. I haven't been in a fight in over 20 years. If you mean how strong I am in terms of weights, I once benched 315 pounds."

"Once, huh?" I asked, playfully.

"Yeah. Once. I did it. I didn't need to prove it again." Robert looked at me and grinned.

"When did you do it?"

"When I was sixteen."

"Wow, that's a lot for any age," I said, realizing he was serious, but trying to be sweet as he boasted about his high school glory years. Still, I couldn't imagine lifting that much weight off any part of my body.

Your profile says you're 30?" Robert asked.

I looked at him and laughed. "Yours says you're 39," I snapped back playfully.

"I didn't mean anything negative by it. Thirty was a good year for me."

"Why was that?"

"It was the year I was able to quit my job and become a writer full time." Robert paused, and looked me over. "Was 30 a hard age for you? I have a feeling 40 is going to be a real hard age for me. I'm not looking forward to it."

"I like my age," I said. "Despite saying a sad sayonara to my twenties, I felt like my current age held a unique advantage. I had lived in two completely different worlds: a world with the Internet, and a world that couldn't comprehend something like the Internet could even exist. People often forgot what the world was like before the World Wide Web."

Robert nodded his head and agreed with me. "I actually enjoyed its primitiveness. It was where *Thomas Guides* sat on our laps instead of our phones. Also, inhaling that unique old book smell whenever we'd open up an encyclopedia we'd plucked from our shelves."

"And who could forget board games on family game night?" I said with excitement.

"How about shopping for our favorite music inside actual record shops?" Robert said with a cute grin. "*Ah, nostalgia*...poison for progress."

"But who didn't love their childhood?" I said.

"Where did you grow up?" Robert asked.

"Right here, in this town Buena Park and Fullerton."

"You never moved?" Robert asked.

"I have another place in the mountains."

"Sounds cozy."

"It is," I said, playfully.

"Your place in town," Robert asked. "Is that the same house you grew up in?"

"Yes, it is. It had been my parents' home before they both passed at different times a couple of summers ago. I was their only child. I own the house now, but I only live there for part of the time."

"The other time you're in your little, cozy, cabin in the mountains," Robert said with a confident *wink* at me. It threw me off. The *wink* is a risky move. If done wrong, you can look extremely strange. Not Robert. He gave me his *wink* and that was all there was to it. He owned the moment. "How often do you go up to your cabin?" Robert asked.

"Every now and then, I escaped to it. *I had to*. After my parents' passing, it was hard living at my house alone for the longest time. Even after repainting and refurnishing the home, and adding a back room with my inheritance, I'd still get choked up living there. Sometimes, when the morning sunlight brightened my room, I half-expected my mom to wake me up and tell me I was going to be late for school."

"I could see how that would be hard. Why don't you sell the place?"

"I don't know. As much as it breaks me to live there, I take comfort in the walls. I take comfort with the house's ambience. My cabin, however, is about a third of the way up the San Bernardino Mountains, right before you hit Arrowhead. In the city of Crestline. It's not the same. It's not home. I like it, but it's not home.

"Crestline? That is where Lake Gregory is, right? Robert asked.

"I like the snow. I have never been in that lake. Whenever snow was in the forecast, I'd drive up for the weekend to stay there. There was something magical about snowfall."

"Except on the rare occasion you have to shovel it from the driveway. I damn near almost slipped a couple of times and bonked my head on the icy concrete last winter when I was up east."

"You spend a lot of time in the snow?" I asked.

"I have a time share on the east coast and some days, the snow is rough."

"You're telling me," I said. "I have to make two or three trips out to my driveway until I get enough snow off my driveway to go somewhere."

I changed the subject. "I was pretty bored tonight before you called."

"Thanks a lot," Robert said.

"I didn't mean anything by it. I was real glad to get out. I had a feeling," I said.

"A feeling?" Robert asked.

"Something in my gut was telling me to go tonight. I felt as if I would be letting a night slip underneath my fingertips."

"Wow, that's a lot of pressure," Robert said, laughing.

"It doesn't have to be about you?"

"That's good. I guess. Wait."

"Look, Robert, I want to take any pressure off of you. I get *feelings* all the time."

"How accurate are your feelings?"

"High eighties," I said.

"Percent?" Robert laughed.

"Sorry, let's both forget I said that." We paused and I decided to change the subject again. "I want to tell you a little bit about me," I said.

"I would love to learn more about you," Robert replied.

"Okay, this might sound a bit weird."

"Try me," Robert said with a bold confidence.

"Well, how are you on interpreting dreams?" I said, with a bit of hesitation.

"I'm not a biblical prophet to King Nebuchadnezzar or anything, but some dreams are interpretable."

I looked at Robert and questioned if I should tell him my dream. It would be a leap of friendship faith. Not too many people know about this dream. I didn't know why I felt comfortable enough to tell him.

"I have this recurring dream," I said.

"I would love to hear it," Robert said.

"My dream is always the same. It's cloudy outside and it looks as if it is going to rain. I'm at an outside market where you can buy fruit and whatnot. At the market, I always pass by a man with a large hunchback. From twenty feet away, he's menacing. Yet, I continue to get closer and closer to him. I stand before him and avert my eyes out of fear, pity. But I'm curious, and I stare at him anyway. When our eyes meet, it's always the same. I'm always blown away at how beautiful and honest the hunchback's eyes are. In my dream, there is a beauty deep inside that man that intrigues me to the point of love."

"Wow," Robert said. "That dream moved me. Let me ask you this," he asked. "What do you think your dream means?"

"That's your job," I said, giggling. "You need to tell me what it means."

"How many people have you told this dream to?" Robert asked.

"About five," I answered.

"And you told me," Robert asked. "Wow, I feel honored."

"What do you think it means?" I asked Robert.

"I think you know what it means. You don't have to ask anyone."

"You think it's that simple to figure it out?"

"My ten year old nephew could figure it out," Robert said, laughing. "Look, Sahara, you don't need me to tell you that maybe at times you have been shallow?"

"You're not the first person to say that," I said. "I don't think I'm shallow."

"It's not that you're shallow all the time, Sahara. Just in some cases. I think your dream is telling you to open your eyes and see all the beauty around you."

I looked at Robert, impressed at how he worded what he said to me. He called me shallow, but yet I found him to be poetic.

"I had always taken away from this dream one belief, or wish, or hope," I said to Robert. "That somewhere out there in the world is a place where my heart would blend together with another into this deep, intense, love-filled bond. What I was looking for was an intellectual and emotional connection that rocked my world. I was seeking the passion of a man's stare, not the beauty of his eyes."

Robert looked at me and was quiet. He slowly took in everything I said. He retained his sweet smile, and peered intensely into my eyes. "I think you're one of the most beautiful women I've laid eyes on."

I pushed my funnel cake aside and wiped off my hands with a napkin.

I said, "Hey...um, you really meant that?"

"Huh? Yeah? Why?" Robert said, very confused.

I took a deep breath and paused. I quit fidgeting for a moment.

"I meant what I said. You're exactly how I imagined you through your profile pic and our conversations."

"Really?"

"Uh-huh..."

I was overwhelmed with this bizarre combination of validation and adrenaline. I took a step toward him, looked him in his blue eyes, and held my stare. Then, as natural as breathing, I fell forward and suddenly, our lips embraced.

Wow! *Could he kiss!* So much passion. Just enough of all the things I liked in a kiss. Force, nibbles, gentleness. His kiss had it all. He just might surpass Bobby Mulholland, my ninth-grade boyfriend, as the best kisser I ever had—or maybe it was the bizarre combination of validation and adrenaline that made it seem that way. No one, I mean *no one* had ever suggested I was one of earth's grandest beauties. I still didn't believe it, but any man who sincerely meant that about me, deserved a kiss.

We both cleared our throats, sat down and tried to act natural. Robert took a napkin and steered my plate that had the half-eaten funnel cake toward me. He finished his vanilla cone in a couple of bites and continued to smile at me. I could tell he was trying to think of something to say. It was as if he was keeping something from me. What? I didn't know. Maybe he was lactose intolerant and doing his best at hiding a silent but deadly gas moment?

Finally, I said, "I still had more than half the funnel cake left. Do you want to share it? It's humongous. I swear the thing is going to give me type 2 or something."

I looked at Robert and he was looking in another direction. He seemed to be fixating on a certain person. I looked across the way to see who he could be looking at. But I saw nothing that seemed out of the ordinary. I saw families and couples rushing to get to their next ride or snack.

Robert looked at me and said something very strange. "I would love to eat three funnel cakes."

"Huh?" I said.

"To answer your question, I would love to eat three funnel cakes."

That was a really weird way to say no to having some funnel cake. Or was he saying yes? I couldn't tell. The man apparently liked his funnel cake.

"You know they asked me if I wanted extra strawberries on it. It was already enough to feed five people," I said. "Please take it."

Robert briefly looked away, then back to me. He made me realize I had funnel cake all over my hands and face.

My embarrassment didn't last long as he said, "You are so much prettier than your pictures," Robert said. "I mean I thought you were pretty in your profile pic, but in person, you're breathtaking."

"Even with funnel cake all over me," I said, smiling.

"Especially because there is funnel cake all over you," Robert said with his sexy wink.

"That just might be the nicest thing anyone has ever said to me." This was getting too serious, and way too fast. The kiss was nice, but I needed to keep it fun. "Hey, do you want to log-ride it up?" I said, trying to be hipper than I was humanly capable of being, but I said it anyway.

He looked at me, puzzled.

Robert had no idea what I'd asked him to do. So, I decided to say it very thirty-years-old-ish. "Robert, would you like to accompany me on the log ride and proceed to have a wonderful, amusing time?"

"That was what you were trying to say?" Robert started laughing. "No, no, no. I'm far too uncool to ever catch onto a phrase like that. 'Log-ride it up.' Do people say that?"

"No. I just made it up." Now, I felt really stupid.

"Well, yes, Sahara. I would like to log-ride it up with you."

"Okay."

Robert stood up and helped me up from the bench. He was very courteous, but it was something I was not used to responding to. I liked being a treated a lady, but not an old lady.

We made our way over to the log ride. This area of Knott's Berry Farm catered to coal miners, cowboys, water rides, and enthusiasts of water rides who didn't mind getting wet on a sixty-some-odd degree night.

Robert held my hand the entire time on the way to the ride. I was a little surprised by his sudden public display of affection, but none of it seemed forced.

As soon as we were last in line, he let go of my hand. I forgot how long the log ride line was. It would be a 45-minute wait, according to the sign. So, he and I were going to get to know each other, whether we liked it or not.

I looked at the people in line with us, teenage couples everywhere, and we looked as if we were chaperones.

As if the log ride was the make-out ride.

Wait! The log ride is the make-out ride.

Everybody from Orange County knew that. I knew that fact, even in high school, where even then it was nicknamed the tunnel of love.

Doubt Robert knows that? I hoped he didn't think that's why I had picked the ride.

He'd said he grew up in Anaheim, the heart of Orange County. I wondered if he thought I suggested this ride so we could continue to make out.

Of course, he doesn't think that. He's too sweet...

I gazed up at him, as he'd seemed to have grown another inch for some reason. He smiled back, reached in his pocket, put a breath mint in his mouth and flashed me a confident wink. Oh, my goodness, he was planning on having a full make-out session on this ride. *Why did I kiss this guy so fast?* I didn't want this to be the type of date where we were really affectionate and we never went out again and whenever I thought back to the date, I would always wonder what the hell happened.

Well, I had bad news for Robert. This wasn't going to be a make-out ride. That kiss back at the food table was special because it had been spontaneous, or enhanced by a bizarre and momentous sugar rush.

I decided not to worry about it. After all, I had initiated the first kiss and it was possibly the best kiss I'd ever had. I looked at Robert and we were forced to be a lot closer than what was normal because we were packed in like sardines while waiting to get on this ride.

Robert and I talked and continued to learn more about each other as we waited in such close quarters. I learned that he collected sports memorabilia. He learned that I was in love with Joey McIntyre from New Kids on the Block from age six to age 12.

I'm having some crazy thoughts about this guy.

Robert then wrapped his arms around me from behind like we had been dating for years. I let him. He knew I'd let him. How a man who I instantly trusted, by instinct, would feel just as comfortable as me and embrace me without hesitation.

The more I leaned into him, the stronger Robert held me.

It was nice. Pleasant. I felt warmth.

I wasn't sure why I felt so comfortable, but I did. That didn't happen too often. Especially this early into a first date.

This date was starting out really weird. Things were just too comfortable, too fast.

Chapter Three

His breath smelled wintery fresh. My breath, on the other hand, was a combination of mouthwash, toothpaste and funnel cake.

Finally, we had reached the front of the line. There were still a few people in front of us.

"I think that sign lied," I said to Robert. "This wait has been much, much longer."

"So you regret spending all this time with me?" Robert joked.

"It was nine hours of nice, sweet conversation," I said.

"It hasn't been nine hours." Robert laughed.

I was still standing in front of Robert, who was affectionately leaning against my back with his chest. His arms weren't around me, but he was leaning on me in just a way that our bodies were gently touching.

I turned around and faced Robert in line. I'd said the words louder than I wanted to. But everyone was far too wrapped up in their own lives to care about whatever I was saying. "Are you for real?" I asked Robert.

Robert looked at me, surprised, and asked, "What do you mean?"

"Is this your *way* with women?"

Robert looked at me and very sincerely said, "I'm sorry, Sahara, I don't have a defined way with women. Until you said the phrase six seconds ago, I didn't know that was another thing I had to worry about in the dating game. I don't date enough to know if any of my instincts are correct."

Robert gave me a look like he surprised himself at how honest and open he was.

"Your charm is your honesty," I said. "Or the belief that you're being genuine when you speak. It doesn't come across as rehearsed."

"You seemed like a seasoned dater."

"Like I said. At one point I was. I used Myspace as a dating site."

"You're on a dating site now." Robert didn't know I was actually on three.

"Yeah, but since my parents passing, I haven't wanted to date."

"Why do you suppose that is?" Robert asked.

I looked at Robert and wasn't ready to give him my truth. We just met. So, instead I laughed about how pathetic my dating life has been. I looked at Robert and thought about what he had said about his dating game.

"If what you're saying is correct," I said to Robert, "you have no idea what works and doesn't work on a date."

"I mean, I know what is the right thing in terms of not making the woman feel like I'm a weirdo."

"Are you a weirdo?" I asked. I was halfway kidding; however, I was interested in his response.

"Of course I'm not a weirdo. Besides being nose deep in my writing, I'm a bit of a sports nerd. I'm really into sports stats and stuff like that. But I'm pretty certain no one had ever classified me as a weirdo."

"Wow, you might have proved you're not a weirdo, but you definitely made a case for yourself as a nerd. You're in luck because I have been classified a nerd most of my life. About halfway through my supposed *nerd* phase, I changed my wardrobe and makeup, just so people wouldn't feel compelled to label me before knowing me. See back then, I was considered a nerd dressed in black...a dreary nerd." It was a little bit fun just being open. Robert made it so easy.

"I collect comic books, too," Robert said. "I think I've beaten you on the nerd scale, by admitting that."

"That's not so bad," I replied.

"But I only collect *Archie* comic books."

"Okay, you win. You're the bigger nerd."

We both laughed.

"Why *Archie*, and why not *Superman, Batman;* you know, the usual?"

"There's a simplicity and innocence that the gang in the comics all have and it's like comfort food. My older sister got me interested in the comic books because they were the only comics around the house. So, whenever I was scared at night, because I felt there were monsters under my bed or inside my closet, or if I felt especially lonely, I would pick up an *Archie* comic and fall asleep reading them. It's not that they were boring; in fact, they were kinda funny, but their simplicity would help me feel safe and comforted and they'd help me fall asleep."

Once again, Robert had a weird look on his face as if he didn't plan on telling me that last bit of information.

"Okay, that's not being a nerd," I said. "That's something you bring up in therapy."

"How did you know I go to therapy?" Robert asked, a little freaked out.

"I didn't," I said. "I was making a joke. I used the term therapy in my joke. You were the one who just volunteered the information that you see a therapist. And for the record, I see nothing wrong with that. We all need someone to talk to once in a while. If you can afford to talk to a professional talker like a therapist, all the more power to you." I took a moment and gave Robert a giant smile and said, "Well, this is about the most un-suave conversation I have had this early on a first date," I said. "We're making a lot of firsts here."

"Suave and me, we're never a good match," Robert said. "Here's a funny story: When I was about fourteen, I had my first girlfriend.

She was an older girl and was this real cool chick. Then right out of the blue, she asked me to go out with her and be her boyfriend. That's how forward this girl was. Of course I said, 'yes.' We were boyfriend and girlfriend for one whole week. Then, once again, out of the blue, she called me up and broke up with me. I asked her why she was breaking up with me. Her reason? She said I wasn't suave. I was shocked, mainly because that was the first time in my life I'd heard the word 'suave.' I had no idea what it meant. I actually had to ask her the meaning of the word, just to show how completely un-suave I was." Robert looked at me and smiled.

I couldn't help but laugh out loud. This guy was priceless. I was completely turned around facing Robert. I was looking him in his eyes and was trying to get an honest read on him.

Was his charm and honesty an act?

I didn't think so. Every once in a while you ran into a guy who was fed up with the bullshit and they just were who they said they were. Most men weren't. To be fair, most women weren't either. Men and women treated a first date like a job interview and they said all the safe words. You sometimes ended the date knowing less about the person than you did when you started.

So, I asked him point-blank. The ride was starting and soon there would be a giant drop and he would be forced to hug me from behind as we went down the water slide.

"Are you a player?" I asked.

"Take a look at my waistline," Robert said. "I'm not exactly a player. I enjoy food a little too much. Plus, sometimes, I stutter."

"I stutter, too," I said, amazed that I had admitted it to him. I didn't think I had ever spoken about my stuttering with anyone besides my parents. "I'm at my worst," I continued, "when I'm excited while telling a story."

"Oh, that is also when I'm at my worst," Robert agreed. "That is why I try to stay calm when a story calls for me to get animated. Animation and my personality are a stutterer's paradise."

"Your waistline is fine," I said, giving Robert a wink. "I like food, too. Oh...we are going to be bad together. Chocolate sundaes and all the bacon you can eat."

"Have you ever had a bacon shake?" Robert asked.

"Are you kidding me?" I said, laughing.

"Nope, I was at this hip place up in the hills. It was right there on the menu."

"And you ordered it?" I said, disgusted.

"Wouldn't you? Just the novelty factor alone."

Robert was just like me and I loved it.

"Did you like it?" I asked, feeling sick to my stomach at the thought of a pork shake.

Robert smiled at me.

"Well?" I was feeling a little gagged in my mouth.

"It was the best damn milkshake I ever had," Robert said, laughing.

"No? Was it? How could it be?" I asked.

"Something about the combination of salty and sweet, I guess."

"I don't think I could drink something like that."

"I'm telling you, it's freaking delicious." Robert smiled at me and paused. I knew he was choosing the right words to say to me. He was an interesting character.

Robert stopped and looked at me and got serious. "Look, Sahara. I'm not a guy who comes into a date with an agenda and try to see how it all plays out just so I can chalk one up on my bedpost at night. I like you. I liked your profile on the dating site. And now, meeting you, you're even more exquisite in person. You seem honest and direct. Both are traits I love."

"It's usually what turns men off about me," I said.

"I love it," Robert replied. "Listen, I don't play games. I feel an initial closeness to you. I think you feel it, too. It's nice when there is that type of chemistry right off the bat. It stinks that the world has jaded us so badly that when we have a true connection, our immediate response is to question it."

"Are you doing the same thing now?" I asked. "Do you feel you and I have chemistry?"

"Yes," Robert said with a tad of hesitation in his voice. "I think chemistry can only be a two-way street."

"Trust me. There are enough delusional guys out there who have no clue."

"I guess the million-dollar question is: Am I a delusional guy who has no clue?" Robert asked.

"You're not delusional," I said. "What you are is...cute."

"I think I like that answer a lot," Robert said, laughing.

I had to follow my instincts and trust this man until he proved himself to be a liar. Unfortunately, many men proved to be liars.

"What if," Robert asked, "I wasn't some guy just trying to get in your pants?"

"You're not? I knew this dress made me look frumpy," I joked.

"I'm being serious," Robert persisted. "What if I was interested in you for who you are?"

"Why can't you be both?" I said. "Desire me and be interested in me."

Robert smiled and nodded shyly. "It's all part of the journey."

"What journey is that?" I asked.

"To fall in love," Robert replied.

Chapter Four

I looked at Robert and I could tell him 'my truth' right here and right now on our first date. I wasn't sure if I wanted to go there. My truth was the part of me I only shared with those I trusted. I didn't screw around with romance. Fooling around was okay if both parties knew the score. But there was a difference in how Robert was holding me and touching me than some guy who just wanted to mess around. He was touching me with tenderness and love, the kind someone had for his significant other.

After a long pause, Robert broke the silence by saying, "I probably only go on a date two to three times a year." Robert looked at me and grinned.

"Am I second or third for this year?" I asked.

"You are actually the first. It's been a slow year." Robert smiled.

"You're telling me you haven't had a date in like a year?"

"That's about right." Robert nodded and gave me a look like, 'Love me or hate me, that was the truth.'

"Wow," I said, laughing.

"Why is that so hard to believe? I'm a regular guy. I have my issues, my baggage, and my insecurities. We all do. I just think there isn't any need to go on dates with people if you know you have no chance of spending the rest of your life with them." Robert tightened his lips as if he'd said too much. I actually loved what he'd said.

We were so engaged in each other's words, the ride attendant had to bark to snap out us out of our conversational malaise. "How many in your party?"

"Um...two," I said, as we hurried and sat in the back of the four-person log contraption. Robert sat behind me and I nestled snugly between his legs.

I had butterflies in my stomach as I wasn't sure if I wanted to kiss him again. The first kiss had been so perfect. A second kiss and who knows...

The ride swished us along as we sat in fake logs with seat belts.

We were coming up on the big drop. We got to the top and slid down with our hands up.

We pulled into the front and got out of our mechanical logs.

No kiss. No copping a feel. Nothing. He was just a nice, sweet guy.

We exited the ride and found ourselves in the middle of what felt like the amusement park's epicenter. We navigated through the bustling Saturday evening crowd. "What now?" I yelled to Robert over all the noise.

"Do you want to go to Cloud 9?" Robert asked.

"Cloud 9? Oh my gosh, do they still have that place here?"

"I actually don't know," Robert said, "but do you want to check it out?"

Cloud 9 was a dance club that was the place to be in junior high and also to a lesser degree high school. I thought it was cute that Robert had remembered it. It seemed he was a sucker for nostalgia, like me.

Robert and I used our subconscious memory in finding the place, even though much of the park, at least visually, had changed. We passed the red and white striped canopy, where the dinosaur ride used to be, and there it was, Cloud 'freaking' 9. Just seeing the outside of the place took me back so many years.

"There it is," Robert said, taking my hand and making our way up to the front. "You want to go in?"

"Do you?" I asked.

"Sort of."

"Just for a moment," I said.

"Okay." Robert dragged me by my hand through the double doors into the dance club. It actually looked very similar to how I remembered it.

Robert held a curious smile as he looked around at the club.

"What's up?" I asked Robert.

"Wanna dance?" he asked.

"Dance?" I laughed. I hadn't gone dancing in years. "Are you sure? We will be the two oldest ones out there."

"Well, that makes us even cooler," Robert said.

Robert led me to the dance floor. And before I knew it, I was dancing with Robert in the middle of Cloud 9 at Knott's Berry Farm.

I moved with the song. I'd never heard of the song before. It was fun to let loose a little bit and be silly.

Then the DJ said, "Let's slow it down," and he put on a slow jam song. My ears had never heard the particular song before, but its slow, sexy beat had me swaying my hips without much thought.

I looked at Robert and I had my arms wrapped around his neck.

He smelled good. For some reason, Cloud 9 made me recognize and realize how pleasing he was to my nostrils. Damn, he had a wonderful, innate way of making me feel comfortable. I hardly knew anything about him, but I felt more comfortable with him in a short amount of time than I had with other boyfriends whom I had dated for months.

The song seemed to last forever—too long—but Robert remained an absolute gentleman the entire time.

After the dance, Robert and I giggled at the satiated bout of nostalgia, and from there we had agreed that one song was enough, since everyone around us seemed young enough to be our kids.

We decided to hit up a couple more coasters. The lines continued to be long, so by the time we finished riding Montezuma's Revenge —one the park's more iconic rides and a cheesy ode to Aztec nation —it neared midnight.

We decided to leave and Robert asked me if I'd mind if he

walked me to my car.

He was so cute.

I told him it was fine. We walked from the Knott's exit to the parking lot while holding hands. We got to my car and I asked the obvious question, "Are you parked anywhere near here?"

Robert laughed.

"What?" I asked.

"I'm on the other side," he said.

"Oh my gosh! Is it? The other side is like two miles away."

"It's okay," Robert said, "I could use the exercise."

"Exercise *shmexercise*; get in my car and I'll drive you to your car," I said. "No one needs to be walking around any parking lots at midnight."

Not even a guy like Robert who can take care of himself.

"You sure?" Robert asked.

"Yes."

Robert walked me to my side and saw me into the car. Then he ran around and got in the passenger side.

I started my car and we backed out.

"This is a cute car," Robert said.

"Cute?" I said. "My car is bad ass," I stated in a teasing tone.

"I meant cute in a real bad-ass kind of way," Robert said.

I smiled at Robert. "So, where's your car?"

"Truck," Robert said.

"Where's your truck?" I said in a deep manly voice like Robert.

"It's on Western Avenue. It's across the street from the park."

"Wow, that's far. I mean for a walk. It's a two-minute drive. But who wants to walk out here in the middle of the night alone?" I pulled into the parking lot and Robert guided me to a navy-blue truck toward the back. I pulled up right next to him in an empty parking spot. We sat there and no one moved. I had expected Robert to get out immediately. Instead, he looked straight ahead through my windshield.

"Can I ask you to do something?" Robert asked.

"That seriously depends on what you ask me," I said.

"It's just a question." Robert looked at me and smiled.

"Go for it," I said.

"Did you have as good a time as I did tonight?"

I looked at Robert and said, "Yes, I did. I had a great time."

I thought he would kiss me, but he didn't. He just looked straight ahead.

"Can I ask you one more question?" he asked again.

"Of course," I said.

"Would you do me the honor of getting out and giving me a hug?"

I opened my door and got out.

Robert walked to my side of the car and he took my hand he pulled me into him gently and he held me tightly. It almost felt like we were dancing again.

Then everything stopped. He looked me in the eyes as he held my hand. He leaned in very gently and gave me a perfect goodnight kiss with just enough passion, just enough intensity, just enough heart.

"Wow, Robert," I said. "That was quite a date."

"It sure was," he said.

"Goodnight, Robert."

"Goodnight, Sahara." Robert kissed my forehead and then went to his truck and waited for me to get in my car.

I got in and waved to Robert, and then I hit the street. I never overthought a nice first date, but Robert was a real cool guy and if he called me up again and wanted to go out, I was sure I would say 'yes.'

Chapter Five

I drove back toward my house. While passing by a toilet paper company's ad on a billboard—don't know what a cute family of bears have to do with the vile act of human's pooing—I remembered that I had run out of toilet paper. I decided to swing into an all-night market. It wasn't the safest place to go at this time of night. But I was out of *TP,* tissues, napkins, and paper towels, and I wasn't about to use my avocado tree's foliage. Even if it was considered 'organic.'

I jumped out of my car and went inside the store. As I stepped inside, I noticed that there were a couple of men inside shopping. No women. The market wasn't too big and had the basic essentials. The guy behind the counter didn't look any older than seventeen.

I gave him a smile and a nod. I think I did it to remind the cashier that I was the sole primped female inside a liquor store in a sketchy part of town.

He gave me zero expression back, and I wasn't surprised. He was probably thinking about anything else but working at 1:00 in the morning.

I went to the back where they kept the household staple items such as toilet paper. I saw some at the end of the aisle on an end cap.

I walked over and stepped up and looked at the prices. They were outrageously overpriced—probably to take advantage of procrastinating suckers like me.

I reached out and grabbed a package of four rolls that were on the shelf in front of me. As I grabbed them, a large, hairy hand intercepted the package right from underneath my nose. I turned around, and the hand belonged to a man with a receding buzz cut, around my age, dirty, and reeking of alcohol.

"Excuse me, but I had it first," I said with a shaky voice. I wanted nothing to do with this guy. Calling him creepy was the most modest adjective I could've used to describe him.

He looked at me, sized me up with his beady little eyes, stopped at my breasts, and held his stare—like some scruffy, desperate predator.

I turned and faced the toilet paper again, and like a dumdum who mustered up a feeling of false courage, I snatched it up, turned away from the man, and made my way to the counter. As I approached the counter, I noticed that an extremely beautiful woman in a black dress similar to mine had entered the store and began to browse. She was stunning. Way classier than me, and like me, clearly out of place in this store...and in this part of town.

I waited my turn to pay behind another man, who also appeared inebriated. He couldn't even properly pick his ATM card out of his wallet. I so wanted to get the hell out of this store, as I knew the drunk man, I had been idiotically bold to, had just finished his shopping and was getting ready to line up behind me.

After his fifth attempt and after dropping loose change from his wallet onto the counter below, he finally said to the cashier, "Well, I have it in cash, so I'll just do that."

I was getting a bit irritated. I just needed to get out of this place and back to my car. The guy in front of me pulled out a twenty from his wallet. Then from behind, his voice, which produced goose bumps up and down the back of my neck.

"Imagine seeing you here."

I ignored him, hoping he would leave me alone. His voice was raspy, and he smelled like he hadn't showered in days.

"Hey, baby, why are you ignoring me? Are you too good for me?" he said.

Now, he was being belligerent and making me nervous. I turned around and made eye contact with the classy chick who had entered the store and who had lined up behind the smelly drunk. Oddly, she gave me a stare as if we had met before, and was eager to tell me something.

"With your nice clothes and nice perfume..." the drunken, belligerent man said behind me. He didn't finish his sentence, and I was glad. I seriously wanted to teleport away that very instant. Far away.

"Look, guy," I said. "I just need to get an item and get home." I didn't turn around, mainly because I didn't want to look at him. Or smell him.

"And where is home?" he asked.

As soon as the drunk in front walked away, I shook my head and laid the toilet paper on the counter, and the second the cashier scanned the bar codes, I picked it right back up.

"Hey, I'll get that T.P. for you!" said the guy behind me. Now, he was standing next to me, completely invading my personal space, shoulders almost touching.

I looked at the drunk and said, "You're not buying my toilet paper. That's just weird. You need to go somewhere and sober up, and you need to leave me alone."

I reached into my purse and pulled out a ten-dollar bill. The cashier handed me my change. I put it in the March of Dimes coin slot on the counter and decided I would leave as fast as I could to get away from this guy.

I walked out and headed for my car. And about five seconds after I exited, I heard the door open and close two different times. I didn't want to look behind me.

"Hi, sweetheart!" the same creepy man said from behind me. "I haven't had a boner in years. It's not that big anyway."

Okay, this just went from creepy to illegal.

31

I thought he wasn't done. That wasn't the weirdest thing a man had ever done in my presence. He said, almost yelling and singing, "You need to know I like to suck my thumb so hard I tear layers of skin off of it. My underwear has a messy poo."

Now it looped back to pathologically absurd.

I turned around and this guy was on all fours.

"Want to hear me bark or meow? I'm good at both," he said.

"I don't want you to do either," I said. "What's wrong with you?" I suddenly became concerned about his mental health. His sexual explicitness turned into the humorous pleas of a crazy man looking for approval.

He barked anyway. He barked like he was a junkyard dog. Then the guy lifted his leg while on all fours and peed his pants right there, in front of everyone in the market to see. While he peed, he sang, "I love to go wee wee with my pee pee!!"

I quickly slipped into my Mazda and locked the doors. I skidded out of the parking lot while still in reverse and fishtailed onto the main highway. My heart rate settled and I made a left on Orangethorpe Avenue to get to my home. I stopped at the light on Auto Center Drive and my heart rate increased again as I spotted another person ominously standing on the curb to the right of me. She looked up at me, and I immediately recognized that it was the brunette woman in the black dress from the market.

There was no way she could be standing out here.

Right as the light turned green, I slammed on the gas pedal, doing my best in shaking what I thought I had just seen on the curb in front of an inflatable gorilla trying to sell me a Honda wearing his bodacious shades.

Something definitely wasn't right here. Sweat poured out of the palms of my hands and all over the steering wheel. I took a couple of deep breaths and told myself that it had to have been a different woman from the one in the market. They just looked alike. That was all. No biggie.

I then drove down a curved street to get to my house, thinking I'd avoid more specters and apparitions...hallucinations—whatever —if I avoided main streets. I eventually reached Dale Street and heeded to a stop sign at a dark intersection, where another figure caught the corner of my eye—a dark and slim figure, like the woman.

Was it the same woman? Don't know, didn't want to know, and kept my eyes on the road as if an invisible driving instructor sat in my passenger seat.

I tried ignoring my paranoia, my sudden fear, and turned right, away from whatever stood across the street. My car went about 100 feet when suddenly it stopped, as if I had applied the brakes, which was impossible because I clearly remembered my foot being on the gas pedal the whole time.

What in the holy hell had just happened?

I turned completely around to see if someone had chained the back bumper. Nothing. Just an empty semi-lit residential street, and whatever stood on the corner of the intersection had now vanished.

As soon as I whipped my head back toward the windshield, and slammed my foot on the gas pedal, I was startled by a set of rapid taps on the window next to me. It had gotten colder that night and my windows had become fogged, so I rubbed the cold frost away from the window and peered through and caught the same lady in the black dress standing on the sidewalk across from me.

I completely went berserk. I screamed louder than I had in a very long time. I was scared shitless. I wasn't sure if I was living in reality or if I was dreaming all of this. *It had to have been a dream.* But I soon found out there was a problem with that theory, as I was very much awake.

I thought I had lost my mind. I hyperventilated at the horrific possibility that I'd never shake this woman from my sight...*ever.*

Chapter Six

I held my breath and looked at the woman standing on the sidewalk to the left of me, still as a statue.

It was definitely her...but how?

My shaky finger pressed the button for the power window, but I mistakenly pressed the button for the passenger-side window. I turned my head toward the passenger-side window as the unexpected sound had startled me again. And like something out of a Japanese horror movie—it was *that* freaky...nothing gets freakier than Japanese horror flicks—the woman in black was there, again, standing on the sidewalk opposite the other sidewalk she had just stood on a second ago.

"I...I don't need any help," I stammered.

"It kind of looks like you do," she said, with the most surprisingly normal voice for the teleporting freak I pegged her to be.

I stomped on the pedal one more time. Nothing, not even a rev of the engine this time around. My car's engine was as dead as the splattered opossum down the road.

What had I done to deserve such a confusing and panic-inducing set of events?

34

"What do you want from me?" I yelled at her through my window.

She didn't say a word, but stepped forward, away from the sidewalk and onto the lawn strip in front of the curb.

"You stalk me, you got me, and now you won't speak to me?" I barked with fear and frustration.

"Of course," said the normal female voice.

"Of course, what?"

"Of course I wish to speak to you."

"Well, I don't know you. I'm all talked out for the night," I said. "I just want to get the hell out of here."

"Don't you want to know how I made that man bark like a dog and then wet himself?"

My mind was going a hundred miles an hour. How would she be able to do that? And, was she the one who was making my car malfunction?

"Don't hurt me. You're not here to hurt me, are you?" I asked.

"I would never dream of hurting you."

"Promise?"

"Promise."

"Can I at least have your name?"

"My name is Paris," she said, with a calmness that lessened the nerves a bit.

Paris was a lovely name. Definitely not a name I'd associate with murderers. A street walker? Perhaps. After a,ll Beach Blvd was just one block away, but I didn't look like your typical John. And if this was her way of getting business, it was only a matter of time before she'd soon be dead or in a jail cell.

"Is that okay if open the door?" I figured, sooner or later, I was going to have to get out and talk to this woman, or flee into one of the homes or backyards.

Frankly, fleeing was the only thing on my mind, but I had to play it cool first.

Paris shuffled back onto the sidewalk and I opened the driver's door. I stepped out and walked around the front of my car toward

Paris. I stepped onto the curb. I grew two inches, but she was still a couple of inches taller than me. Definitely a precise 5'8".

We both dressed similarly, but she liked her dresses long and satiny. I liked mine at the knees, but with mixed fabric. Few could pull off the shiny satin look—I wasn't one of them. Our makeup was exactly the same, but her hair reminded me of my days before I went corporate. Pitch black, not a natural highlight in sight.

"Look, Paris," I said. "You're definitely freaking me out right now. Who are you? What do you want? My mind is playing tricks on me. Did you lace my funnel cake at Knott's or something?" I continued to look Paris in the eye sheepishly, and continued, "What's going on? Please tell me I'm not losing my mind and that you're not just some crazy demon terrorizing me."

"I'm quite the opposite, sweetie. I want to help you," Paris said.

"What makes you think I need any help?" I asked.

Paris smiled at me and said, "You're a prime candidate for help. You turn guys crazy, and then you run out on them."

"I know. What the hell was that back there? That guy peed his pants and didn't have a care in the world."

"I was surprised you ran off. He was defeated, and you didn't trust your senses. You had no reason to skid out of the parking lot like a bat out of hell; you could've crashed into a poor unsuspecting driver."

"Senses? My senses were to run. I ran off because that insane man wasn't my problem. I hope he doesn't hurt himself, but he still isn't my problem."

Paris winked at me and said, "That guy was a pig and he got what he deserved. It was actually really funny to watch. He'll be fine...that's if you're sincerely worried about him?"

"What do you think happened to him?" I asked. "Was he on drugs?"

Paris smiled and then an even a stranger event occurred before my eyes—stranger than the happening where she had teleported all over orange county, following me, like some mystical pinball. A small ring of stardust-like material appeared to surround Paris as she briefly gazed up toward the sky, and then pulled her eyes to the ground as if she were paying reverence to some kind of invisible, all-knowing force. A neat little illusion for sure.

She then locked eyes with mine, and with soft intensity said, "No drugs. I mean, he was drunk. Inebriated for sure. But what if I tell you he was under a spell?"

"A spell? Like magic?" I asked, with a giggle. "What kind of magic are we talking about here? Like a magician? Like that Criss Angel dude?"

"What do you think?" Paris asked.

I nodded my head, reaffirming my suspicion that Paris was some traveling illusionist who decided to waste her talents on me in the middle of the night, in some random Orange County suburb. "You should really think about taking your act to Vegas, you know. I don't even carry cash, so it'll be difficult for me to give you a tip right now. Do you take PayPal?"

Paris shook her head.

I paused, narrowed my eyes and asked, "So wait, all of this isn't some sort of trick?"

Paris crossed her arms, smiled, and shook her head.

"Uh...are you saying this is real?"

Paris shook her head enthusiastically.

"Witchcraft magic?"

"If that is what you wish to call it, sure," Paris confirmed. "Witchcraft."

"You're saying you're a witch?" I asked.

"Yes, I'm a witch." Paris looked at me like she was waiting for an insane reaction.

I might have felt insane inside, but I still managed to remain calm. "Okay, I think I know about this Wiccan stuff because I had an identity crisis in high school, and tried it after failing at becoming a vampire and zombie first—didn't have the guts to test the whole coming back from the dead part. But no matter how much I tried to conjure a demon to do my homework, or will a dead plant back to life, nothing seemed to ever work for me. Yeah, I've never seen weird stuff happen until tonight, but I still think it could be sleight of hand."

"Sleight of hand?" Paris asked. "Are you still suggesting things were done in foolery?"

"Were they?" I asked. "You have to admit, it's a logical question for a logical world."

"Why would I want to trick you?" Paris looked at me indignantly.

"I know that sounds insane, but you calling yourself a witch is even more insane. How did you get that man to act like that?" I asked.

"It's called the Creep Spell. It's a spell where a guy says and does the opposite of what he wants to do and has no control over stopping it until the spell rubs off."

"How long does it take for the spell to rub off?"

"When I say it does."

"Is he still under the spell?"

"I released him from it, once you were far enough away and I knew he wasn't able to know what direction you went in."

"But, he'll never figure it out? Will he? He'll just think he went insane for three minutes?"

"That is correct."

What was I saying? I was implying that what this crazy woman was telling me was true. However, if she were crazy, she would've kidnapped me and put me in her windowless van by now. But that hadn't happened, and the feeling of danger had lessened before I even knew it. In fact, she seemed quite normal. Friendly. It was her soft, trusting face.

"Let's say that lout back at the liquor store was an immortal or a warlock; he might have had a clue what happened to him. But no man of mystical means would allow himself to be so piss drunk as to be taken over by a spell."

"Immortals? Warlocks? Seriously? Did you bring the 10-sided die? Cause I didn't."

"Let me ask you a question. Before you ran into me in the market, did you have a funny feeling about tonight?"

With healthy skepticism—okay, truthfully, the doubt had been diminished by now—I replied, "I did have a feeling about tonight. I mean I have lots of feelings, but I thought it had more to do with my date with Robert. Look, I'm not that much of a Doubting Thomas, alright? I've always believed that this earth gives off a kind of power. I guess you can call that power *magic*."

I took a seat on the curb and shook my head. Paris just seemed so cool, calm, and controlled as I ridiculed and doubted everything she had thrown my way. Either she was really a witch, or someone who was so delusional she truly believed in her own bullshit. "Are you telling me that warlocks are real? Immortals, you said?"

"Yes, there are *immortals* around us," Paris said, smiling, gesturing air quotes. "They still can die, but they must be killed a certain way."

"Are you implying vampires and werewolves...wooden stakes, silver bullets and all that jazz?" I asked, lightheartedly.

"Let's take things one step at a time and not overwhelm ourselves too fast," Paris said.

This was a lot of information to digest. *I'm still not sure if I'm being absolutely messed with.* I looked at Paris and I had some questions that needed honest answers. "You seriously did a spell to make that guy act like that? Are you two working together?" I asked bluntly. I was just going to say it. If this is some sick con, I needed to know right away. "Did you know that guy back there and plan on doing this?"

"Wow, you really don't trust people, do you?" Paris said.

"Well, if you trust people too much, you always end up getting screwed in the end. It's one of life's simplest and most important lessons," I said. I then paused, looked around the neighborhood, and realized how desolate it felt. A car had not passed us by or through the intersection since my Mazda decided to suddenly stop. "Paris, you seem nice and all, but I really need to go home,"

"How do you explain seeing me at two different street corners?"

"I don't know...I'm getting scared," I said. I then began to scratch my head. It would usually itch whenever I'd get overwhelmed with nerves. "Fine, I'll continue to listen to you...answer your questions if it means me getting home sooner. Tell me Paris, how?"

"*Magic,*" she said.

I sighed and then let out a chuckle that easily could've awoken a nearby slumbering resident, but again the neighborhood remained eerily quiet; not even a leaf blowing in the wind.

Paris gave me a sincere, almost loving look. "There's nothing to be scared of. You can trust me. I know it's hard to trust someone you just met. But I'll ask you one thing: What is your heart telling you to do?"

"I don't know if I want to trust you. I don't know if I want to continue knowing you," I said. "I'm trying to stay calm here, but this is getting weirder and weirder with everything you're saying."

I'd always had a sensitive, empathic side. It was very easy for me to tell by their body language if someone was hurting inside or had recently experienced loss. My last statement seemed to have bothered Paris a lot for whatever reason, as she recoiled slightly and her caring smile flattened. *How am I supposed to act?*

"Sweetie," Paris said. "I'm a witch of the highest caliber and it wasn't a coincidence that I met you tonight. Destiny told me to meet you. I want to reach out my hand to you and offer you a glimpse of my world."

"What exactly is your world?" I asked.

"It's beautiful. Unlike what you read in books or see in movies. That's all fiction. Most witches are some of the most beautiful souls and women you will ever meet. I want you to open your mind, body and soul to a world that will uplift you, and give you the kind of power you always knew you had in you."

"What is a witch of the highest caliber called?" I asked.

"*Most High Witch.*"

"Creative..." I said, sarcasm oozing out of every one of my follicles, and I had some hearty follicles too. It took two waxing sessions to make sure my arm didn't look like Robin Williams' before my date with Robert.

I continued. "And how did such a name originate?"

"It's the name our coven chose."

"Your coven? So there's more than one coven. With multiple identities?"

"Sweetie, every witch has her own identity and her own agenda. We're not soldiers. We're witches." Paris looked at me and smiled. "Honey, look at you. You're practically trying to dress like me. But I could tell there's more wanting to come out. You've compromised against your own will. I know you've subconsciously wanted to have this encounter for a long time." Paris looked at me almost like a loving sister.

"Look, Paris," I said. "I have never wanted to be a witch. Or, at least, I never seriously thought it could happen. I wear black mainly because it's slimming, not because I want to fly on a broomstick."

"You know, there is no one quicker on a broomstick than me. Or as cute-looking on one for that matter."

"Flying broomsticks are real?" I asked. "Let me guess, you own a cauldron too, and you're not cooking menudo in it either, right?"

"Magic is real. It's all around us. It oozes out of our very nature. We're all hurting. We're all celebrating. And magic allows us to have some control, so there is less hurting and more celebrating."

"I haven't thought about it like that," I said.

"Plus, you can make jerks look stupid, and what is greater fun than that?" Paris said, laughing. "Let's get off the street and go somewhere where we can talk. Would you like to get out of here and grab a cup of coffee?"

I looked at Paris and I wasn't sure. I really just wanted to go home. But she had gained my trust, in a way some television pitchman gained my trust in convincing me to spout my credit card number to some stranger on the phone. And she seemed real genuinely eager to do this, to really help me. Why? Hell if I knew.

It had been a long time since I'd done anything like this; you know, follow some stranger who had promised me the world, or at least some form of personal improvement. Kind of like Anthony Robbins, except in a female form, and teleporting around town all while promising me magic and the secrets to a magical realm. *Much better than risking scorched and melting skin on the soles of my feet by walking on hot coals, right?* I felt scared, intrigued, and a little adventurous.

"I know Norm's is open," Paris continued.

41

"Okay," I said. "Norm's it is." I was now fascinated. If anything, this would be a night to remember. I mean, how could anyone possibly pass up steak and eggs, with a side of hash at one in the morning?

Chapter Seven

There she was, Paris, *The Most High Witch,* sitting in my passenger seat. Probably on my chewed-up piece of passion fruit, sugar-free gum. But she didn't have to know that, or maybe she knew, but didn't want to disturb our newfound *magical rhythm.*

With a snap of her fingers my car had started up again and we headed toward Norm's. *The* spot for witches and their newfound apprentices, apparently.

I was still taken aback about the whole spell concept. It was a scary thought. "You're telling me," I said, "the finger snapping where you turned my car back on was a magic, spell thingy?"

"Yes, I am telling you all of that," Paris said. "Want to test me?"

"Do I want to test you? How am I supposed to do that?"

"Ask me for anything under a hundred bucks. I'm not a genie."

"All right. I want a Slurpee from 7-Eleven," I said.

"A Slurpee?" she said in surprise.

"Yes, a 7-Eleven blueberry Slurpee."

"This is your test? A Slurpee?"

"I'm thirsty," I said. It was a very dry night.

"Okay," Paris said. She thought about what she would say and then she said, "Many ways, many days. Show Sahara she don't need no man giving her a blueberry Slurpee in her hand."

The casual urban lingo had thrown me off, but it was charming to say the least. Suddenly, soon as I blinked a sixteen-ounce blueberry Slurpee appeared in my hand. It was in a 7-Eleven cup and it was freaking cold.

"Am I dreaming?" I asked Paris. "Have I died?"

"You're not dead, Sahara," Paris said to me. "Magic is real. The second you embrace it, it becomes your lover."

"My lover?" I asked. I didn't know why, but that embarrassed me.

"Yes, magic will intoxicate and give you feelings of passion, desire and the other things that a lover might give you."

"It's just a Slurpee," I said. "Getting a blue tongue out of it is as intimate as I'm getting with this thing."

"I'm speaking about the Magic behind the Slurpee. You know what I'm saying and for some reason you want to avoid it. You're resisting the Magic and all that it holds because all your life you have been taught the opposite."

"Can I drink this Slurpee?" I asked, avoiding the deep sentiment by Paris. I needed to digest what she said to me.

"It's a Slurpee. Blueberry, my favorite too. Knock yourself out," Paris said, smiling.

I took a sip and the Slurpee quenched my dry throat. Very tangy. Probably the most fun I had experienced since giving Robert his going away hug.

I was just about to take another sip when it dawned on me that I had just witnessed an actual witch perform actual magic before my mascara-caked, bloodshot eyes. I was damn tired and beside myself. "Can you drive?" I asked.

"Your car...right now?" Paris asked.

"Yes, I'm not feeling well."

"I'll drive," Paris said.

I pulled over and both of us got out of the car on the side of Commonwealth Boulevard and switched sides. As soon as I sat down in the passenger seat I looked at the clock on my dashboard. It read 1:30 a.m.

What the hell am I doing out this late? And with a flipping witch?

"Instead of Norm's Restaurant, do you mind if I take you somewhere else?" Paris asked.

"Is this where you drive off to a weird, distant spot and kill me?" I said, half-kidding. "I mean, I was completely kidding."

"Look, Sahara. I like you. If I was going to kill you, I would have done it a long time ago. I don't waste my time with any drama. All you been doing is giving me drama."

"Do you kill a lot of people?" I asked.

"I haven't killed anyone. That isn't what I do." Paris looked at me and shook her head.

Yeah, I'm the one who sounds like they're making no sense...

"What do you do?" I asked.

"I balance out the bullshit," Paris said. "If I see a guy mugging a woman, I'll do a spell that trips him up and he falls to the ground. Or, if I see an old man who needs help getting out of his car because he's handicapped, I might give him a momentary strength spell. I look out for others. I look out for those who can't look out for themselves."

"You're like a witch superhero?" I said.

"No, I'm just a witch. You can leave any kind of superhero out of it. I've done too many things I'm not proud of."

I wanted to ask her what she meant by that. I mean after all, I was trusting this person with my car minutes after meeting her. But this was a highly unusual circumstance. But still, I was weary. That was my nature, to trust and then question myself until I was weary...even after I had convinced myself she was an actual witch, hopefully not of the wicked variety either.

I continue to slurp while she drove my car. "You look like a witch but you don't talk like what I would have suspected. I can almost hear a hint of a country drawl in your voice."

"Born in Mississippi," Paris said.

"Of course, you were. You're a witch from Mississippi?" I said it with sarcasm and irony.

"Just because I'm a witch doesn't mean I'm evil," Paris said. "We are brought up and taught that witches are evil, fake beings. Both couldn't be further from the truth. Most witches are some of the most tenderhearted souls you have ever encountered. And you can see for yourself, we're as real as the sun. I'm not saying there aren't others who use the Magic for their own gain and self-interest, but that's their journey. I chose this journey. The journey I'm on right now is a fantastic one. I'm just wondering if you like any part of it?"

"Is it a cult?" I asked.

"No, it's the opposite. You call your own shots. Not to say that some witches don't stick together and form covens. But that's because at the end of the day, we all need someone to have our backs. But we pride ourselves on being individuals."

"I have another question: What makes you think I want to be a witch?"

"Like I said, I had a feeling and I went with it. If I was wrong, I'm sorry. You can drop me off anywhere you like, and I will never bother you again."

Paris had called my bluff.

I eyed her as she carefully drove my Mazda. Her eyes focused on the road, but filled with sincerity. Not an ounce of cynicism narrowing them. She could've left me right now, wrote it off as no big deal and moved on with her magic-filled, *witchy* existence.

The question is...can I? Now that I have seen this power, the power of witchcraft, do I want to turn my back on it? Or do I embrace it? Do I make it my lover?

I was a single woman who worked a dead end job. I used to love it, but now, I dreaded going to it every waking morning. I had a dysfunctional, unbalanced dating life. I had absolutely nothing going for me, but now? Now I had the opportunity of actually becoming a witch? Who wouldn't want to be a witch? Honestly, I was tired of being a recovering nerd. I wanted to be the one in control. Then, without thinking, the words came out of me: "Okay, I'll do it," I said. "Make me a witch. I want to be a witch!"

Paris smiled and looked at me. You could tell she still sensed some doubt, but I gave her a look that showed I was determined to make my own decision.

She nodded.

"So, how does this happen?" I asked. "Do I drink a potion or something?"

"Why would I have you do that?" Paris asked, laughing.

"What is the ritual of becoming a witch?" I asked.

Paris smiled and said, "There is no ritual. Being a witch is like choosing to be a poker player or a construction worker. You start out with a learning curve, but you are constantly piling on a hands-on experience. Becoming a witch is a skill."

"A skill? Now, I'm totally confused," I said.

"There isn't anything to be confused about. Becoming a witch is a personal choice. You have a 100-percent say on how intense you want your witch experience to be. Some people go full throttle and take it to the max. Others, like myself, try to make an imperfect world a better place. Both are admirable ways of being a witch."

I was liking this more and more. I liked having control. I didn't want moons and ocean tides determining if I became a werewolf or zombie or not. "So, do you have a coven?" I asked.

"Where do you think I'm taking you, sweetie?" Paris said. She smiled at me. "I have a real good feeling about you. The last time I had this feeling, I was right on."

"Where's that witch now?" I asked.

Paris looked like she had a hundred things to say about the subject and then, she just stopped and composed herself and said, "Her name was Abigail. She was a good friend and she let magic consume her." Paris paused. "She was a phenomenal person, and something happened. Everything stopped."

"What stopped?" I asked.

"She was learning so much that she eventually surpassed me in power. Then one day, it was as if the lights went out. She just stopped doing anything, and became dead inside. Almost catatonic." Paris tried saying something else but couldn't, and started to choke up.

This woman, Abigail, apparently meant a lot to her.

"And the idea is, you control the Magic," I said. "You don't let the Magic control you?"

Paris smiled at me and said, "That is exactly right. I couldn't have said it better myself."

"So, what's Abigail's story these days?" I asked.

"You are a little too green for me to go into the details of Abigail. Just know, someone's core character will never again be overlooked by me. If we ever talk about the black side of the craft, there you go. A tragic example, if I've ever known one."

I looked at Paris. Tears ran down her face. There was a love there. I felt badly because I knew better than anyone what it felt like to be screwed over by a friend.

"Abigail isn't talked about much at the coven," Paris said mysteriously. It sounded like a warning.

"No problem. I'll never bring her up ever again."

"Even though I was wrong about her intentions," Paris said, "I wasn't wrong about her sensitivity to magic. So, you might be vetting me right now, but I'm also vetting you."

"How fun. Two people sitting in a car judging each other."

"I'm not judging you," Paris said. "I'm wondering if I've still got what it takes."

"What it takes to do what?"

"Be someone's mentor," Paris said.

"Why would you question yourself over one bad seed?"

"You'll know soon enough about Abigail and you will understand my regret." Paris looked at me and said, "So, by me bringing you to my coven, I am making a giant statement to my peers. I haven't mentored someone in three years, not since Abigail, so they will be extra interested in you; mainly, though, because of what happened last time."

"Great," I said. "It wasn't weird enough training to be a witch. Now, I have a whole witches' coven afraid that I'm going to become the next super-evil witch?"

Paris looked at me and smiled. "I feel you should know exactly what you're getting into, even from a social level. If you are truly serious about taking on the craft, there's a dark side to all of this. It does no good to hide it from the newbies. All I can say is, sometimes the risk is high, but knowing that you're on the side of goodness makes the fight worth it."

"Do you know for sure that you're on the right side?" I asked. "I'm pretty sure if someone would ask Lex Luther, he'd say he was on the right side, and Superman was on the wrong one."

"This is real life, Sahara. There are no super villains. There are just really bad people who use the craft in a selfish way that it was never intended to be used. You will learn all of this. The last time, I picked a psychopath to mentor. So, I, too, am a little gun-shy."

"How can you be so sure of me?" I asked.

"I'm not, but you're the best risk I have come across in a very long time."

"So, that's what you do? You're just a mentor who'll be mentoring me?"

"Of course. I found you. As good a fateful connection as it gets," Paris said.

"And that is important?" I asked.

"It's probably the most important," Paris said. "When do you think was the first time I saw you tonight?"

"In the Quickie Mart," I said.

"It wasn't," Paris said.

I got scared, and was afraid to ask the question.

Holy shit! How long has this woman been watching me?

"See, that fear that is right there," Paris said. "What you are feeling at this exact moment?" Paris asked. "That fear is going to mess up this relationship. It doesn't matter when I saw you. If you can trust my character, you can trust my intentions."

"When did you first see me?" I asked.

"Let's just say, tonight I saw you cozy up with a rather large man." Paris smiled at me.

"You think he was that large?" I asked.

"He wasn't skinny." Paris laughed. "But that's okay. He seemed into you and he seemed like a real considerate guy. He's a safe guy. But you're too young to be with a safe guy."

"You don't know me," I said. "You don't know what I want. What if I'm fed up with the whole dating game and Robert is exactly what I'm looking for?"

"Is he?" Paris asked.

"We've only been on one date, and I'm too much of a realist to believe you can know something like that after one date."

"Okay, let me ask you this," Paris said. "Is there a guy in your life that you think is so hot that the very thought of him makes you...well, let's just say, weak in the ankles?"

"You mean knees..."

"No, ankles. Ovulation tends to affect ankles, not knees. Discovery Health Channel taught me that."

"Oh, okay. Maybe," I said.

"Is he someone you wouldn't dare talk to? But the very sight of the man makes you rather moist?"

I laughed out loud. I really didn't think of guys like that. In my mind, I imagined how perfect it could be, but I'd never dare date outside my weight class.

"There's a guy," I said, with a shrug, "but he's way...*way* out of my league."

"I'm telling you, you can have *any* man fall in love with you. Every single day, he falls in love with you all over again. You see, with magic, if you want something bad enough, you'll find a spell that connects with you and if it's a perfect match, you can get all the toys you want underneath the Christmas tree."

"But I couldn't do that. It'd be too weird, knowing he was under a spell. Especially a spell I put on him. It almost doesn't seem fair to the guy. What happened to making the world a better place?" I asked.

"You're still doing those things that make a difference, but you're also not living in poverty while you're doing it. What you need to understand is that all magic comes from a specific place in the universe. That Slurpee you have in your hand came out of 7-Eleven's Slurpee machine. That is also one of 7-Eleven's cups."

Right then, I thought I was going to throw up. I had been inhaling the Slurpee ever since she gave it to me. I rolled down the window and I threw the Slurpee outside. The cold air felt nice against the night sky.

Paris continued. "So, when you want something, you need to be very careful in how you ask for it. Because you might be taking a child's last blanket." Paris smiled as she got off on a street near the city of Temecula.

"Where are you going?" I asked.

"Ortega Highway."

"Where's that?"

"It's a highway that cuts up and over a mountain. Not the safest highway. Especially at night." Paris laughed.

"Sounds lovely," I said.

Maybe I was with the crazy woman.

Chapter Eight

Paris drove the Mazda inland, down the 91 Freeway, where we eventually hit Interstate 15 towards San Diego. We eventually exited a poorly lit off ramp lined with creepy willow trees. We finally reached civilization and drove through a small city named Lake Elsinore. The French Riviera it was not, as it was just a small desert town built next to a man-made lake named Elsinore.

I thought she knew where she was going, so I trusted her. Realistically speaking, I had no choice; she was a witch, but if she wasn't, and was just foolin' me, I'd probably be able to take her if things got weird. "You do understand, Paris, that I'm being very trusting."

"What you need to understand, Sahara, is that this is your journey. This is your ride and you can get off the ride wherever and whenever you want. You can tell me right now that you have second thoughts and you don't want to go on this adventure, and an adventure it is."

Was she bluffing? I didn't know. I knew one thing for sure, I felt that something special was going to happen on this night, and maybe Paris wasn't as shallow as she seemed.

"I want to stay on this ride. Both figuratively and literally," I said.

"You sure?" Paris asked.

"I'm sure," I said, as sure as I'd ever been. "Just one thing, okay? I need to *trust* you."

Paris looked at me. We locked eyes, and she didn't say anything at first. Finally, she relented, "I'll always be here for you. You can *trust* in that. As long as you want my friendship, I will be here." Paris grinned.

I appreciated how she spoke to me. So certain. So knowing. No one had ever said that to me before. I liked the idea of having this high level of loyalty and friendship with someone.

"I do believe in magic," I said. "I always have. I don't know why, but it's an innate feeling that I know in my heart of hearts that magic is indeed true."

Paris looked over at me and she stared at me with her deep brown eyes.

"What's wrong?" I asked.

"Nothing's wrong. I just love how raw and honest you are. It's refreshing after all the lies I'd experienced."

"Abigail really did a number on you," I said, trying to relate to Paris on some level. Paris nodded and looked ahead as if she was thinking about something specific.

A moment passed and she said, "Okay, we're about twenty minutes away. Do you have any questions for me?"

"Actually, I do, I have like a thousand questions," I said.

"Okay, give me the first question that most concerns you."

"Was Knott's Berry Farm the first time you ever laid eyes on me?" I looked at Paris and I wanted to get a read on her, if she was being honest with me.

"Yeah, that is the honest truth. I followed you, because I knew you were going to need a little magic. "

"How did you know that?"

"Sometimes I just know. Call it a feeling. Who was the guy you were with?"

"It was a date. His name is Robert?"

53

"I thought, at some point, the two of you might need magic."

"Why was that?"

"Call it a feeling," she repeated her previous statement. "What do you think of him? You were pretty cozy."

"He's a fascinating person, there are not too many people who see the world the way he does."

"Which date were you both on? The tenth date, twelfth date? What?"

"Tonight was our first date."

"No freaking way!" Paris seemed surprised.

"Why do you say that?"

"His body language told a whole different story. It seemed like you two were real comfortable being around each other. That doesn't usually happen until many dates later. And that was your first date? So where'd you meet him?

"The Internet."

"Aw, the Internet. As much as it's changed the world, it's now the best way to get a date. Even for a witch."

I laughed because she was right. It was unfortunate, the world we lived in, but that was the way it was.

I had no idea how large Lake Elsinore was, but I knew we were still driving around the dimly lit, sleepy town. To my right was absolute darkness, but with the occasional light reflecting off the water. The lake was humongous, and our drive seemed to last forever.

I continued where I had left off. "We wrote emails to each other a couple of times and talked on the phone twice. Tonight, I just wanted to go out and meet a guy, have a few laughs. Nothing serious. But I've met a real interesting guy. I'll be honest, I don't think I've ever felt as comfortable with another human being before, besides my parents."

"Wait, what? You mean he feels like your parents? Are you not attracted to him?" Paris said with certainty.

"No, I feel an attraction for him. It might not be as animalistic as some of the attractions I have had, but there's something definitely there." I thought about Robert and wondered what he'd be thinking if he knew I was in Lake Elsinore with a witch.

"How old is he?" Paris said.

"He's thirty-nine!"

"How old are you?"

"How old are you?" I asked Paris back.

"I'm thirty-six." Paris said without hesitation.

"Okay, I'm thirty," I said.

"Are you one of those women who believe in true love?" Paris asked.

"Why not?" I said.

"Have you ever had it?" Paris looked at me and wanted to know my answer.

"I've seen it in others," I said, "like my parents."

"Have *you* ever fallen in love?" Paris asked me slowly.

I thought about it and, although I had said, 'I love you,' to a couple of boyfriends, I had never actually been in love.

I looked at Paris and laughed. She wasn't trying to make me emotional. She was trying to make a point.

"So, you are saying with magic, I can have an amazing deep love with the man of my dreams?" I asked.

"Magic is whatever your heart desires. Anything and everything will be literally at your fingertips."

"Call me romantic, but I want a guy to fall in love with me because he loves me all on his own accord. Why are you giving me this power?" I asked.

"It really isn't my decision. Fate leads me to a place and then my intuition finds the person. You need to understand something, Sahara; fate led me to you. Fate had taught me to find you all these years. I didn't know it would've been you specifically, but now that I know that is you, I feel overwhelmingly inclined to help you. For some strange reason, I care about you and your outcome very much."

I looked at Paris and hugged her inside the car. She had spoken to my heart. She made me think and feel things I had never imagined were possible. Had I found that amazing friend I'd always wanted?

"Fate wants me to connect with you. Ask fate why she chose you," Paris said.

"Fate is a she?" I asked.

"Everything beyond here, and us, is a she," Paris said.

We were now going up a mountain, along a narrow road, and I feared if I continued to converse with Paris, I'd mess up her concentration. Her eyes needed to be on the road. So, I just quit talking.

After fifteen silent minutes going uphill, we reached a large group of cabins on the left side of the road. It was some type of church summer camp.

"Yeah, summer camp," I joked.

"No, you are going to visit my coven: The Witches of Ortega Mountain."

"Do you guys make that salsa too?" I asked.

Paris pulled my car into a dirt paved parking lot.

"In all seriousness though, is this where you guys coven?" I asked. I didn't know if coven could be used as a verb, but it did sound better than *witched.*

"On the outside, it doesn't look like much. That's the way we like it. But once you open the doors, you see something quite different and it affects each person differently. Mother Earth shines on our coven with great delight. She is very proud of us. We see her blessings each day."

"Is Mother Earth like God for witches?" I asked.

"God is whatever he means to the individual. Mother Earth is all her own. We are all part of a perfectly-made puzzle and until we can make all the pieces face the same way, we will continue to use magic until each piece fits."

"Sounds noble. I love it. I also love that all this seems like it's for a great cause. It makes it more personal. It's what I have always needed...a sense of positive community."

"Hold on," Paris said. "Let's get out and go inside a few of these cabins and buildings. As I take you on this little guided tour," Paris said to me, "I don't want to talk. I just want you to take everything in. At the very end of it, I'll answer any questions you might have."

"It sounds hauntingly serious," I said.

Paris smiled. "It's a place that is special to a lot of people. I hope it becomes a special place for you."

Paris seemed so authentic; I hope I wasn't just another number for her and her coven.

We both got out of the car. It was still night, and I had no idea of the time. I just knew I was about to experience something I had never experienced before. Whether it was going to be glorious or the literally the end of my life, the commingling feeling of dread and excitement had me on edge.

Chapter Nine

Paris was right about the overwhelming sensual experience I'd receive every time we stepped into a new cabin.

Each cabin contained a different set of witches working on potions and scales. They all seemed very hospitable, but at the same time, I felt they all gave me a watchful eye.

The whole experience was overwhelming...baptismal, in fact. The smells, the colors from the lights and the music—it was all so mesmerizing, overloading my senses as if I were on the greatest mind trip of all time.

The single room cabins had no beds. They were more like work stations, each with their own cozy feel. From the colors to the chants and the music throughout the experience, I'd never felt more at peace and the feeling of communion than I had on this night.

After visiting each of the small cabins, Paris and I walked toward the parking lot. Although I thought Paris had shown me the coven in its entirety, she still seemed somewhat eager to show me something else.

"Once you decide 100 percent that this is what you want," Paris said, "you and I will get a cabin assigned to us."

"Here? Assigned? Already?" I asked.

"No, not already," Paris said. "I need more than words to show me that you're committed. Words are just triggers for the spells. The decision to use a spell and live with its consequences, are the actions required that tell me everything I need to know about a person. Your demeanor will demonstrate how comfortable you are with the journey."

"Do you have to check in and out of here somewhere?" I asked.

"No, Sahara. Quit being so silly. Wicca, in itself, is an individualized experience, and is given to us at no cost. A gift that must be treasured and never taken for granted. Each person guides their own path and doesn't rely on others. We don't rely on each other, because we are all capable, but if things get particularly hairy, we're there for one another."

I nodded. It was the most I could do as I was still in awe of the whole experience.

"Even though we are all individuals, no sister in the coven can bear false witness to one another. It is the worst thing you can do in the sisterhood and is punishable by banishment from the coven."

"Sounds pretty harsh."

"I'm not talking about exaggerations either. When a sister who is part of this coven confronts you, you must tell her the truth."

"You guys take honesty and integrity seriously."

"You have to be among family. Without it, you have nothing to stand on. The stuff we don't want people to know, you don't talk about."

I was very intrigued by the rules of the coven. I prided myself on being a real honest and open person. If this was as far as the coven's code of honor went, I was definitely game.

"It sounds all so intriguing," I said to Paris. "But you promise you don't worship Satan? I know it may sound like a silly question, but it's just a nagging thought brought on by my old-school and somewhat conservative upbringing."

"Sweetheart. Satan wasn't a witch. We do believe there is a darkness out there that is direct opposition of good. We just don't call it by one name like the devil or Satan."

"Look," I said, "I've seen things in this world that are unexplainable. Maybe magic is the answer for the unexplainable. But I want to tell you that what I've seen you do tonight with Magic, and what I've seen so far here at the Coven has wiped away any doubt I might've had about the existence of the craft."

"Before you say all that," Paris said, "I want to show you something." Paris gave me an enticing look and then she led me to a giant chapel-looking building that was in front of all the cabins.

"This used to be a Mormon camp and this was their Mormon church," Paris said, before opening the chapel's large, decorative doors. She led me into the chapel. A breeze swooped deep inside me and gave me a joy I hadn't felt since I was a kid tasting ice cream for the first time. It was one of the most beautiful, most settling places I had ever seen. A purple glow made everything look ethereal, and the most chilling music played, from an unknown source inside the chapel, loud enough to make you think you had entered heaven itself.

Paris continued to lead me deeper into the chapel to a small stage at the front.

On the stage I saw this giant book, a seemingly mystical and radiating book. "What is that?" I asked, pointing at it as it glowed brightly back at me.

"*The Book of Shadows*," Paris said, as she grabbed and held my hand for comfort. "It's where witches express their love in writing. We share our hopes and dreams with one another. We write out spells that will uplift one another. Others write out rituals to remind us of our place within the universe."

I stood and stared. A glowing dust seemed to rise out from its cover and up into the air. Tiny particles darting through the purple haze like drunk fairies. I felt its power. I could sense something supernatural reaching out to me and embracing me emotionally.

There was another tiny breeze that was stronger as I got closer and closer to the book. "May I open it?" I asked.

"Are you an individual?" Paris asked.

"Of course I am," I said, laughing.

"Then you can make an individual decision. If you're afraid that it will get all *Raiders of the Lost Ark* in here if you open the book, then the answer to that question is no."

"I just don't want to make a mistake," I said.

"You won't, sweetie. Open the book. Go to the first page where there is nothing written. I want you to write down all your hopes and dreams. Spend a few minutes writing. Take it very seriously. We believe all dreams can happen. There's always a way with magic."

Paris's words brought tears to my eyes. I had never experienced a religious or spiritual experience before, but this felt damn close. Because I had bought into her rhetoric, and suddenly been injected with a burst of idealism, I actually trusted her words that my dreams were about to come to life

I walked up and took the beautiful pink pen that was to the right of the book. I held my breath as I laid my hands on the very large binding. It was at least a yard long. I touched the cover of the book and the instant I touched it, something came over me emotionally and spiritually. It was love. It grew inside my soul, resonated like thunder, and enveloped my entire being.

I opened the book and went through it rather fast. I figured most stuff in this book were spells and rituals that you needed to work your way up to. Finally, toward the back of the giant book, I saw the empty page Paris had alluded to. If I intended to write a lot of thoughts, it had to be done with my best penmanship, as there were no lines on the pages. Luckily, I'd always been known to own mad calligraphy skills—just ask any of my relatives who have received birthday cards from me.

I held the pen in my hand. Something came over me because I began to write out my dreams. It was the first time since I was a little girl that I believed that dreams existed. I wrote from my heart and I left it all on the page. I wrote, "*Dreams are something I've always been afraid to have. I'd always misread my dad. He always seemed angry, or he seemed disappointed about something I'd done. And I always knew deep, deep down that I was the cause of that anger, disappointment and resentment. Neither one of my parents*

61

gave me a reason to dream or to believe in the unknown. They were practical. They raised me to be practical."

Paris nodded for me to go on. I continued, *"This is my wish and this is my dream. All my life, I never gave myself permission to be exactly what I was born to be. My wish is that I can express exactly who I am to the core. I want to be able to love in a harmonic existence. I want to be able to cry out of happiness. I want to feel loved, and I want to offer my love to my family, friends and significant other."* I looked up from the book and said to Paris, "I feel like I'm just rambling on."

"Sahara, open your heart to the book. Let your true self be reflected on the page."

I nodded and looked back down at the giant page and began to write where I left off.

"I want to live in that innocence within myself. But, what I truly want is for someone to receive my love and not reject it eventually. I just want to love and to be loved unconditionally—forever."

I shut the book and felt pretty exposed. It wasn't like I had signed it. Still, I had left my raw self-right there on the page.

It was time for us to go. I had absorbed so much, and needed some time to reflect.

Paris and I walked back to my Mazda in the camp parking lot.

Paris, with my keys still in hand, walked to the driver's side door. I flashed her a sleepy and tired smile. She nodded and returned the gesture, letting her know I was fine with her driving me back home, and that she had earned my trust—in spades.

Chapter Ten

After I woke up from a much needed nap, we didn't talk much on the way back to my house. The silence and the early morning desolation on the highway gave me ample time to reflect. It wasn't until we were a mile from my home that I decided to say a word. "Can I ask you a question?"

Paris looked at me and said, "She does speak after all."

"The silence was nice. I thought we were both enjoying it."

"What's your question, Sahara?"

"Okay," I said, "how are you getting home after you know...you drop me off at home?"

Paris stayed silent and grinned as she made a right onto my street. I was surprised at her sudden bout of coyness.

"Fourth house on the left?" I said.

Paris pulled into my driveway, put the car in park, and handed me the keys. We both stepped out of the Mazda and met at the back bumper.

"So, what now? Where do you live?" I asked.

Paris flashed me an impish grin. "I have this friend that I stay with around this area after a late night, or after an assignment."

"Friend?" I said. "Paris, you naughty girl, you. A friend, huh?"

"He is someone who offers me a place to sleep when I need it. Are we intimate? It's none of your business, sister," Paris said, with a playful wag of her finger. She then lowered her eyes and took on a more submissive posture, sagged her shoulders, and suddenly realized I had been quite vulnerable and trusting during our little escapade. Paris decided to return the favor. "Okay, fine. We're intimate sometimes, okay?"

"Doesn't sound like he looks twenty-one," I said. "Mr. Butler is a rather seasoned fella."

"You're right, he's closer to my age. Though, on occasion, if I'm picking off a menu, a medium-well New York steak is always a good choice. But lately, you're right, I've liked things with a little more pizzazz, more energy. A little more youth. So, I'll have the venison with a scotch."

"Scotch? Gross."

"Not a hard liquor fan?"

"Just not a fan of the drinks they order in westerns. Hate scotch, whiskey and gin."

"What do you like?"

"Tequila and vodka. They sit better in my stomach. I only drink maybe three times a year." I paused and looked at Paris. She didn't seem like she was in a big hurry to go anywhere.

As I looked at Paris, I felt that on some level I was somehow being played. But I didn't care. It had been a long time since I had a boyfriend or a best friend come over and stay at my home.

"Would you like to stay here until you get caught up on sleep?" I said to Paris.

"You don't mind?" Paris asked.

"I don't mind," I said.

"That would be great. Just tonight and I'll be gone in the morning."

"You can stay as long as you like, I'm serious," I said, and immediately had flashbacks to my first day of kindergarten where I made friends with Susie Vargas, and promptly had my first sleepover the following weekend. "You're safe. I want you around.

You're the closest thing I've had to a real friend in a long time. It's kind a refreshing connecting with someone so soon, so fast."

Paris looked at me and gave me a sweet, genuine smile. "Yeah, me too. I think I made a pretty cool friend tonight."

"Do you have trouble opening up when it comes to emotions?"

"I don't like to do it. Life can be sad. Life can be exciting and filled with romance. Love is whatever you want love to be. I'm a fan of love. Not a fan of betrayal."

"I know about betrayal," I said, "referring to my ex-boyfriend."

"So, you never want to be in love?"

"What's made you think I haven't been? I am thirty, after all."

We both walked to my front door and I took out my keys and opened the door.

"I have so many books I want to share with you," Paris said to me as I walked in and began turning on every light I saw. It was a habit of mine when I came into my house.

"I like books," I said. "I'll let you borrow my Kindle."

"You don't have these types of books, I guarantee you that."

"Oh yeah, *those* types of books," I said, thinking about the glimmering one at the chapel, instantly making me excited and nervous. "Where would you go to get such a book?"

"After we sleep," Paris answered, "we'll hit a bookstore."

"Bookstore?" I said jokingly. "You can't just download it to your Kindle or Nook?"

"A bookstore is the only place you're going to find the kind of books we're looking for," Paris said.

Before deciding to escort Paris to my room, I gave her one last steely, still playful, glare. "Anyway, my bedroom is in the back and it has a bathroom. So, you can sleep anywhere you want. I have a bed in another room. I have a futon in another. The other room is packed with books, bean bags, blankets, but has a TV."

"Got cable?"

"Not in that room," I said.

"You mind if I just sleep on the floor in your room with some blankets?"

I looked at Paris and felt comforted by the thought of sharing a room with someone who I could chat with well into the morning. It has been a long time since I had a sleepover. "I don't see a problem with that." I didn't know if she snored or had any other annoying bedroom habits, but I wasn't going to worry too much. Throwing stones in glass houses and all that stuff. My last *real* boyfriend said I suffered from late night, ninja flatulence. *As if...*

I nodded my head toward the room and paced into the hallway, but Paris stayed behind. I turned around and said, "What you waiting for? I'm pooped; do witches not need sleep?"

Paris replied, "Allow me to make you breakfast before we go to bed?"

I looked at Paris and it had been so long time since anyone cared if I went to bed, or ate breakfast, or lived, or died. And to top it off, she wanted to make me food. I was as hungry as I was tired so I walked her to the kitchen and I sat at my table and watched Paris make me a three-egg omelet with bacon, and while managing to put together a fabulous hash brown dish with a potato and an onion I thought had gone bad in the refrigerator.

We ate, laughed, and acted like *besties* until the morning sun blazed in through the kitchen window.

We eventually put our dishes in the sink and headed to my bedroom to get some well-deserved sleep. I immediately crashed on my bed, and Paris came in and set up her pillow right next to me on the floor.

Something odd happened before we went to sleep, though. I knew Paris had nothing on her when she came into my home, not even a purse. She stepped into my bathroom, still wearing the black dress she had on with the high black stockings, and three minutes later, she stepped out of the bathroom wearing a tight little white football jersey that had the number 11 on it, with a pair of pink sweats.

"How did you..." I said. "Never mind, I really dig those sweats, but doesn't sleeping in that jersey make you all itchy?"

"Nope," Paris replied with a smile.

"Didn't know you were such a sports fan," I said.

"What, aren't you?"

I paused and didn't respond; instead, I snuggled deep inside my plush comforter. My bed was absurdly and unnecessarily large. I had a California king. I knew the carpet in my house had a hard, rough surface. So I threw her down a couple of blankets I had up on my bed. However, a few minutes after I had turned off the lights, and we said our goodnights, I heard her tossing and turning on my carpet.

"Paris!" I said.

"Yes," she answered.

"Would you like to sleep on the bed with me?"

"Are you sure?" Paris said.

"Yeah, all my friends used to sleep in the same bed with me when they used to spend the night. I mean, it's been a while since anyone has spent the night, but I didn't mind then, and I sure don't mind now. Also the thing is huge. You'd actually be farther away from me than you are now on the floor."

"What happened to your friends?" Paris said. "They don't come around too often anymore?"

"Let's just say it's just one of those things where everyone reaches a certain age, and life expects you to all of a sudden grow up, move on...to another state, or a state of mind...you know, like raising a family...the American Dream." As soon as I finished my bitter pontification, Paris got up and climbed over me and got in the bed and lay next to me.

Was this weird? I'd just met this woman tonight and I was already trusting her to sleep next to me in a bed? She had a way. A poetic way that spoke to my heart when she wasn't being crass. And I knew if I allowed myself to take this person in, I might open up to something that I never knew existed within myself.

"Question?" I asked Paris.

"Yes," Paris said.

"Do you like girls?"

Paris laughed, and rolled over toward the wall. She never answered, and never put a move on me. I immediately felt like a lame homophobe. Going without real human interaction for a long time, really made one a paranoid, socially awkward shut-in. I seriously hoped to lighten up. I was being recruited to become a witch, for goodness sakes!

I had to disavow all sense of prudishness.

Chapter Eleven

I woke up, got out of bed, and was dead set on making some coffee. It had been a long sleep for both of us. As I got out of bed, my narrowed and blurred eyes couldn't believe the time displayed on the alarm clock. Because I had slept well into the late afternoon, I decided that it was going to be a lazy Sunday afternoon before going to work tomorrow.

I hated my job. I'd always wanted to make a living as an artist. A painter. That's my true passion, but due to real life and all the responsibilities that came with it, my passion had been relegated to a hobby. The walls of my home were covered in half-painted works. I'd been told my stuff was too poppy. I didn't know a painting could give people the same feeling that reality TV did. But I was damn proud of my work.

Paris came into the kitchen, looking as groggy as me. I gave her a cup of coffee. She sat cross-legged in the middle of my living room floor and gleefully sipped from the cup.

I looked at Paris and was jealous that she remained beautiful despite not showering and waking up with a face full of makeup after eight hours of restless sleep. Not me though. When I woke up, I looked like a drunk gargoyle.

"I never asked you about last night," I said to Paris. "How do you go about making a living?"

Paris laughed. It was very similar to the laugh she gave me before she rolled over and went to sleep. I decided to press the question. It was as if she relished in her own mysteriousness. I wasn't going to let her get away that easy. "Do you have a job?" I asked again.

"The answer to that question is no," Paris said.

"So, let me get this straight. You have the power to do a spell that makes a man act and wet himself like a dog, and you've decided not to parlay that into some money-making venture?"

"I survive by the earth. The earth tells me I'm okay with my decisions when I happen to run into a person as wonderful as you."

Wow, that was about the nicest thing anyone had ever said to me. "You barely know me," I said, embarrassed. "You also told me you haven't done anything like this in years."

"I haven't," Paris said. "But you're wrong about one thing. We once knew each other. It was in a different life. Two people don't hit it off as well as we do, unless something cosmic is going on. There was no reason for me to be at Knott's Berry Farm yesterday. But a kid gave me an adult ticket that someone in his family wasn't using. He just offered me the ticket in an Albertson's grocery store. Some people might tell the kid, 'No, it's okay. Thank you, anyway.' Not me. This child offered me this ticket to a place I hadn't gone to in twenty years. I saw it as a sign that Mother Earth was leading me to someone. The earth took care of me. The second that I don't have a place to live or to have to beg for food, I'll know then I'm off my destiny's path."

"It's so weird," I said, looking in Paris'sdirection. "You say things that I have only felt, but couldn't articulate. I've been a prisoner of my own pain for years. But hearing you tonight reminded me of the woman I used to be. The lady I always wanted to become! Somewhere, I got off destiny's path. I've been living on automatic for years. And I didn't realize how much I was dying inside, until last night at the coven camp."

I looked at Paris and I had a vulnerability that I only gave to men.

Paris smiled at me and said, "I think this is what they call fast friends."

Paris and I both ate a bowl of Froot Loops. Since it was so late in the afternoon, the sugary, colorful puff rings served as breakfast, lunch, and dinner.

Right after we each downed our third bowl, we got ready to head on over to her special little bookstore she had promised to take me to. Well, that's if you called slipping into a pair of sweats, T-shirts, and putting one's hair into a bun *getting ready.*

***

She took me to this herb and natural medicine shop in Anaheim that apparently had a very interesting book section.

As soon as we entered, Paris immediately grabbed seven big books off one of the center shelves. It had to have been $150 worth of books.

"I can't pay for all those books," I said.

"I would never dream of asking you to do that. My treat," Paris said.

When we got up to the counter, Paris gave the lady a credit card and a signature. That was all it took for me to be the new owner to seven of the most bizarre looking books I had ever seen. Five different books of spells, *The History of Wicca,* and a book on inspirations, with pages filled with optimistic quotes and incantations.

I had work the next day. I told Paris I need to get home. She told me she was going to stick around the shop and eventually ask her guy friend, the seasoned USDA Spartan, to pick her up.

I gave Paris a hug, and exchanged phone numbers.

"Give me a call, alright?" Paris said, with a pair of smiling eyes. "And get some reading done."

"I certainly will," I said.

It felt awkward leaving someone behind that I'd rapidly developed a connection with. The fear that one of us was going to feel as if a relationship that developed this fast, wasn't worth pursuing further entered my mind. Why would someone pursue something so unnatural, so ordinary, and so jarring?

I drove away from the bookstore alone with all the heavy books that Paris had just purchased for me at the herbs and natural medicine shop stacked on the passenger seat.

As soon as I got home, I dusted off an old corner bookshelf I had in my garage and decided to drag it to one of the empty corners in my living room.

Ever since I got my Kindle, one of the rooms became filled with boxes of books I hadn't decided where to put. Someday I hoped I'd put together a library in there.

I loved books. I always had. I read everything from fantasy to Harlequin novels, and J.R.R. Tolkien was my favorite. But I also loved a lot of the modern indie stuff that had become available on Kindle and Nook in recent years.

I laid out the seven giant books on my coffee table, before setting up the old bookshelf in the corner of the room, and decided to look through them that same evening.

I stared at them as they gave off this creepy vibe. I just sat there, listless, realizing how bizarre and surreal the past 24 hours had been. A witch had spent the night with me after taking me on the trip of my life, promised to transform me into someone like herself, and handed me a set of books from an herbal shop that I had always passed on the way to work; all while proclaiming ourselves best friends.

What the hell was I doing? What had I gotten myself into?

At least I didn't feel so alone anymore. But at what cost? Obviously it was an answer that needed further exploring.

Chapter Twelve

I heard a familiar sound in the bathroom. It was my cell phone going off. It hardly ever rang. No one ever called me on the weekdays, then I thought about how I gave Paris my number.

I grabbed the phone and I looked down. It was Robert. He waited one day to call me? Most guys waited three days. I couldn't believe I was obsessing over some stupid, arbitrary dating rule that originated from some mid 90's flick.

I thought if you generally liked someone, why not call them the next day if that's what you felt like doing?

"Hello," I said.

"Hi, Sahara. This is Robert."

"Hi, Robert," I said, more excitedly than I wanted to. I wanted to come off as if I had plenty of options, even though I didn't, and I'm sure Robert probably knew as well.

"Hi," he said again, stammering and fumbling his words somewhat. It was rather cute. I stayed silent and waited for him to get everything out.

"I...I was just calling," he said, "to tell you hi, and umm, wondering what you were up to."

So cute.

"Well, Robert," I said, "I was going to watch a little TV and head to bed, but probably toss and turn for a few hours before eventually falling asleep as I usually do."

"Why do you have a hard time falling asleep?" Robert asked. "You've got insomnia?"

"No, it's just that something crazy happened, but nothing I couldn't handle. It all kinda happened after our date."

"Did you go see someone else?" Robert asked.

"No, a woman kind of imposed herself on my life. It's a long story, and I might tell you about it another time. I'm still trying to digest everything that has happened to me."

"It sounds serious," Robert said. "Like a scam artist or something?"

"It is serious," I said, "but it's not a scam or anything like that; well, I hope she's not scamming me or anything."

"That's good. Let me know if you need anything," Robert said as genuine as anyone could be. I believed him. I knew it wasn't just lip service. This was a really good guy.

"Well, the reason why I called you is, I was wondering if you like to do something this weekend. We don't have to do anything crazy like go to an amusement park. I was thinking dinner and either a movie or we could head out to Brea and see some stand-up comedy if you're into that kind of thing. Two of the last *Last Comic Standing* finalists are headlining, but I'm not sure which ones. But I remember all those guys being extraordinarily funny."

"I like that show. I watch it whenever they have a season. They skip a lot of years. You never know when that show is coming on again."

"True."

"Let me ask you a question. If we could go out and do anything you want, what would you like to do?"

"Pretty much what I asked you to do with me this weekend," Robert answered. "I love good comedy and I love great food. Not a bad night."

"But if you could take me anywhere, and knew I'd be excited no matter what, where would you take me?"

Robert said, "I'm not going to drag you to a sporting event if you're not a fan of the team or the sport. I learned my lesson the hard way with that one."

"Is your team playing the Lakers?" I asked. "That's my team."

"No, they are playing the New Orleans Pelicans."

"Is this professional basketball?" I asked. I wasn't ignorant to sports names. My dad was a huge sports fan before he passed. I always knew which teams were good, but I never quite followed any team like I did whenever the Lakers were in the playoffs. I had never heard of the Pelicans in any sport. I thought Robert might be messing with me. I'd check the Internet tonight.

"It's not a brand-new team. It's just a brand-new name. Don't worry, I won't take you to a Clippers game just yet."

"You really are a sports fan?" I asked.

"I usually don't talk sports too much on a first date. I used to think it made me look manly. I realized all it made me look like was an oaf who only talked about sports. I am well-versed in a lot of subjects. I just like sports more than those subjects, but I'm not an idiot."

"I think you're an extremely smart and insightful man," I said. "You recognized it and changed," I said. "I think that takes a lot of growth."

"Thanks," Robert said. "I do love sports, but I also love plays and musicals. I love all types of movies. I'm willing to try and do new things, even if at first thought they're scary." Robert laughed and took an extremely long pause on the phone. Robert was selling himself as if he was a car dealer trying to get me into a deal that was too good to be true. He didn't have to do it. All I was really ready to do was take him up on his initial offer of a calm, easy, and long test drive.

"I think dinner and a show is great, but I also think going to the Staples Center and watching a Clippers game is great."

"So, you're saying you're going to go?" Robert asked.

"I have some things already planned this weekend, but let me see if I could fit us in and I'll get back to you. Is that okay?" I asked.

"Of course it is. I'm the one asking you out on a date inside a week. I have to assume you have other plans, too."

"I'm glad you did," I said.

"I thought it was worth a shot."

"I'd love to go. Look, I'm tired and I think I might need to go to bed now, just to ensure I don't have a restless night before another maddening day at work."

"Of course," Robert said. "We'll talk later."

"Of course," I said.

"Okay, goodnight, Sahara," Robert said in a sweet, deep, sexy voice.

"Goodnight, Robert," I said.

I ended the call, rolled over and began to think about Robert and his ability to grow on me—so quickly.

Thinking of him was pleasant; in fact, it was so pleasant, that as soon as I laid my head on the pillow, before I knew it, I was in dreamland.

Chapter Thirteen

I woke up at 6 a.m. and I was starving. I opened my eyes and immediately craved a sausage and egg croissant at this place called Timmy's in the city of La Habra. Best breakfast anywhere. It was a mom and pop place about fifteen minutes from my house and I didn't have to be at work until 8:30 a.m.

I decided I would just run out and grab a croissant sandwich to go. I'd take it home and eat it while catching up on some DVR shows that I'd missed due to the suddenly bizarre turn of events in my otherwise mundane existence.

I decided to put on a pair of black sweats, a black T-shirt and pair of black sneakers. I realized how black and witchy everything I owned was. It's funny how Paris's subtle influence revealed how unaware of myself I really was. Hell, my entire wardrobe screamed modern witch. The only thing missing was witch's hat for good measure. I didn't own one and I was pretty sure a hat wasn't a necessity for the gig. Paris didn't wear one, why would I?

As soon as I had turned on my Mazda I noticed my gas tank was nearly empty. I'd forgotten to put gas in my car for almost a week and the last time I had a full gas tank was when I drove around the desert the other night with Paris.

There was an Arco near the restaurant and I decided to pull in and put twenty dollars' worth of gas into my car. I remembered when you used to give the guy a twenty and almost get more than half of it back as change after you filled up your car.

I got out and saw a woman filling up her pink Volkswagen bug. She caught my eye because she looked so much like me, but she was wearing a loud green dress. Maybe that was why I noticed her. It was a bit eerie. I felt like I knew her. It reminded me of my encounter with Paris.

I quickly filled the tank up. Closed my tank lid and hurried back into my car.

I pulled out and headed toward the boulevard. The pink bug, that had the woman that looked so much like me in the hideous green dress, quickly pulled out in front of me, essentially cutting me off.

I almost honked, but I didn't want to elicit another awkward and strange encounter. We both drove out onto the boulevard and I pulled up behind her at the turning light on the intersection. The restaurant with the yummy croissant sandwiches was across the street from the gas station. I immediately thought, *wouldn't it be funny if she turned into Timmy's parking lot?*

She made the U-turn, forcing me to slam on my brakes, and predictably turned into Timmy's parking lot. *Of course...*

Timmy's didn't have a drive-thru as it was a little breakfast bistro. The thought of standing in line behind my hideously dressed doppelganger unnerved me.

I pulled in and parked on the same side of the parking lot as the pink Volkswagen bug.

I slowly got out my car and nearly peed my pants when my green dressed twin approached me from the side hastily, and blurted, "Are you following me?"

I gave her a look as if to say, 'I'm just as freaked out as you.'

"Oh, I'm sorry. I was only teasing you." The woman sensed my fear, and reveled in it.

"I saw you at the gas station and I was like, 'Oh my God, that woman could be my sister...possibly even my twin.'"

I looked the woman in her eyes. Her eyes were brown as mine were green. But her face was so familiar. Too familiar. I wasn't sure if I was losing my mind. I just smiled at the woman and wanted to get my sandwich and not deal with making a new friend like I did the other night.

"Do I know you?"

"Aside from the fact that we're a few chromosomes off from being twins?" the lady joked,.

"How can you be certain?"

"I'm just am. I'm really good with faces."

"Much better than me, I suppose," I said, laughing.

The woman then gave me a strange, sharp look.

"How do you know Paris?" she asked.

I was thinking this girl might be her girlfriend and she was stalking me. What if USDA Spartan was a lie and instead, her *friend* was this chick?

"How do you know Paris?" I asked, throwing the question back at her.

"One question, one answer." Then this lady winked at me with her right eye.

Oh my God, she was doing a spell on me. She too was a witch. *What the hell is going on?*

"I'm going to repeat my question. How do you know Paris?" she asked me.

"Paris is a witch," I said, against my will. "She thinks I have potential and she wants to train me."

"To be a witch?" she asked.

Suddenly, I understood what was going on. I didn't want to tell this woman anything. I was getting a sneaking suspicion that I was talking to Abigail. The actual infamous, treasonous, dark-side resident, Abigail.

This lady who I suspected was Abigail saw that I got my senses back and forced me to speak again, with what I assumed to be a forceful spell. "One question, one answer," she said, again winking with her right eye as if she were experiencing a nervous tic. She took a deep breath and asked me another question.

"Is Paris training you to be a witch?"

"Yes, she is," I said, against my will.

"You know if you use the spell five times on the same person, it backfires. I bet Paris didn't tell you stuff like that."

"Paris hasn't trained me to do anything yet," I said.

"Why did you tell me anything? I didn't put a spell on you?"

"Because that's what you do if you think the person you're talking to might be able to use the information you're telling them."

"You're very trusting. I like that," she said.

"The way you say it makes me think you don't like it for the same reason that most people like my honesty."

"You are so green. I could just eat you up." She pursed her lips, and then said with a straight face, "Then I want to spit you out."

That sent a shiver down my spine. "Abigail?" I asked.

"You already know about me? Paris is so obsessed with me that she talked about me with you." Abigail chuckled. Not like a witch, but in a creepy way, nonetheless.

"Why did you come to me and how did you know where I was going? You were ahead of me both times."

"I remember being as green as you, but I hungered for knowledge, and sought it as if it was the secret to eternal life, unlike you." Abigail looked me over and said, "You have an ambivalent aura."

"That's bullshit," I said, finally standing up to the garishly dressed bully.

"So, you understand what I mean?"

"Yes," I said. "You think that I don't feel as passionate about the craft as you once did. Obviously, it's you who doesn't care about the benevolent roots of witchcraft, I do. Because look at you, you're wicked. So wicked you're bad, bad, bad."

"Bad? We don't call our side bad. We just choose to use Black Magic, but we don't consider ourselves bad. We just have differing philosophies from those who think they are practicing the good side of magic."

"So, you are aware that witches are on two sides?" I asked.

"Are they?" she said. "Or are we all on the same side and some witches haven't embraced Black Magic because they're afraid? We all don't have to be enemies. That's Paris'sside that drew the red line. Our side didn't. Because of her, there is a split in the witch community."

"Don't you dare bad mouth Paris! Don't implicate her in this so-called division. She's looking out for everyone. She cares about the craft, obviously more than you ever will."

Abigail began to get angrier as I continued to defend Paris. There was something between them that had seriously gone sour, on a personal level. "I'm done speaking with you. I need more time to figure out what our dear friend Paris is up to and whether I should confront her, diplomatically, of course." Abigail gave me a strong stare accompanied with a contrasting kind smile. She turned on her heels and walked back toward her car, but stopped and stared at me one last time and added, "Wiser is she, wiser is he. You won't remember me until the next time we speak."

Chapter Fourteen

After ghoul green had sped out of the parking lot, I went into Timmy's and ordered my sandwich. I decided to eat it in the car, as I didn't want to come out to a keyed car. Unfortunately, that was all I remembered that morning. See, apparently, I'd fallen asleep after my third bite.

I opened my eyes, and was still in my Mazda with my seatbelt on, parked in the spot I had pulled into, with a half-eaten croissant sandwich on my lap. I looked at my gas tank. It was filled up about a third of the way up. *Had I filled my gas tank completely?*

I looked around for a receipt, and after searching under both seats thoroughly, I decided to place the warped thought at the back of my mind and finished what was left of my sandwich before heading back to work.

Work was rough that day. My brain was foggy and I felt as if I was on autopilot the entire day. I couldn't wait to get home.

Luckily, I did get home without incident. I was so tired when I got home from work that night, I ended up crashing on my love seat. I slept from five in the afternoon till 3:30 in the morning. The only reason I got up was because someone had been blowing up my phone mercilessly.

I wanted to throw my phone against the wall, as I had woken up with the stiffest neck.

I didn't recognize the number, but it was in my same area code.

"Hello," I said a little wearily, but damn, I was grouchy.

"Sahara. Good morning." It was Paris.

"Seriously? It's almost four in the flippin' morning." I moaned. I didn't mess around.

"I had a premonition that you were well rested," Paris said confidently.

I was, with stiff neck too...bizarre.

"I want to show you something really cool this morning. Can you meet me at your gym at 5:00 a.m.?"

"Really?" I said.

"Can you make it?"

"Do you know where my gym is?"

"Is it that giant one on Beach and Orangethorpe?"

"That's the one." I paused and sighed into the phone. "Are you being serious? I have never been to my gym before 10 a.m."

"It'll be a first," she said cheerfully.

"You want to meet in a couple hours, so we can work out at five in the morning?"

"Yes."

"You know I have to go to work."

"What we're going to do will only take twenty to thirty minutes. If it takes longer, trust me, you'll be happy."

I had no idea what Paris was up to. "Okay, I'll be there."

"I'll see you there. Also, fix yourself up a tad."

"Is there anything else?" I said to Paris.

"Just be there, and don't chicken out."

"I'll be there," I said.

We ended the call with a goodbye and I rolled over and got up from my loveseat and headed to bed for another half hour of sleep.

***

I got up and made myself a bowl of Special K. It instantly became my favorite cereal once I decided to buy into Kellogg's advertising campaign that their version of a chocolate-layered version of Special K cereal could be good for you.

After breakfast, I rinsed my dish in the sink.

As soon as I was done taking a shower, I decided I'd just wear my work clothes to the gym. I couldn't find my workout clothes, and made the decision that if I did decided to work out, it'd be the lightest workout in the history of workouts. Like a couple of leg lifts and a walking chat on the treadmill at level 1.

I drank my five-hour energy drink, scurried out of the house, and got in my car.

I pulled into the gym's parking lot. I couldn't believe how many cars were parked in the spots at this horrid hour. Other people loved their exercise. Boy, did that make me feel like a slug.

As I entered the parking lot, I made eye contact and nodded at Paris, who was standing at the gym entrance.

Since the lot was full, I had to park in the back.

As I walked past the ocean of parked cars, so I could meet Paris, my eyes and neck zipped toward the physical specimen that quickly approached Paris from the other side of the lot. It was Donovan. Paris smiled at him as he entered the gym, and turned to me, flashing me the heartiest of grins after seeing my reaction.

"I'm pretty sure your guy just showed up," Paris said.

"My guy?" I asked. "Are you talking about that guy I mentioned to you?"

"Yes," Paris said, "And by the way, gorgeous doesn't even define that man. That was just about the most beautiful man I had ever seen. And oh my God, he was wearing a tank top with the cutest pair of shorts on. Nice and tight."

Donovan was the only known element for me at the gym that morning, the reason for Paris meeting me there was the ultimate unknown.

"Sahara, can you walk by him when he's benching his serious weights? When he's by himself, of course, and give him your best smile and sexiest strut."

"I can't do that," I said. "How embarrassing."

"Just got to trust me on this," Paris said.

I was pretty positive Paris was planning on doing some magic to get this guy to notice me. Once he noticed me, then what?

"You want me to just walk in there and act like some sort of bimbo in front of Donovan?" I asked.

"Not a bimbo. I want you do your most elegant, classiest, sexiest strut."

"A sexy and classy strut."

"That's all you have to do, sweetheart."

I took out the gym I.D. from my bra as I never bothered to pay for a locker.

"Crap, how am I gonna get you in?" I asked Paris. "You got a membership too?"

"No, why would I have a membership?"

"Yeah, you're right."

"I'll just wait go around back and watch you through the window."

I stepped inside the gym and walked to the front counter and showed my card to the young lady who almost looked like she was asleep.

I headed back to where they kept the free weights and the machines, as it was the only area of the gym where I had ever seen Donovan.

I turned the corner and walked into the free weight section of the gym. The worst part about this section was the three-wall mirror. I saw Donovan lying on the bench and boy, did he look fantastic. His tan glistened, even at this hour of the morning. His long gorgeous dark brown hair just draped over his shoulders like a Greek god. He was wearing bright red sneakers. They were off-putting, but cute.

Paris quickly came into the view on the other side of the window that faced the main street away from the parking lot.

Donovan's piercing blue eyes stared straight ahead, stilled and showing off the fierce concentration it took to finish his next set of reps on the bench. I turned around and saw Paris mouthing something through the window. "Walk past him," she pantomimed.

85

I turned around and Donovan hadn't looked anywhere in my direction. I then held my breath and walked past Donovan just as Paris had instructed me.

I flashed him my best coquettish look and was shocked that I had the nerve to even do that. Our eyes eventually connected and he gave me the cutest, sweetest smile. *Oh my God!* I nearly tripped over one of the dumbbells.

I had to commit to an awkward bunny hop. I stopped right in front of the dumbbell free weight racks and gathered myself, thinking he thought that I was just another chick that was trying way too hard. I then glanced up at Donovan, through the mirror. He stared at me with narrowed eyes, but I couldn't tell if he was interested in me, or was confused by my goofball flirtations.

Did I have toilet paper stuck to my shoe?

I looked down and that wasn't it. He continued to stare. I had to do something. I couldn't just stand here and not do anything. I was wearing high heels, for goodness sake.

I looked at the free weights and tried to act like I knew what I was doing. I was at the heavy end of the rack. *Are you kidding me? Someone could lift a 200-pound dumbbell with one arm?* That was insane.

I decided to mosey over and walk down the rack. I got to where they had the smallest weight; the 20 pound bells were the lightest weight. I wasn't exactly a workout girl, but I had always been a bit strong compared to my friends growing up. I grabbed the 20-pound dumbbell and decided to put both my hands over it and raise the dumbbell over my head and do a triceps exercise that a trainer had once showed me.

The second I lifted the dumbbell over my head, I felt someone behind me. I was looking at the floor. I could see his feet. He was wearing red shoes. It was Donovan.

"I got you," he said.

He got me. What does that mean? I think it meant he was going to spot me. I had gone to this gym for three years and nobody had ever offered to spot me.

Okay, what was Paris up to? Can love spells really work?

I did five reps, and he helped me with the last one. I was so embarrassed. I was dressed for a work meeting and I was over here trying to get a triceps workout in before work. I must have looked like an idiot.

I put down the weight in front of me and slowly turned around and looked at Donovan in the eyes. He was a lot shorter than I thought he was. He was only 5'7" or 5'8". But it was 5'8" of luscious man.

"Thank you," I said.

"No problem, I thought you might need a hand." He smiled at me in a super sexy way.

What was going on?

"That was very courteous of you," I said. I had no idea how to talk to him.

"I'm always up to help a beautiful woman." He smiled at me and it felt so genuine and honest. If this was a love spell, it was a good one. Because he was acting the way I would have only dreamed of a man this hot would act toward me.

"I've seen you before," Donovan said. "You work out on the machines and run the treadmill."

He was exactly right. He had seen me before. I didn't know why he took stock and remembered me, but it made me feel good to hear it. I just hoped it was for good reasons.

What the hell am I saying? I'm talking to Donovan, the gym god.

"I like your dress. I think frills are sexy. I'm not sure how effective a workout outfit it is. Don't get me wrong, it's a sexy outfit."

I nodded my head at Donovan, hypnotized at the fact that he thought what I had on was sexy.

"I'll be done with my workout in thirty minutes. Do you want to hit a juice bar and have some breakfast?" Donovan asked me just out of the blue.

"A juice bar to have breakfast." That was officially the first time I had ever heard that phrase, but I needed to stop being such a smart-ass. This gorgeous man had just asked me to breakfast. "Okay, I have work at 8:30. It's about a half hour away from here. So, I will need to leave around 7:30."

"No problem," he said, winking at me. "I'll meet you up front in about a half hour. I'll take a quick shower."

"Take your time," I said. I wanted to think about Donovan's hot steamy shower where he was lathering up his beautiful abs and chest.

Donovan shook my hand and said, "My name is Donovan, by the way."

"I...my name is Sahara," I said like a fifteen year old meeting a teen idol. "It's very nice to meet you, Donovan," I said, trying to sound as grown up as I could.

"I'll see you in a bit," Donovan said as he walked back to the bench press he was working out on.

I turned and walked completely out of the gym. I took a moment and just had to laugh at what just happened. I had just talked to *Mr. Gym Hottie* like we were old friends. And meeting for breakfast? What the hell?

I walked over to my car and found Paris sitting in it. "Did I not lock my door?" I asked.

"No, it was locked. Really securely, I might add," she said. "It took a couple of spells, until I got it right. So, hats off to you, young grasshopper."

"What happened in the gym?" I asked Paris.

"It looked like he asked you out."

"Was that your spell? That he would ask me out?"

"What spell?" Paris said.

"Oh, shut up. You can't expect me to believe that you didn't do a spell."

Paris laughed and completely dropped the subject. "Where is he taking you?"

"He wants to go to a juice bar for breakfast."

"Oh, what a beautiful meathead he is," Paris said fondly.

"He actually seemed extremely nice. So, whatever you did, Paris, you made him a gentleman."

Paris smiled and made a funny show of dusting off her hands. "My work is done."

"You did do a spell? I mean, of course you did a spell. But what kind of spell?"

"Look, real early in a mentor's relationship, she or he is supposed to put a spell on the person they are mentoring and see how they deal with it. Dealing with spells that have been thrown at you either by the dark side—or even by a friend, in this case—is something you need to deal with right off the bat. I'll come over to your house after work if you like. We could go through some of the magic spells."

"Sounds like a full day. But okay, come over," I said.

"I'll bring fast food," Paris said. "What do you like?"

"Fast food?"

"Yeah."

I thought about it and said, "Everything."

Paris laughed and said, "I'll see what I can do for dinner."

"That's very sweet of you."

Paris walked off. She was done talking to me and making my morning go haywire by throwing a spell on Donovan.

She literally just walked away from the area and disappeared into the sea of parked cars.

I guessed I was on my own again, but felt it was temporary.

Chapter Fifteen

I waited in my car in front of the gym and redid my makeup. I looked down and realized I received a text. It was from Robert.

'I woke up thinking about you. I just want to wish you a good day. Any word about this weekend?'

Such a sweet guy, but I had a completely different date going on in about five minutes. Robert had to wait his turn.

I stepped outside and walked to the front of the gym. Right on time, Donovan walked through the front door entrance. He looked breathtaking, as he wore a white button-down shirt, unbuttoned lower than it should have, which was accented with a pair of light blue jeans, and thank goodness he got rid of those hideous red shoes. He had these cute brown shoes on with white socks. A wonderfully manicured man and vision to behold.

His eyes caught mine and he gave me one of his amazing giant smiles. "Hey, Sahara," he said. He walked over to me and gave me a big hug and swept me up as if I was a little bag of potato chips instead of the curvy woman I was. Anyway, I felt like a bag of potato chips as he lifted me in the air playfully. He set me down and

I laughed. I liked his playfulness, but that's not something I wanted to do on a regular basis with anybody.

"Let's not do that again," I said.

"No problem, love," he said. Even his voice sounded like blue suede.

"Who would you like to drive?" I asked.

"Oh, I don't have a car," Donovan said, as if he didn't just tell me something really weird. A grown man with a modeling job should have a car.

"You mean your car isn't here?" I asked.

"No, I don't own a car," Donovan said.

"Are you a big environment guy?" I asked.

"Not at all. Drill, baby, drill," he said. Donovan made the hand motions of a drill drilling into the pavement.

Wow, he's kind of funny. I wasn't expecting that.

But this guy didn't have a car and he didn't feel the need to explain it. I heard from enough people that he was a model. So I knew he had a job. *Why doesn't he have a car?* I didn't know. Now, I was embarrassed to ask him. I figured I would learn more and more about him as our breakfast date went along.

"Okay...well, my car is this way." I began to walk in the direction of where my car was parked. I looked over my shoulder to see if Donovan was following me, and he wasn't. I was super confused.

I continued to my car and was about to feel horrible when I looked in my rearview mirror and I could see Donovan waiting on the curb and looking in my direction.

Holy shit! This guy thinks I'm just going to drive over there and pick him up. Who the hell was he?

I looked at the rearview mirror and I saw him crack a smile. That was all I needed to see. I backed up my car and then pulled forward toward the front of the gym. I parked alongside the curb.

If he thinks I'm getting out and opening his door for him, I will leave. Hot or not, I will make a stand.

He leaned down and I unlocked his door from my side. He opened it and got in. I was about to tell him he could pull the seat back when I remembered how short he was.

"So, where is this juice bar?" I asked.

"It's at my house," Donovan said.

"Seriously?" I asked.

"Nah. It's around the corner. But if you want one of my special smoothies, you can only get them at my house. And I swear, that's not a euphemism."

I laughed. That was now two funny things he'd done. Apparently, he had some semblance of a sense of humor.

"Are you inviting me to your house at 6:30 in the morning for sex?" I asked.

Donovan looked at me and smiled. "Look, I seriously would love to make you one of my original smoothies and ask you what you think. I'm thinking about marketing them, but I don't have much of a clue how to do the marketing part."

He seemed honest. He didn't answer my question, though. But I could figure any man was up for sex at any time of day, especially, when it was strange. Men called certain sex 'strange' meaning they hadn't had sex with the woman before. The whole concept pretty much proved to me that any man would sleep with any woman once. I hoped that was not true. There had to be good guys out there. Donovan was probably not one of those guys. However, he was the man I was currently on a date with—he looked like he was sculpted by Michelangelo.

"We can go to your house for a smoothie," I said. I did like the fact that he said house. Now the question was...a frat house or some regular house where ten male supermodels lived?

"Look, if you feel uncomfortable, we can do a smoothie at my house on another day. Or, I can make a big batch tomorrow morning and bring some down to the gym."

"You would sincerely do that?" I asked. That did not sound like something a guy who waited on a curb to be picked up would do.

"Yeah. I make an amazing smoothie. I want to get it patented, so I can sell it. The more people who try it and love it, the more people who will be on board once it goes national."

"Ah, franchising. You're speaking my language. Donovan, do you know what I do for a living?"

"No, I don't. I'm sorry."

"Don't be sorry," I said. "I'm not trying to make you feel bad. I'm telling you I'm head of marketing for the company I work for. It's a national pizza chain. Once you get your drink to where it's ready for distribution, come see me. I would love to help you with a marketing plan."

"Wow, you would do all that for me?" Donovan asked. "You don't even know me."

That was the exact same thing I'd said to Paris.

"I don't have to help. I just thought if you needed it..."

"No, I'm not saying that. I deal with a lot of haters. I'm not used to someone offering something generous like you just did without a catch. Is there a catch?" Donovan asked.

"There is no catch. You seem very passionate about this smoothie you make and whenever I see that kind of passion in my line of work, it usually leads to sells. And who knows, maybe you can buy yourself a car."

Donovan just laughed about my car comment. Didn't say why he didn't have one. He just said, "Thank you," to the rest of the things I said.

"Sometimes, it's more fun helping people than it is making money."

"Look, if you help me market it and it blows up, you're getting paid right along with me."

"That's sweet. Who knows, when the time comes, maybe we will draw up an agreement. But let's take it...I don't know...ten minutes at a time."

"You offered and I got excited," Donovan said.

"You should be. I'm a great marketer when someone has your passion. But first things first. Let's take this one step at a time. Now, where do you live?"

Donovan then began guiding me to his house. While he did this, I just smelled him. He smelled wonderful. Under no circumstances would I sleep with him. If he didn't start making that smoothie immediately, I would leave. I mean, it was his house. He was already home. I could leave whenever I wanted.

"Take a left at the light," Donovan said. "Then make another sharp left and drive down to the end of the cul-de-sac. My house is at the end."

I was praying this guy lived alone. I didn't want to deal with roommates or worse yet...parents. I pulled into his empty driveway and parked. He had a basketball hoop up above his garage. He had a cute little house.

"Are we in Fullerton or Anaheim?" I asked.

"Fullerton," Donovan said. He hadn't yet gotten out of the car. I wasn't sure what to do, so I just opened my door like gangbusters. Was I going to open his car door? No, I was not.

Once I was outside my car, I walked up to his house. Dominic got out the passenger side and took his time and strolled over to the front door and opened it. It was unlocked, so he must live with somebody.

"Who's here?" I asked.

"No one. I live alone."

"Your door was unlocked?" I asked.

"And...?"

Talk about making a girl feel unsafe. There could be killers and murderers in his house. But Donovan was pretty manly. He could probably do a lot of damage. Okay, he lived alone like me in what also looked like a three-bedroom house.

I went into the kitchen and my man, Donovan, was a man of his word. He went straight to his blender. He cleaned it out with water. It already looked clean. I thought that was courteous of him to clean it further.

Donovan went to his refrigerator and opened it. I looked inside and all I saw was health food. Of course, that was what he had. He didn't get that body eating Wetzel's Pretzels and Ding Dongs. (Both

94

were delicious, by the way, and might make an appearance in my refrigerator from time to time).

Donovan pulled out fruit, nuts and vegetables.

"Please don't put any vegetables in my smoothie," I said. "Vegetables are gross enough without drinking them in liquid form. I can't see how anyone could do that."

"You need to trust me," Donovan said.

"Trust you? I met you forty-five minutes ago."

"But yet, you stand in my kitchen," Donovan said.

He had a point.

"Okay. I will try it, but I don't want to watch you make it. I think if I see any vegetables go in that blender, I'm going to hurl."

"That's fine. Why don't you have a seat outside on my backyard patio and I will bring you the smoothie?"

"Promise me, you will not put a roofie in there," I said. Like I said, I didn't mess around. I asked people straight out.

"I wouldn't even know how to get a pill like that. Nor would I care to look into it." Donovan sounded as sincere as anything he had said to me so far. "Are you allergic to anything?"

"Okra."

"Very well. You will not get any okra in your smoothie."

I stared down Donovan and I cracked my own smile and said, "Okay, I'll be outside."

I walked through his back door and onto a couple of steps that led down to his backyard. His set up was way different than my backyard.

His backyard had a lot more exciting things going on. He had a Jacuzzi that looked amazing, even at this time in the morning. But in the middle of his yard, he had a trampoline. It was really cool. Even though I didn't get Donovan's permission, I walked over to the trampoline and took off my high heels. I got onto the trampoline and bounced a bit. This was fun. I jumped higher and higher. The higher I jumped, the more I imagined what it would feel like to fly around on a broomstick. I still wasn't sure if what Paris said to me was true or if she had just been teasing me.

I stopped bouncing and decided I wanted to have my smoothie on the trampoline. So I sat cross-legged, the way Paris had in the middle of my living room the other day. Here, I was doing something very similar.

I exhaled and I looked up at the morning sun. It felt really nice. So far, this was really great. Donovan was such a gentleman. I was anticipating something weird would happen at any moment. I guessed I was going to have to wait and see.

Chapter Sixteen

In about five minutes, Donovan opened the back door to his house to get to the patio. He had two pink smoothies that were in see-through glasses that allowed me to see the color. He had even put cute little umbrellas in the smoothies. He looked out and saw me sitting cross-legged on his trampoline. "Do you want to drink your smoothies on the trampoline?" Donovan called out.

"Only if you also join me on the trampoline?"

"I have to admit," Donovan said, "I have never eaten on the trampoline, let alone drunk one of my smoothies on it. This might be a little bit different."

He walked over to the trampoline and kicked off his brown shoes before he got on. "Oh, thank you for taking off your high heels," Donovan said.

"Of course," I said.

Donovan smiled at me and he squinted his eyes against the sun and looked as hot as any man had looked, ever. He handed me one of the smoothies he was holding.

"Thank you," I said. I set it on the trampoline and used the trampoline to hold my drink. I was praying it wouldn't spill all over Donovan's trampoline.

Donovan did the same thing. "I sure hope they don't spill," Donovan said. He scooted even closer to me so we were about three inches apart.

He leaned back,looked back toward the sun, and this time, he did it with his eyes closed.

I was trying not to be awe of this guy's looks. That was so not me. But this dude was insane looking. I'm attracted to men like Donovan, but I don't where it goes from there. I'm not just going to sleep with him and be a one night stand.

"So, do you own this house?" I asked, trying to stop focusing on things that haven't happened yet.

"It was my parents' house. They died when I was ten years old. I was sent to foster care, and when I was eighteen, the house was mine, and so was a little bit of cash."

"Your parents died when you were ten?"

"Yeah," Donovan said, trying to not allow himself to get emotional. He didn't strike me as a guy who would ever just break down and cry.

"Did they die at the same time?" I asked. It was a morbid question, but I was a morbid girl.

"No, it was at different times."

"But both happened when you were ten?"

"Yeah," Donovan said. He gave me a look as if to say 'let's change the subject.'

"How old are you?" I asked.

"How old do I look?" Donovan asked. He got this question a lot and he liked to say, 'How old do I look?' and women would say twenty or twenty-one because he could pass for that age. But I was smarter than the average person when it came to reading age. Why? No idea. But I could usually almost get it on the dot.

"I want to preface this by saying," I said, "I have two answers on how old you look."

"Go on. I'm fascinated," Donovan said. Of course he was. We were just focusing on him at the gym, and I had listened to the gossip.

"Okay, just going on your skin, face and body. I would say twenty-one. But going by the deepness of your eyes, I can see years. So, I say you're twenty-seven."

"Wow, twenty-seven. That is the oldest age anyone has ever guessed." Donovan was insulted.

"I said twenty-one, too," I said, trying to specify that I had two answers.

"Basically, you said at first glance, you'd say twenty."

"Twenty-one," I said, correcting him playfully. I was pressing some buttons. This was a little more fun than I thought it would be.

"But you said after seeing me up close, you now say I look twenty-seven. So, that means up close, I have never looked older."

"Do you see how crazy that sounds?" I said to Donovan. "You are older. So every day should be the oldest day you have ever looked. Lifting weights and dieting doesn't make you actually go into the fountain of youth."

"I know," Donovan said honestly. "The answer to your question is twenty-nine. You guessed my age, only two years younger."

I couldn't help but laugh out loud. This guy was upset at me for an age that was still younger than what he was. This just might be the biggest prima donna I had ever run across. He might be a little high maintenance, but there was something else about him. He was a lot more complex than people gave him credit for. What I gave him credit for.

"Well, are you going to try my smoothie?" he asked.

I looked at Donovan and he was too calm to have put anything weird in it. I took a sip and it was sweet and tangy. Wow, it tasted incredible. It tasted like a smoothie Sweet Tart. "This is good for you?" I asked.

"Yes, only made with natural ingredients and no added sugar."

"That's amazing." I tasted the smoothie again and it tasted even better the second time. "Donovan, this is really good. And you say this is your own special recipe?"

"Mine and nature's."

"Wow, you need to get this patented and on the market. It's incredible."

"Thanks," Donovan said. He actually seemed a little embarrassed that I liked his drink so much. That surprised me. I thought he would act arrogant about it, but instead, he acted extremely humble.

"What time do you go to work?" Donovan asked.

"8:30," I said.

Donovan pulled out his cell phone and said, "Well, that gives us around twenty minutes to chat. Do you want to bring the smoothies into the living room?"

"We can chat out here just as easily as inside," I said, not allowing him to get me inside his home. Who knew what kind of sexual superpowers this guy had? I'd probably have my panties off the second I entered the door.

"Okay," Donovan said. "Do you mind if I take off my shirt? I'm a little hot."

You're a lot hot, I thought. I didn't see any harm in it. I mean, I needed some kind of reward for not just running into his house and sleeping with him the first time I came over.

"I don't mind," I said.

Donovan then did one of the hottest things any man had ever done to me without realizing they were doing it. He probably knew he was doing it, but still it was hotter than hell. Donovan stood up on his knees while still on the trampoline. Because we were sitting so close together. His stomach was at my face level. Donovan then slowly and methodically unbuttoned his shirt. And his insane abdominal muscles were about two inches from my face and boy, did this guy smell good. He sat down again. He was just wearing his light blue jeans and white socks.

I leaned back and felt extremely overdressed. But these clothes were staying on.

"What are your passions, Sahara?" Donovan asked.

"What exactly do you mean?" I asked.

"Instead of asking someone what they like to do, I like to ask what their passions are. You tend to hear amazing stories. It makes for much better chit-chat." Donovan smiled at me and his answer surprised me. But I would answer his question.

"My passions include many things. Not one passion defines me, but yet they all blend together to make up who I am," I said.

"That's a vague, beautiful answer," Donovan joked. "Give me one of the things that defines you."

"I paint pictures. Lots of pictures. If I could do it for a living, I would. I have half-finished ones on my walls, too. Someday, I will finish them all, but I enjoy the process as much as the result."

"That's what I'm talking about," he said.

I looked over at Donovan and he seemed genuinely interested. I didn't know how much of this was a spell, or if he was even under a spell anymore. Of course he was. The hottest guy in Orange County had asked me over to his house for a smoothie. *Like that happens to me every day.*

I decided I would put this spell to the test. "So, Donovan, why did you ask me over today?"

"Like I said, I have seen you before in the gym. You remind me of someone who meant a lot to me a very long time ago. So, I guess you could say I've been crushing on you from afar. But I never saw the chance to come up to you and introduce myself. So, when I saw you in high heels wearing a sexy black lace dress, trying to do a two-handed dumbbell behind the neck pull up..."

"The exercise I was doing is called all that?"

"Something like that. They change the names to workouts constantly. Anyway...so, when I saw you dressed for success and you needed a spotter, I jumped up at the chance. I knew it was an easy way to meet you."

I was mesmerized that this beautiful man was talking about me. It was hard not to get caught up. He sounded so honest. I would think his voice would be cheesy and everything he would say to me sounded like a really bad pick-up line. Instead, he made smoothies and was an orphan at ten. I was captivated by him. I wanted to kiss him. But how did I kiss this guy and just show him it's one kiss? He was probably so slick that the second our tongues touched, he'd be undoing my bra strap. I knew I had to wait till goodbye and even with that, I was taking a chance. There was no certainty that he would be going in for a kiss.

"I think I should head off to work," I said, surprising myself. I guess I wanted to see if that kiss goodbye was going to happen. I stood up and walked to the door of his house. As I entered the inside, I scurried to the front door. I knew if he just touched me inside his house, I couldn't be accountable for what would happen next. I got to the door and opened it. I walked over to my car door.

I could hear Donovan following behind me.

I stopped by the driver side of my Mazda. I turned around rather sheepishly, not knowing how close behind me Donovan was. He was a good four feet. Perfect distance. Not too close and not too far.

"Thanks for the delicious smoothie," I said.

"You could have taken it with you and enjoyed on the way to work. I can go back and grab it?"

"No, don't do that. I mean your smoothie was out-of-this-world delicious. I just need to get going, but I had a lovely time. I really did."

"Don't sound so surprised. I'm not some predator who devours women."

"No, you're not. You are quite a gentleman."

"Is there any other way to be?"

"Trust me, the way you look on the outside, you could be the poster boy for the way it shouldn't be. But you surprised me and I'm sorry for judging a very beautiful book by its cover."

Donovan and my eyes met. He was barely two inches taller than me so we were practically eye to eye. I didn't care. He was just as beautiful on eye level.

Donovan stepped into me and took both my hands. It was a very sweet, safe gesture. He stepped closer and gave me a very gentle kiss that lasted about three seconds. It was nice. A little passionate. A little innocent.

But very nice.

Chapter Seventeen

I escaped the clutches of Donovan's sensual arms just long enough to get inside my car. I sat down and put my seatbelt on. Donovan made a motion with his hand to roll down the window. I sighed and rolled down my window halfway down.

"Can you roll it all the way down?" he asked.

I looked at Donovan in a flirtatious way as if to say, 'are you up to something?' I felt safe in my car. So, I rolled it all the way down. Donovan crouched down to get to eye level with me.

"Let's go out this weekend?" he asked.

"Okay," I said, without even considering the alternative answer of, 'I'm busy' or 'no.' "Which night?" I asked.

"How about Saturday?"

"Saturday, it is. I guess I'll be picking you up."

"Yeah, is that cool?" he asked. For some reason, I expected him to follow his last comment with a comment like, 'Don't worry, I'll pay for everything,' but he did not.

What he did do was lean and kiss me gently on my lips. Not a long kiss. It was shorter than the last one, but just as nice.

I looked at Donovan and said, "Goodbye, Mister."

"Goodbye," he said.

I rolled my window up before he could go in for another kiss. I didn't think I could handle kissing this guy one more time, as I might just call off work and spend all day here. But I couldn't do that. I would not do that.

I backed up my car and he looked on and gave me a wave with his right hand.

I hit the road and made my way to my job in Whittier. I just took I-5 and I got there in twenty minutes.

I got to work in my six-story building. I was the head of marketing for a local pizza chain in southern California called Manifesto's. Most of my day was coming up with new ways to market pizza. At first, it was a little bit fun. But now, I wished I was solo...a consultant. Then businesses would come to me, and pay me for a marketing job. That would keep my job fresh and fun. This type of job made me hate the very sight of pizza. I considered asking the powers that be if I could telecommute for a while.

After working a rough eight-hour shift, I was extremely sleepy and couldn't wait to get home.

I pulled into my driveway and parked in my garage. I could hear my TV playing from the garage. I didn't remember watching TV and leaving it on. I felt a little bit scared.

I went to my door and it was unlocked. I know for a fact that I had locked it. I opened my door and peeked in my head, making sure that most of my body was outside the door so if I had to bolt to the street, I could.

"Hello?" I called out.

"It's just me, sweetie!" *Paris.* Somehow, she'd gotten inside my house without a key. Of course she did. She was a witch.

I stepped inside and Paris had moved my living room furniture all up against the wall.

"What is going on?" I asked.

"We are going to need some space inside so we can start practicing our magic."

That's right, Paris was coming over. My life had gotten extremely weird, extremely fast. I could barely keep up. And to think this all had started with me wanting to go on a date on Saturday night with Robert.

Robert...wow. I hadn't answered him about this weekend. I already made a date for Saturday. I got pretty caught up in Donovan. I needed to remember which guy had the spell on him and which didn't. Robert really liked me for me. That was a big plus. Donovan just made me sweat and melt and he was rather charming if that was even his real personality.

"We need to have a talk," I said to Paris. "Could you turn off the TV?"

"Oh, sure, sweetie." Paris clicked off the TV and looked at me.

"Look, I barely know you," I said. "We can say we're cosmic sisters all we like, but the truth of the matter is, I have known you less than a week. We need to set some boundaries. Just because you're mentoring me, that doesn't mean you can just walk in my house when I'm not home."

Paris looked at me with a distraught look. "I'm sorry, sweetie. I just figured you wouldn't care, but now I know you do, so I won't do it again."

Great. Now I felt bad.

"Look," I said. "I have had a packed day and I am completely exhausted. I might be a little grouchy."

"Grouchy? After some morning fun with Donovan, I thought you'd be electrified."

"There was no morning fun. I mean we had a nice time, but not the kind of time you are insinuating."

"Uh-huh," Paris said.

"I'm telling you the truth," I said.

"So, you went inside his house for what reason?"

"How did you know I went inside his house? I haven't told you any details about our date. You're starting to freak me out, Paris."

"Relax, baby girl. I might have followed you to his house, but that was it. After I saw you go inside, I left it alone. I was just excited for you. Not in a stalker way, but in a big sister way. Please believe me."

I wanted to believe Paris. Everything she said could happen, but she was a little too much up in my business for my liking. That was where I needed to draw the line.

"Okay, listen," I said. "I like you, Paris. I'll be honest. I'm afraid to trust you. So many people have screwed me in my lifetime, it's hard for me to trust anyone. I need to make a line in the sand right now. You need to not be so up in my business. I don't know how else to say it...other than that."

Paris looked at me and gave me a warm, loving smile. "I'm sorry. I got excited and that is the truth. It has been a long time since I've wanted to even be friends with a woman. But here you were. I saw a lot of me in you." Paris paused and it seemed as if she was stopping herself from getting emotional. "I'll pull back. I'm sorry for getting too involved."

Man, she was a world-class manipulator when it came to guilt. Or she was just so much more honest than I gave any human credit for? "Look," I said. "Before we steer too far off the tracks, I have a question for you. I know you put a spell on Donovan. I want to know what kind of love spell it is. Is this guy going to fawn all over me because he will be so in love? I'll be honest. It feels cheap. Although, he's sweet and says all the right things, I just don't feel as confident around him because I'm not sure what is real and what isn't."

"Are you going to see him again?" Paris asked.

"Yes, this weekend," I said, a little bit embarrassed.

"Very nice. Trust me, he'll be a gentleman."

"What kind of love spell is he under? There must be a ton of different kinds."

Paris smiled as if this was a teaching moment for her. "I'll tell you this," she said in almost a creepy witch way. "He is under a spell, but I won't tell you which kind. That is going to be your first assignment. You need to recognize what kind of spell is being used toward you."

"Really? We're going to do it like this? With riddles and rhymes?"

"It's not like that," Paris said. "Just trust the process."

"Okay, I'll trust the process. I'll give you ninety minutes of my time and then I will need to go to bed and I have to catch up on sleep."

"All right," Paris said. She grabbed the book that was on the very top of the pile of books I had stashed in the corner of my living room. "This book is a good starter kit. It will guide you and teach you the basics until you're ready for more intense magic."

"Okay," I said. "Do I need a wand?"

"Yes, you do," Paris said. "I happened to bring one for you from my personal wand collection. I want you to have this wand. It's my gift to you."

Paris went over to a backpack that was on the floor. This was the first time I noticed the backpack was even sitting there. I wondered if she did magic and I didn't see it.

Anyway, she pulled a pretty pink sparkly wand out from her backpack.

"This is yours," Paris said. "Remember the power isn't in the wand. It's in the ritual."

"Thank you very much for this gift," I said. "I have no idea what that you just said, but thank you."

"Sahara, the wand is an accessory. The true magic comes from our words and our hearts."

"Is that how you do a spell?" I asked. "With words? And heart?"

"More often than not. Sometimes, you can cast a silent spell with just movement. But your heart is always a part of it."

Silent movement? Words and heart? There was a lot to learn. "What will we be learning today?" I asked.

"I'm going to teach you a spell that is not in the book. This is my spell. It's an aura-cleansing spell. This is a spell you can do for yourself as much as is needed to give you positive energy and have life possibilities open up to you."

"You're going to teach me an aura spell. Something that I cannot see."

"You won't be able to see it. But when magic makes you feel a certain way, that's when you truly start believing."

"That's beautiful," I said.

"Don't worry, Sahara. I will be teaching two other spells today, too. I will teach you a basic love spell and a basic money spell. Both should come in handy for you immediately."

"Okay," I said. "What do we do first?"

Paris walked over to me and took me by the hand and led me to the middle of the room. "I want you to sit cross-legged on the carpet with me."

"Okay," I said. I sat down on my faded white carpet and Paris sat right across from me. She was so close to me that our knees were touching.

"Look at me, Sahara."

"I am." I looked across to Paris.

"We all have bad mojo that attaches itself to us throughout the day. It's just tired spirits trying to bring you down. An aura cleansing is like showering up right before the big game. Our big game is practicing magic. Think of it as stretching out your soul."

"Okay," I said.

Paris exhaled really slowly and then said, "I'm going to show you the spell. It's very simple. It's very direct. It gets the job done."

"Okay," I said again. I was getting a little bit nervous now. I knew she had the ability to do magic and now I had a front-row seat.

Paris began to speak with authority, "Cleanse me. Wash me clean. Bring me peace and show me love."

Paris held her posture. She was cross-legged with her hands in the air. She wasn't using her wand.

Then I felt a breeze come through the room. At first, it hit up against the curtains, then it blew past us and then out the window.

"Is that all you have to say?" I asked.

"It doesn't have to be a Shakespeare sonnet for it to be a spell," Paris said.

"Very nice. So, are you all cleansed now and could get away with wearing a white dress on your wedding day?"

"It's not like that, Sahara. And marriage? Gross. What has happened to me is, I have been cleansed of all evil and worthless mojo."

"Mojo?"

"Spirits."

"You really believe that?" I asked.

"What's there not to believe? Everything about this world is staring everyone in the face. Everyone is so worried about proving whose god is greater instead of doing the things that was asked of us by the Creator, which is to feed the poor, tend to the hungry and love thy neighbor—principles that witches live by. It isn't something that had to be written in a book."

"Not a cult?" I asked.

"You choose this whole process. If you never want to do anything, you never have to do it. My job is to help you find your way."

"Why did you choose me?" I asked.

"Like I said, Sahara. You remind me of someone else I knew...very externally. Now it's your turn to do the spell. Just remember the three simple sets of words. 'Cleanse me. Wash me clean. Bring me peace and show me love.' And then hold it."

"Hold it?"

"Sit completely still. You are waiting for an answer and when you feel that bit of wind touch your breath, you know you have been cleansed and your aura is squeaky clean."

I felt silly. But I definitely saw some power moving with Paris's spell.

I was going to do this. "Cleanse me," I said. "Wash me clean. Bring me peace and show me love." As the words came out of my mouth, I felt how important the words were and how if you said something like this out loud that you better be a good person or that was some serious crappy karma.

I held my pose and just allowed my heart to be open. I held it and I held it and I was just about to say something, when I felt the breeze come through the room again. The breeze came right up to my lips and I inhaled the wind and just breathed.

The air was exhilarating. I could feel power in the breeze. Then something remarkable began to happen inside of me. I felt every worry, every concern just melt away in a sea of goodness. I was getting lightheaded, but filled with joy.

"I do feel like my aura has been cleansed. Wow."

"It has, Sahara. Now, you are a vessel that can be even more susceptible to magic. You see, you didn't know it, but you just passed the biggest test."

"How so?" I asked.

"Mother Earth blessed you. She came down and breathed on your face. That doesn't happen to everybody. I've seen some strong witches and warlocks in my day that never had that happen to them the first time they threw out a spell."

"What does that mean?" I asked.

"It means my intuition is right. It always is. It means you are going to be a perfect candidate for this kind of work."

"Cool," I said. I didn't know how else to take someone saying I'm a natural at being a witch.

"So, let's talk about basic spells," Paris said. "Basic spells include the luck spells, minor love spells, minor money spells, health spells and protection spells."

"That's a lot of spells for just a beginner," I said.

"That's not even the tip of the iceberg. Every one of the spells that I mentioned has over 500 different kinds of specific spells. Don't get me started on combinations. Once combinations are introduced, then the amount of spells that there could be is practically endless. But today, I'm going to teach you three. You have already learned one, and it appears that you're a natural."

"Okay," I said. "What is the next one?"

"The next one is called a money spell. The spell eliminates all negative energy that is stopping you from having success in regard to money. This spell won't make you rich. It will just not ever allow you to be poor as long as you use it as a go-to spell when needed. This is also a simple spell that you can do whenever you want some positive financial energy."

Paris was sitting cross-legged in the middle of my floor. She closed her eyes and said the following spell, "Shelter, food and love. Provide me with all the above. Let me be rewarded for the work I deserve, and let me reward others for what they preserved." Instead of holding the spell in a frozen pose, she snapped both hands twice into the air, almost as if she was cheering in a crowd.

She opened her eyes and said, "That's the spell."

"Wow," I said. "That didn't seem like anything."

"Money isn't just going to fall out of the sky. Some spells allow life to give you what you deserve and this is one of them. Sometimes it takes time, but it opens up avenues for you for sure. Trust me. I'm a living example of how you can survive on this spell."

"Okay," I said. "Could you write this spell on a piece of paper so I can read it and memorize. I'm a better visual learner." I walked into my kitchen and grabbed a piece of paper and a pen that I had on the counter and came back to the living room and handed them to Paris. She took her time writing each word of the spell as if it had its own special significance. It was very poetic to watch.

Finally, she was done writing and she handed me the paper. "Don't just read the spell," Paris said. "Memorize it and really own it."

"Own it?"

"Make it a part of you. If you do this, I promise you that you will see amazing things begin to happen to you in terms of feeling financially secure."

So I read the spell enough times that I memorized it. When I felt like I owned it, I said the spell out loud. When I was done, I felt a power go through my body as if I would be magnetic toward positive endeavors.

The feeling was intoxicating and liberating. I felt a freedom I had never felt in my lifetime. It was a carefree freedom that feels like everything would always be okay. The worst was behind me.

"What's the third spell?"

"I'll write it down for you on the back of this paper. And this is a spell you have to own. Or you can look pretty silly in front of a person that you want to answer one question honestly. But let me warn you. You do not want to abuse this spell. There are things we all just don't need to know about each other and I learned the hard way. Let's just say I was dating a Cher impersonator… but I had no idea that he was doing that until I asked what he did the following night. So, try to keep it in the moment."

"Okay," I said. "Is this a really long one?"

"Nope, one of the shortest spells there is." Paris wrote more words than I thought she would write on the back of the previous paper I had given her.

She handed me the paper and I looked down at what she wrote. 'One question, one answer.' Then she wrote in parentheses: (Followed by a wink with right eye).

"Seriously. That's all you have to do?"

"Amazing, isn't it? It was always there at your fingertips and you never knew it. You know you have never said, 'One, question, one answer,' and then winked at the guy with, specifically, your right eye."

"No, I can say I have never done that." That was when it dawned on me that magic had always been around me, I just didn't know how to control it. But it was there. I always knew it. This thought was very overwhelming and tears burned up in my eyes.

"What is wrong, sweetie?" Paris asked.

"Let's just say the world is finally opening up to me, just like you said."

Chapter Eighteen

Paris stayed over and she spent the night again and lay on the other side of me all night. I had to be honest, I liked her being here. It felt like I was safe again, the way I used to feel when my parents were alive.

The rest of the week went by in a hurry, and I never got back to Robert about our date. I wasn't sure why I hadn't or why I was procrastinating talking to him. A strong part of me wanted to see him this weekend. I just hadn't called him. I was having too much fun with Paris. To Robert's benefit, he wasn't blowing up my phone or my emails trying to get an answer. He was just waiting for me to give him an answer. I liked his patient heart.

Paris spent Tuesday, Wednesday, and Thursday night at my house. On Wednesday and Thursday, she introduced me to new spells. We did a luck spell, and a protection spell. Paris didn't know it, but she was already part of my protection spell. It had been a long time since I felt anyone had my back like this woman had shown me in such a short time.

I got up and went to work on Friday.

When my work week ended, I decided to do my little special treat I gave myself if I didn't miss a day at work for the week. I knew that seemed ridiculous, but I'd had a problem with not going to work in the past. All work was for me was going to an office building and I got paid for doing so.

I pulled into the bakery parking lot. I parked in a spot right next to the handicap spot in front of the bakery. The name of the bakery was Hot Treats, and that was exactly what they were. They made all these delicious desserts and they heated them up and when they served them, they were hot and delicious. My favorite was the chocolate éclair with vanilla ice cream at the center. This was so delicious that I literally only allow myself to have this treat three times a year because it was so insane tasting. I could eat two every day, at least until they made me sick.

I stepped out of my car and on the ground were three hundred-dollar bills. I looked around and there were no cars or people in sight. I picked up the money and sure enough, it was real money. I didn't know what I should do. I wanted to keep it and there was no real way to report this as found so they could find the person who lost it. The reality was, if a person lost three hundred dollars, they wouldn't report it, unless it was attached to their wallet or purse.

So, finders keepers. I put the money in my purse. I didn't want to spend a lot of time standing in a parking lot with the money exposed, even if I was practically the only person in this shopping center.

I went inside the bakery and ordered my éclair. I got it to go and I could heat it up in my microwave if it got too cold. What I was worried about was the vanilla ice cream. They had different kinds of chocolate éclairs to choose from. So I picked one that had nice vanilla custard in the middle. Within a couple of minutes, my éclair was ready and I walked outside. As I walked around my car, I could hardly believe what I saw.

Three more one hundred-dollar bills.

Now, this was getting serious. Did I park over a gold mine? I quickly put the bills in my purse. I dropped to my knees and looked underneath the car. There were no more. Sure, I felt a little disappointment, but six hundred dollars was officially the largest amount of money I had ever found. I've found a five dollar bill floating inside a toilet once...yeah, I grabbed it.

I got in my car and headed home with a smile on my face, knowing I had some fast money that I could spend on useless stuff I'd otherwise feel guilty spending my own money on.

I got home and knew Paris was still at my home. She was going to teach me one last spell before going home and supposedly visiting that dude, who, for some bizarre reason would never say his name. It bothered me at how secretive she was about him, especially after I had confided in Paris everything about me.

After a bit of small talk, and more attempts at trying to get her dude's name, Paris had me stand up and taught me a health spell that was simple enough. You say it when you are injured or feeling sick.

After the lesson, Paris, fell silent.

"What is it, Paris?" I asked.

In a soft voice, she said, "This entire week, I've seen an evil surround you. At first, I thought because you're a newbie and sometimes that happens. But normally, that lasts for about a day."

"Evil?" I said. "What evil?"

"Sahara, it's been three days and I still sense and feel it around you. You have a lot of darkness that surrounds your aura and I'm not sure where it's coming from. I'm going to recommend you do the aura-cleansing spell multiple times a day until this evil moves away from you. I want to teach you one more spell and unfortunately, you won't know if it works until Black Magic is used against you, but because I sense and feel this darkness around you, I think I need to teach one more spell today."

Paris taught me six short lines. I said them out loud because there was no Black Magic being used against me. I wanted to see if I could feel the power of the spell.

I said out loud, "I take back my power. At this very moment...this very hour."

Then a power was released from me and it swirled around the room in a breeze. I felt a comfort in knowing I had this spell and I could use it whenever I needed to.

115

Paris felt the breeze too and seemed pleased.

"That'll do it for the day. Remember, only use the spell when someone is using Black Magic against you."

I looked at Paris and I was a tad curious about what kind of power Black Magic had. I had seen what happened when regular magic was at play. I just wondered how menacing and powerful Black Magic was.

I had a strange feeling that I would soon find out.

Paris looked at me long and hard and then gave me a warm smile. Was she reading my thoughts? Or just maybe she sensed my curiosity.

We finished for the day and Paris told me she would be going to her guy's house. She said they were going up to a weekend trip in Arrowhead.

Okay, that was a little more information. Maybe it took Paris a while to open up about her own love life or whatever was going on between her and her guy.

I had a feeling Paris liked this guy a lot more than she let on.

After Paris left, I put my phone on my coffee table, and collapsed on my couch in the living room. Doing magic spells was tiring. I was expecting to get a phone call from Donovan and possibly Robert, but Donovan was so weird. He might think the ball was in my court and I needed to call him to finalize our date for tomorrow night.

Maybe that is why I am holding off speaking to Robert?

As I lay on my couch, I turned on my living room TV. It was a flat-screen. I think that was all they made these days. Or at least, that was all the big stores sold. I went through my recorded shows that I had on my DVR. I had some favorite shows and I was behind on a couple of them. My TV show watching was as eclectic as my current music interest. I watched every kind of show. I guess it came down to writing and believability.

Believe it or not, believability was important to me in regard to reality shows. Some shows I knew were completely scripted. And then, there were other shows I just knew were real, like *Survivor* or *The Real World*.

My favorite comedies ranged from dark humor to slapstick. I thought a sense of humor was one of the greatest traits we had as individuals. I thought the world was funny. Sometimes, dark humor made me laugh, and sometimes, silly slapstick humor gave me the giggles, depending on my mood.

I loved crime dramas and game shows, late night TV, Fox News and MSNBC. That was what a person slowly became when they gave up dating and just committed to being single—a TV aficionado. I had developed weird navel gazing about myself and my love for TV was very much about learning to know myself and understand myself better through my choices and interpretations of shows. I did the same thing with novels and was a voracious reader.

Tonight, I was watching a stand-up comedian on Comedy Central when my eyes felt very heavy. Extremely heavy. I hadn't even opened my éclair bag yet. I had put it in the refrigerator. I was thinking, why didn't I tell Paris about the luck spell working? I was meaning to, but I never did. That was my last thought I remembered before I was knocked-out, sound asleep.

I slept on the couch all through the night. I didn't go to the bathroom once. Just ten hard hours on that couch. I woke up, wide awake, at 4:00 in the morning and boy, did I have to use the restroom.

I was surprised that my phone never went off. I looked at my phone and I had no calls, no messages. That was weird. I felt a little sad about that. Maybe I wasn't as popular as I thought I was.

I was the one who hadn't officially gotten back to Robert and it was already Saturday. I still wasn't sure why I didn't confirm. Maybe a part of me felt bad about dating two guys in the same weekend.

This was extraordinarily early to be up on a Saturday morning. I hadn't done this since I used to get up at six in the morning to watch *ThunderCats* on Saturday morning cartoons. Did they even have those anymore? Saturday morning cartoons on ABC, CBS, and NBC? How could they compete with Cartoon Network? Still, that was an awesome part of my childhood.

117

I decided to make myself some coffee and go outside in my backyard. I didn't have a pool or Jacuzzi. But I had a cute red wooden bench under a canopy. I decided to grab a more advanced spell book and I took it outside to read through it.

I sat down with my coffee and with the porch light on, I could read my book rather easily.

I opened the book I picked up from inside and turned to the first page. The name of the book was *Spells for Others.* This was apparently a book about spells you can only do for other people and not yourself. This should be fascinating.

I skimmed through the introduction of the book and I liked what I read in the preface. It talked about how the intent of spells were to balance the good against the bad and only the witch could choose which side she were on. I remembered Paris telling me most witches chose to be on the side of good, because people were inherently good.

The book talked about when you used magic for someone who was outside the craft, how their natural reaction was one of four things: the person was lying and was trying to con someone, the person was nuts and I wanted nothing to do with them, or I believed them, but that was not for me, lastly, the reaction was...they believed and yes, this was exactly for me.

That was my reaction. The last one. I believed this was me to my core. I had a little of all of them and maybe the con one was a close second, but mainly, I believed because I felt this was my salvation.

Wow, I couldn't believe how excited I was to get into a book.

The book was broken up into personal stories, reasons for doing a spell for others, and the actual spells themselves. I couldn't believe anyone could just buy this book off the shelf. Granted, the bookstore was hidden behind a number of buildings and seemed the only clientele were women and men interested in witchcraft. It was probably a 'who you know' kind of place.

I began reading the first page. It was a personal story of this witch's name, Camella. I read her story and I couldn't help but feel like I identified with a lot of who she was before she became a witch. She then talked about balance. How balance was so crucial to the world's existence, so therefore, magic couldn't work outside that balance. When magic did work outside, it was usually Black Magic.

I read three more stories that were similar. The last story was the most fascinating. It was about a man who chose a life of being a warlock, so he could help others. It seemed bananas, but once I read his story, I saw how magic affected each of us differently, and sometimes, the only answer out there was to do something extraordinary and become a warlock.

I skimmed to the middle of the book.

There was an entire section on reasons why it was necessary to do magic for others. It talked about how to use magic for others when they couldn't do it themselves. And the book talked about how you guided them over this one hump that was preventing their happiness. Their whole world would open up to them.

Wow, that seems pretty intense.

I was thinking about the spell Paris did on my behalf and how much I noticed my world opening up to many possibilities.

I skimmed to the back of the book where the spells were broken up into categories. There were main spells, known as the beginner spells, and then underneath each of those spells were more specific spells. The stronger you became as a witch, the closer you could get to having immediate magic at your fingertips. It was about the most exciting bit of information I had ever read.

I read the spells in my head and purposely didn't read them correctly. I was afraid one of them might work, even if I didn't say them aloud. It was amazing that just one word out of order made it so a spell couldn't be active.

I started to think, *What if I didn't say them out of order? What if I allowed myself to do a little bit of magic on my own? After all, Paris says over and over again that this whole thing is a personal choice.*

I had an excitement building inside me. I was terrified as much as I was thrilled.

However, I had a haunting feeling, something I couldn't quite explain.

I was reading a section about how to move objects with a spell. I decided to see if I could do this without Paris in the room. It was a Telekinetic Spell.

I read the preface to the spell and the book of spells said, at first, to try the spell on really light items like a plastic fork or a pencil. Once you got the hang of moving smaller objects, you could gradually move bigger and bigger objects with the spell.

This was a little scary. I didn't have Paris here as a safety net. But I was craving doing my own spell as if it was a drug.

I decided to grab a pencil from my coffee table inside.

I decided I was going to try a Telekinetic Spell. I flipped in one of my advanced spell books and turned to one of the strongest Telekinetic spells that existed. It was called The Gravity Spell 101.

The book said you needed to be a High Witch to perform the spell. That was one level below what Paris was. Paris was a Most High Witch. I was going to risk some weird stuff happening if I tried to do this spell and something happened that I wasn't prepared for.

I read the spell almost twenty times in my head. I was trying to memorize it and "own it," like Paris had said. The second I owned it in my head, I decided I would say the spell out loud to try to move the pencil I had placed on my backyard table. The table was made out of wood. It was the color of Donovan's shoes...that first time I met him, back at the gym.

I took a deep breath and I got extremely afraid again and questioned if I should even do it. Power was such a temptress. I craved to see what I was made of more than I feared the unknown.

I looked at the pencil and said the spell as I had memorized it.

"The moon and the sun and the stars were placed once upon a time. I command the energy in you to move without rhyme."

The pencil was supposed to at least move a little bit. Nothing happened.

I waited a good ten seconds to see if that pencil would move and there was nothing.

Maybe I'm not cut out for this after all?

I looked at the spell again and looked to see if I'd said it correctly. I think I added an extra 'and the' when saying the spell out loud.

So, I looked at the pencil and once again, got very excited. I commanded the pencil again, this time, saying the spell correctly.

"The moon, sun and the stars were placed once upon a time. I command the energy in you to move...without rhyme."

Suddenly, my entire wooden table flew across my backyard in a rage of fury and crashed into the cement wall that connected my house to my neighbor's. The table shattered into many pieces. The force that it went into that wall was insane. It cracked the cement but it didn't break down the wall. That was one tough wall.

Holy crap! What did I just do?

I wanted to be petrified by what just happened, but I wasn't. I was actually very turned on. It gave me a thrill like no other to be able to do what I just did.

Then something happened to me. I began to crave power. Reading these spells made me hungry to receive as much power as I could. Next on my list was to master potions. Paris hasn't mentioned anything about potions. I was so tired of being mediocre. Then a dark feeling came over me and I tried to fight it off, but I couldn't. I began to crave learning at least one Black Magic spell.

None of my books had any Black Magic.

Suddenly, I realized what I was thinking and I did get afraid. I was afraid that I wanted the dark powers. I decided to take a deep breath and to go back inside.

I decided to stop and to go inside and digest what had just happened and debated on telling Paris about it.

Chapter Nineteen

I sat outside on my patio and watched the sun come up. As usual, I drank all my coffee, before heading inside for my customary hot shower.

I got out, dried myself off, put on a T-shirt and sweats and decided to catch up on *It's Always Sunny in Philadelphia*. Such a disgustingly raunchy show, but hilarious, and I was almost done with season three.

Then, soon after I had composed myself after watching a sweaty and naked Frank slime out from the inner depths of a leather couch, I began to obsess about magic again. But not the type of magic Paris had bestowed on me, but I began to wonder about the black stuff...the forbidden stuff. No matter how much I tried to put it out of my head, the power of magic, in general, was becoming quite intoxicating.

My obsession led me to the computer. I went online and researched everything Paris taught me, as well as the books she purchased for me at the herbal shop. After quenching my sudden lust for knowledge, I felt I needed more, so I trawled the inner depths of the Internet searching for every single bit of information regarding Black Magic. I probably would never do an actual Black Magic spell. I just wanted to see one, a real one. Not from YouTube, where any geek with a computer, and a little knowledge about post-production software could pretend to actually cast a spell; no, I wanted to see real magic in action, in person. I eventually found a website that claimed to sell real spells. They didn't claim to have Black Magic spells lying around. But I guess it was true when they said you could find pretty much anything and everything on the Internet, if you knew to where to look, of course... or had some elite *Google-Fu* skills.

What led me to this store was the following term, "Black Magic Spell Book bookstore California." Thanks to the all-powerful, and all knowing breach of privacy Google specialized in, the search revealed a local shop that claimed to have a forbidden spell or two in its inventory.

There was a store in Westminster called Esscenxe. Westminster was not very far from where I lived. I had no idea what else they sold. But I got their address and put it into my GPS.

The store opened up at 9:00 a.m. so I had plenty of time to get there. I took my time and put on my usual wardrobe.

I got to Esscenxe with a little bit of time to spare. The store was surrounded by various shops, all catering to the local Korean community. I might've been in Koreatown; then again, I remembered Koreatown was in L.A., and Little Saigon was in Orange County. But I knew for sure the signs were in Korean; the same type of lettering was displayed in front of one of my favorite restaurants that served bulgogi, a type of marinated, grilled beef that tasted as if it were handed down from the heavens.

I parked my car and walked a few feet to the store. It was another herbal medicine shop. I wondered why they kept that a big secret on their website.

I stepped inside and was greeted by horrid dark lighting. I could barely see anything.

A woman greeted me behind a counter. I looked around the store. Vitamin bottles everywhere. Five shelves, filled top to bottom with natural cures, ranging from cod fish oil to colloidal silver, whatever the hell that was.

I stepped up to the woman and had no idea if she even knew that the store she worked in had been implicated on the Internet as a Black Magic peddler. I started to get the sinking feeling that the site may have been a hoax and probably was a bait and switch tactic so customers would buy their herbal remedies.

But the shop that Paris had taken me to was also an herbal place.

The woman at the counter looked to be in her late forties/early fifties. She had jet-black hair with large streaks of gray. Or was it gray with streaks of black? Either way, she was a rarity. An older woman who refused to chop her short.

"Hi," I said to the woman. "Can I ask you a crazy question?"

The woman looked at me and without missing a beat, she said, "I'll probably have a strange answer."

Was that her way of letting me know it was safe to ask anything?

I drove through morning rush hour traffic to be here, so I might as well ask the question. "I'm looking for a type of book," I said.

"What type would that be?" she asked in a condescending way. She was just waiting for me to ask. I didn't know why I was afraid of asking. Maybe, I thought once I asked, I had let another person know I was interested in Black Magic. "I'm looking for a book..." I said, stammering a bit, "a book about...that would...uhh...have Black Magic spells in it."

Oh my God. I said it.

"I see," the woman said. She knew I wanted to ask about Black Magic books the second I walked in here. The black attire probably gave it away.

"It's through the door," she said.

"What door?" I asked.

"The one you came in from," she said.

"That's to the parking lot."

"Is it?"

I wasn't sure if this woman was just messing with me or this was some potentially screwy Alice in Wonderland moment.

I decided to take a leap of faith, so I opened the door and expected to immediately feel and see the sun.

But there was no sun; in fact, as soon as I opened the door, I realized I wasn't outside, but inside a reasonably large bookstore that had nothing but books, or was I inside a Black Magic spell? How could I be here? Was I in a different dimension?

The room had a wooden décor. The only source of light was from the couple of fluorescent bulbs above.

I browsed the books on the shelves.

I assumed they all dealt with Black Magic. Feeling slight unease, I looked around. There were two other women shopping and another woman behind the counter, a different cashier than the one I encountered as soon as I entered the store. I wasn't sure how I was going to ever get to the parking lot again.

This cashier was much friendlier and much younger. She had blond hair and was rail-thin. Unhealthily thin. I think the gray-haired lady outside was like a guard dog, and her job was to keep out the riff-raff.

The cashier smiled at me as I walked up closer to her.

"Hello," she said. She looked to be around my age, maybe younger. Probably younger. "Can I help you find something in particular?" she asked me.

Okay, here it is. Showtime.

"I'm looking for a particular kind of spell book," I said.

"Any type of spells, in particular?"

I said, "I want a spell book that will show me how powerful my magic has become."

"Hmm," she said. "So, you're saying you want a book that will challenge you?"

"Something like that," I said.

The lady came out from behind the counter and very swiftly grabbed three books that were in different locations of the store and brought them up front and laid the books in front of me.

All three books were rather small. Almost pocket-size, compared to the massive books that Paris had bought me.

One book's title was, *Ruling a Man for Life*. Okay, that was just extremely wrong. All I could think was that a Black Magic witch's scorn must be the worst scorn there was.

"I don't think I'll be taking this one," I said, handing back that particular book.

I looked at the next book and it had the smallest title I had ever seen on a book: *Warrior Spells*.

"What's this one about?" I asked.

"Sometimes, things get ugly and you need to be able to fight witch to witch. This book will teach that to you."

"It helps you fight?"

"Attack and defend," the woman said.

"I'm definitely getting this one," I said. The next book I laid eyes on was titled: *How to Defeat a Warlock*. "I guess this book is self-explanatory," I said to the lady.

"Men fight an uglier game. This book will help you think the way they do and keep you five steps ahead."

"Is it a book of spells?"

"Sort of. It's more of a power book."

"Power?"

"It shows you how to handle yourself in any situation you may come across with a warlock, including techniques that harness pure, unadulterated brute strength."

"I'll get this one, too," I said. I wasn't sure about the warlock book, but the lady was really pushing me to get it.

Both books cost me seven dollars. This place was ten times cheaper than the place Paris had taken me to.

I handed the money to the blond cashier.

I then asked the cashier, "How do I get back to my car in the parking lot?"

"The same way you came in," the cahier said.

"Okay."

The lady didn't give me a bag and she didn't give me a receipt. I turned around and the same two women were still shopping in the store.

I stepped out through the double doors, expecting to be back in the herb shop; instead, I was smacked in the head with sunlight. I was on the sidewalk in front of the shopping center parking lot. My car was to my left.

I got in my car and made my way back home. I laid the two books on my passenger seat. I often looked over at them on my drive home.

This time I didn't. A sense of guilt kept my eyes glued to the road ahead.

Chapter Twenty

I put the two Black Magic spell books I got from the secret Black Magic store in my empty room where I kept my books. I decided to hide them underneath some stacks of other books—didn't want Paris to find them.

I had a feeling she was beginning to pick up on sudden fascination and possible addiction to all forms of magic.

I just wanted to know what was on the other side. I wanted to know what I was up against if I was ever attacked with Black Magic. That was why the warrior spells seemed so appealing. I decided to grab the warrior book and take it outside to my backyard.

I wasn't quite sure what had happened in that store. But I saw some serious magic at work. That was certainly a power unlike anything I had ever imagined, something I could definitely employ if I ever wanted to mean business.

I flipped through the warrior book. It was filled with different types of combat spells. No, I never wanted to attack anybody using Black Magic, but I wanted to learn how to protect myself. So, I decided I would teach myself two different spells from the warrior spell book.

Now, defensive spells were used whenever one was attacked. Except that three fourths of the book were attack spells. I flipped to the back and tried to find a defensive spell that seemed to be the strongest.

I found one particular spell that looked promising, and it was guaranteed to work "98 percent of the time." Who guaranteed it? Who knows, but those were as good odds as any.

As I began to read over the spell, I felt a sense of authority. It took maybe five minutes to memorize it. A short incantation, thankfully. Actually, all warrior spells seemed to be short, especially the attacking ones.

Anyway, I decided I would say the spell out loud in its entirety. I wasn't being attacked by anything, so it seemed to be a safe thing to do.

But it is Black Magic. I don't know how intense this spell could be.

I started to get nervous and a little scared to say the spell out loud.

But gathered my nerves and said, "Menacing spirit, I speak against thee; take back your attack, or you shall face the wrath within me."

I decided I would only learn one attack spell, but not say it loud. The spell was very simple: "Lose control. Face your fate."

This spell was supposed to knock someone backward off their feet. Another spell I saw was something I didn't want to use—to take half a person's soul and add years to my own life. The things that were clearly evil didn't attract me. What attracted me was learning how to protect myself. I didn't want to seriously hurt anyone.

Suddenly, I heard my doorbell ring. It startled me.

It seemed weird that anybody would ring the doorbell. The only person who had come over to my house in months was Paris.

I went into my living room and walked to the front door.

I looked through the peephole and I could see a redheaded woman that looked like she could be my sister. Maybe she was selling Girl Scout cookies...for her daughter, of course.

I was in the mood for a couple of Samoas so I opened the door.

"Hello, Sahara," the lady said to me.

Before I could I respond, I instantly felt lightheaded. Flashes of light blinded me and suddenly I became deathly afraid.

It was Abigail, and she had slightly changed her appearance, which is why I didn't recognize her through the peephole.

"Why are you here?" I said. "How'd you know I lived here?"

"Aren't you the polite hostess?" Abigail said. This time, she was wearing a hideous guacamole-colored dress. It was the same type of cut as the horrendous bright green dress she had on last time.

Was this her deal? Wearing ugly green dresses?

"Why are zapping me with these dainty, annoying spells? Please, get lost."

"That is a shame," Abigail said. "I usually make a better first impression."

"I heard."

"You have?" Abigail asked.

"I heard how you used Paris. You made her think you were on her side. You made her think you weren't actually wicked."

"Wicked?" Abigail said, entering my house without being invited in. One thing was for sure, she wasn't a vampire. Vampires waited to be invited in before they killed you.

"Where are you going?" I asked.

"To your backyard," she answered.

"Why are you doing that?"

"I heard you were playing around with the dark stuff, and a little birdie told me you visited my favorite store in Westminster. Just to let you know, Irvine's got one too, and it is pretty much the same deal, but the one in Irvine does have the spell that traps your enemies inside a prism, where they eventually go insane looking at themselves from multiple angles."

"Will I get trapped inside a spell?" I said.

"Is that how you feel?" Abigail asked. "Do you feel like you were held against your will?" I followed Abigail into my backyard. She turned and faced me and my backyard cement. I had cement where the richer houses in the area had pools in the exact same spot. "Or, did you do everything you did voluntarily?"

"As far as Paris is concerned, that is none of your business," I said.

Abigail started to get very angry. I could see it in her eyes. I could almost feel her rage. "You are very strong," she said.

"Why would you say that?" I asked.

"Because you can already feel me. You feel my presence when I'm around you, but you don't know what it is. Only someone who is very sensitive to both magic and the spirit world can do that."

Abigail's statement didn't affect me the way I thought it would. I felt a sense of pride. "That doesn't mean I would choose to do Black Magic."

"You know, it's nearly impossible to double dip. There are only a couple of us that can do that around these parts."

"Is Paris one of them?" I asked. "One wouldn't know because she only practices good, wholesome, funny magic."

I was taken aback by the intense feelings she had toward Paris. I had no idea what had gone down when they had parted ways, but it must've been rather traumatic. The hostility they had for each other was beyond petty.

"Why are you here? Why are you tormenting me?" I asked.

"Tormenting you? Honey, you have no idea what torment is."

"Is that supposed to scare me?" I said boldly to Abigail. I now knew three spells that I could use to fight her if I had to.

"No, I wasn't trying to scare you. It was a just a tiny little warning, something you can stick under your cap and ponder later. Oh, wait, I forgot, you won't be able to."

"Why not? What are you saying?"

"Why do you think you couldn't recognize me until I spoke to you?"

"A spell?" I suddenly got very scared and realized that was the evil that Paris had sensed around me. Apparently, Abigail had put me under a rather strong spell—a forgetting spell, and who knows what else.

If only Paris were here, I'd ask her how I could combat such a nasty spell. Abigail had done me wrong, my short-term memory was severely diminished.

"Why have you come here?" I asked.

"I'm here to match Paris's offer. I will mentor you and teach you spells that will grant you the power you've always sought after. Aren't you tired of life and people kicking you down? Don't you want to get back at everyone who has wronged you? Let me tell, what I can teach you is...*better than sex.*"

"Don't think because you compared it to sex that it makes it more enticing." Better than sex? I shook my head. There was no way I'd take Abigail up on her offer, no matter how tempting it sounded. Paris not only was my mentor, but became my friend. "Thanks, but no thanks. I like the team I'm on," I said.

"Do you?" Abigail asked. "Is that why you wandered into one of our secret Black Magic stores and bought two books?"

"That is so creepy that you know all of that," I said.

"What you see as creepy, I see as an opportunity to teach one of the most promising witches to come around in a long time. You do understand that you have a power that is far greater than that preschool crap magic Paris is teaching you." Abigail paused and continued. "She hasn't even taught you what potions can do. I want to show you everything, all that is mind-blowing."

"Mind-blowing?"

"Yes, mind-blowing. There's a spell so powerful, you literally feel like your head is going to explode, like that movie *Scanners*, because it's just that strong! I won't hold anything back. Quick, easy lessons; you'll learn fast, and my potions are highly addictive and foolproof. Black Magic and potions are a match made in heaven, there's none of at preparatory crap involved like Paris's feel-good potions. Sahara, would you please consider being my apprentice?"

"Apprentice?"

"Yes, when you practice sorcery, that is what you are. But I am done speaking to you. I know deep, deep down that you want to come over to my camp. You can fight it all you want. But next time, if I don't get a decision, I'm not going to be so friendly."

"This is friendly?" I said. "You threatened me."

Abigail stared at me and said, "Wiser is she, wiser is he. You won't remember me until the next time we speak."

Chapter Twenty-one

I woke up on my couch. I had no idea how I ended up crashing on it, but considering the crowd I was hanging with of late, it was certainly a welcomed inconvenience.

Learning, fighting, and conversing with witches definitely made my life way more interesting than it was before. The memory lapses, fits of missing time, and being at the center of a mystical relationship turned sour, was beginning to wear me the down.

I eventually remembered why I woke up on the couch. Eager and without much needed training, I played around with some of the spells from the books I had purchased from Esscenxe. I was lucky I didn't end up getting killed or turning my neighbor's home into a mud hut. Magic was definitely the reason why I had blacked out and ended up on waking up on my couch.

Something definitely happened between the time I evoked the spell in the backyard and the moment I woke up on the couch, because as soon as I stood up, I noticed my clothes were in tatters. But what?

I wasn't sure what havoc had ensued.

I picked up my phone. It had been a while since I received a call from either Robert or Donovan. I debated calling Robert, as I missed his sincerity, and his kindness, but decided against it.

I took a shower, changed my clothes, and played around with more benign spells in the backyard before I received a phone call around 11. It was Robert. I almost didn't pick up his call. I felt somewhat guilty about Donovan, and since Robert was so damn nice, I felt I needed some time coming to terms on how I felt about him. But I yearned for his pleasantries, and who wouldn't want to talk to someone who hung on your every word.

"Robert," I said, "I was just thinking about you."

"Yeah, me too. I mean, of course I was thinking about you, it's why I called you. Yeah...uh, yeah, that's one of the reasons why. But listen, remember how I had asked you if you wanted to go out sometime this week. Well," he said, clearing his throat, "I just wanted to let you know that I gotta postpone. I forgot I was going to a writer's conference. It actually started yesterday, so I've missed quite a chunk of it already."

"Okay," I said. I wasn't sure how I felt about him cancelling a date with me, even though I hadn't committed to a second date. I bit my tongue. Robert did the courteous thing by calling me. He definitely didn't have to do that. Internet guys were usually pretty rude post first date when they weren't interested. Not Robert though, he was more eager to see me after our first date, and more thoughtful too, when you compared him to other guys.

"You know," Robert said. "My flight doesn't leave until 4:00 p.m. You wanna meet for lunch somewhere?"

He was making an effort to see me one last time before he flew out of town, how could I say no? "Where's the conference?" I asked.

"Chicago. I'm only going to be there for the dinner tonight and the book signings tomorrow."

"Where do you think you want to go to lunch?"

"If you're interested, we could meet at a place downtown, or I can pick you up, I mean, there will be plenty of time after lunch and my flight. I'll be able to drop you off, what do you think?"

"Why don't I pick you up instead, Robert?" I said.

"You don't have to do that. I can pick you up."

"You can pay for lunch. I'll drive."

I wasn't sure exactly why I was *jonesing* to drive. But I wanted to get out on my own accord. I had had a long freaking morning.

"Can you text me your address?" I said. "Then I'll put it in my GPS."

"Sounds good. Can we do this soon though?" Robert asked.

"How about in a little more than an hour? It shouldn't take me that long to get ready." I had already done my makeup, but I still need some freshening up, I thought. I didn't want Robert to remember me in an awful light before he skipped town for a couple of days.

"Okay, how about 12:30 then?" Robert said.

"Yep."

"Okay, I'll see you then."

"Bye, Robert."

"Bye, Sahara."

As I spent the full hour getting ready—didn't expect it to take that long, but wasn't surprised it did as I wanted to look my best for Robert—I started to realize that I had wanted to see Robert all along, but was too afraid to accept his offer or of asking him myself.

I spritzed on some perfume and realized I had only fifteen minutes left if I was to make it to Robert's house on time. If there was traffic on the 91, I would've been screwed.

I put myself together and grabbed my purse and got into my Mazda. I made it onto the on ramp with ten minutes to spare, and luckily, traffic was very light.

The GPS informed me that I was twenty-two minutes from his house. Unless my Mazda all of a sudden doubled its horsepower, I was going to be at least ten minutes late.

After risking a ticket by illegally driving down the carpool lane, I made it to his house in ten minutes. I parked my car in his driveway, and from the outside, his house was one of the largest one-story homes I had ever seen. It seemed to extend itself to the other side of the block. He'd said he was renting. But still, the rent in these parts, for something much smaller, wasn't cheap.

I walked to Robert's front door and knocked. I peeked through the small glass-stained window in the center of the door and could see Robert holding a pink carnation, looking as handsome as he did the other night.

"Hi," he said as he opened the door, a giant smile widening his face.

"Hello."

"You look amazing," he said. I virtually wore the same thing I had worn on our first dress. But this time in satin, and with a subtle purple and lime green trim. Apparently, Robert liked the look as well, as it was confirmed by the sparkle in his eyes.

"Does my chariot await, milady?" Robert asked.

"Chariot? You're in a time crunch, my friend, I brought forth a 4 cylinder demon on wheels from the future," I said.

"Don't worry, we've got time, but if we continue to stand on my porch, then our lunch date will be nothing more than a short power lunch. Plus, I got two alarms. One on my watch, and one on my phone, and oh yeah, my tablet too. Three alarms; enough to keep us aware of our limited time if we get engrossed again."

"That sounds a little OCD to me," I said.

"I think we are all OCD a little, or we wouldn't remember to get anything done." Robert got embarrassed. He smiled and drew back a little. He apparently thought I was implying that he was gushing over me and that wasn't what I was implying. I was making a joke.

"All right, let's go," I said. I walked over to my car and got in the driver's side. Inside, I pushed the door open for Robert.

Robert put on a pair of stylish sunglasses, which I felt definitely complemented his cherub-like, but otherwise cute face. He had a lot of confidence for a big man. Heavier guys tended to be a bit insecure and would come across as shy and self-conscious. But not Robert. I wondered if he had always been kinda thick, or if his weight gain had been a recent happening. It didn't matter to me though, because it didn't seem to matter to him. He was as confident with himself as Donovan, and they couldn't look any different, but interestingly enough, they shared the same brashness and insecurities.

Quite fascinating.

"You know your way around these parts," Robert asked.

"About ten years ago, I was a pizza delivery girl in this area. The tips weren't bad too. I was bringing in more money than friends I had who were waitresses at upscale restaurants. People out here loved their pizza, and they were very grateful to get it from me. A ten-dollar tip wasn't uncommon, actually."

"Nice. What was the name of the pizza joint?"

"Frank's Pizza."

"Oh my God, I love that place," Robert said.

"Either way, that is why I know the area," I said.

"Cool beans," Robert said.

'Cool beans' was an idiom we both shared. Funnily enough, it was a term I'd use whenever the person I was having a conversation turned into a dullard. I had hoped it didn't mean the same for Robert.

"Yeah, cool beans," I said. I looked into his eyes if he took it the same way as me.

"Yeah, I have no idea now what we're talking about," Robert said, laughing.

"Beans," I said in my silly way. "We are talking about beans and why they are cool." I was trying too hard. Saying 'cool beans' wasn't funny, and I refused to move on.

But Robert laughed out loud. He had my kind of sense of humor, which was a gigantic plus in my book.

I turned right on Harbor and parked behind one of the buildings facing the boulevard.

"Where are we going?" Robert asked.

"I thought you knew," I said.

"You were the one that just kept on driving to this area. I'm not familiar with food places down here because they go out of business so frequently. It is a little hard to keep up."

"I know a place," I said. "I haven't been there in years, but it's pretty cool and I think you'll dig it. Amazing sandwiches, my friend, like totally amazing."

"You're a foodie?" Robert asked.

"I'm a foodie," I said.

Chapter Twenty-two

I walked with Robert to the sandwich place. It was in an establishment that had a two-way entrance with a cashier on both sides. We were coming from the back of all the stores and restaurants that were on Harbor Boulevard. I wasn't sure if this place was still there, but I remember it being so damn good, I had a sneaky feeling it was.

Robert walked alongside me, forcing me to go at a faster pace. He knew he was short on time, and probably wanted some quality time with me. I thought it amusing.

We walked down an alley. Not some scary alley in a bad part of town, it was a red brick alley that looked more like a place you'd play an instrument for tips. I didn't remember it looking this nice the last time I was here. The city had done a nice job of making downtown more welcoming.

After a two minute walk, there it was. Chow's Deli. And the graphic of the owner's red, fluffy Chow-Chow was still in the center of the window, wearing the annoyingly-cute checkerboard chef's hat.

"Here it is," I said. "It's still open. So, not every business closes down as frequently as you think in this part of town."

139

"I stand corrected." Robert said, with a humble smile. A jerk would've looked annoyed.

I hopped in through the back entrance, over a couple of steps. It kind of reminded me of Donovan's backyard. I should really stop thinking about Donovan with this sweet man next to me.

"Let's find a spot to sit," I said to Robert. "If memory serves me right, it's self-seating."

Robert and I found a booth near the middle of the sandwich shop and sat across from each other.

A cute, little, dainty waitress came up to us who couldn't have been older than twenty-one. She had long brown hair, which I liked, but her makeup was a little too Miss America for me.

"Hey, guys," the waitress said. "Welcome to Chow's Deli."

"Chow's Deli?" Robert asked. It wasn't the first time he had heard the name. I think he was trying to flirt a little with the waitress.

"It's playfully named after the owner's dog, Rufus," she said. "Sadly, he passed last winter."

"Awwww..." we both said. Robert looked sincerely touched.

"Chow is actually the owner's nickname, too," I said. I remembered that from back in the day when I would come to this place all the time.

"We get mistaken for an Asian restaurant all the time," the waitress said. "We get calls asking for lo-mein specials all the time, but this place couldn't be more the opposite. You're in hoagie heaven."

"Two drinks first, please, as I want to give my friend here some time to look over your menu," I said.

"Take your time. What would you like to drink?" she asked.

Robert looked over at me, allowing me to speak first. "I'll have Dr. Pepper."

"We have Mr. Pibb," she replied.

"Even better. Most places don't have Mr. Pibb, so I'm stuck with the second-best thing, which is Dr. Pepper," I said, looking at Robert, embarrassed and expecting a reaction to my juvenile thinking.

The waitress didn't add to my response and jotted down my order. She turned to Robert and gave him the biggest, friendliest smile. "And you?" she asked, bouncing on her hip.

"I'll have the same," he said.

"Mr. Pibb it is," she said, as she made brief eye contact with Robert, smiled, spun around, and walked away from our table.

Had I said something to piss her off, or had she just flirted with Robert in front of me? I think Robert may have actually played along too.

I gave him a questionable look. I knew I needed to address this immediately or it would eat away at me all during our lunch date.

"If you want," I said, "we can get her number for you. But I doubt she'd date someone twice her age."

"Rrrrearrrr!!!" Robert said like a cat, implying I was being jealous. "I was just being friendly. I was actually trying to make you laugh. I really wasn't flirting with the waitress. I would never dream of flirting with another woman when I am on a date with you. That isn't me and I apologize if it seemed that way."

Damn, that was the perfect thing to say. He was right. I was being unnecessarily jealous. What the hell?

"So, Chicago," I said, changing the subject. "It seems kinda odd you'd forget about this convention; they usually cost a pretty penny, no?"

Robert smiled and said, "The truth is really embarrassing. It's one of those things that may come across as weird. I think it's better if you don't know."

"Okay, now you have to tell me," I said. "I didn't realize I unraveled a secret."

"You're funny," Robert said, then he made a squealing sound.

"What was that?"

"It was me," Robert said.

"I know it was you," I laughed. "Why did you just squeal like a hyena?"

Robert paused. He seemed rather apprehensive, but eventually said, "I didn't go to the convention on time because you told me you would get back to me before the weekend. So I waited until I couldn't wait anymore. Then I felt like a pathetic loser when you never called back."

"Wow, Robert. I didn't know. I am so sorry. I've been dealing with a lot of changes this week."

"It was hard. I'll be honest with you." Robert looked at me, as if he didn't want to say anything else that would possibly embarrass him.

"That is like the sweetest thing a man has ever done for me," I said, all while acknowledging how much of a selfish diva I was being. But thankfully Robert never quit, as he still called me and managed to score a last minute date, giving me the benefit of the doubt. He was a great guy. I still believed he was flirting with that waitress, though.

"I know, I'm not too suave, remember?" Robert said.

"You're two things that are better," I said to Robert and I meant every word. "You're honest and you're open. Those qualities beat suave any day. Don't get me wrong, a little suave can go a long way. But what you have is substance. That is the kind of thing that women realize they need."

"That's refreshing to hear," Robert said.

Robert stared at me as if he was looking right through me.

"What?" I asked.

"You have a good heart," Robert said, sadly.

"Why are you distraught?" I asked.

"I just see what's coming."

"See what coming?" I asked.

Robert then squealed again. I was starting to think he might have Tourette's. Robert took a deep breath and laughed. "I'm not sure what is going on, but I feel compelled to answer your question."

"Okay," I said. Now, I was absolutely fascinated with this man.

"I see the writing on the wall. The inevitable will happen soon."

"What's the inevitable?" I asked.

Robert looked at me with pain in his eyes. He still looked somewhat apprehensive, but he was speaking from the heart anyway.

142

"You'll just stop calling me. Watch. That's the way it works in the dating game. Whenever you like someone, they dismiss you. You'll have ten other girls interested, but the one you pay the most attention to, eventually dismisses you."

"Dismiss?" I asked.

"Because we're not really dating. We are two people who saw each other's profile on a dating site and agreed to go out and do a lookie-loo. To be honest, I'm shocked we're on this date."

"Why are you telling me all this?" I asked. *Talk about a sudden downer.*

"I have no idea. But it is weighing on my heart," Robert said.

"Look, just relax. Let's talk and get to know each other better. Let's not talk about things that haven't happened." I didn't know any other way to put it. This guy was burning down the house before we'd even bought the property.

"Okay," Robert said. "What kind of sandwiches do you recommend?"

"They have an amazing meatball sandwich—extremely filling. I'm probably going to go with my second favorite sandwich here; their Monte Cristo. It's out of this world. "

"They make Monte Cristos here?" Robert asked.

"The best ever." I meant it too.

"Bennigan's had the best one I ever ate," Robert said. "It's been years since I had a really good one."

"Well, you will love the way they make it here. It's heavenly."

The waitress came back and we ordered. I watched Robert the whole time. He passed the smell test this time. We both ordered the Monte Cristo with fruit. We knew the sandwich was going to be enough calories to last us all day.

"They usually bring the sandwiches out inside of five minutes," I said to Robert.

"That's about how long it takes Subway to do it right in front of your eyes, so you can see them not spit in the food. But I would imagine making a Monte Cristo would take longer."

"My motto is simple," I said. "I try not to say things that make anyone want to spit in my food."

"I guess that would be the easiest way to go about it," Robert said, laughing. "I'm usually great with waiters and waitresses."

"I was a server for Coco's in my twenties. It was all about good service back then. So, when someone gives me good service, I appreciate it."

"I'd tip ya an extra five percent," Robert said, jokingly.

"Funny guy," I said.

"You're too nice, Sahara," Robert said.

"So are you," I said. "That is really important these days. There are a lot of bitter daters who treat the dating world like they are ordering at a restaurant. I'm all about authentic, genuine people and you seem to be that way."

"I'm not usually this open," Robert said. "It actually surprises me how honest I'm being. I feel like I'm going to throw it all out there and you will either fall madly in love with me or you will run for the hills."

"Those are two pretty extreme choices," I said, laughing. "Maybe I'll be okay with something in the middle."

"In the past," Robert said, "I felt I loved too hard and chased the woman away."

"That doesn't sound like a bad thing. To love hard..."

"You do on a conceptual term. But when it is staring you in the face, it's a lot to handle if you're not in a place in your life to take that on." Robert once again gave me the same pathetic look like he had said too much.

"I guess it is when the person feels it's the right person for you. You want the person you're in love with to love you hard right back," I said.

"I think you're right," Robert said. The waitress came back and gave us our drink refills. I watched Robert as she put the drinks on the table. He went out of his way not to look or talk to the waitress again. The waitress left and Robert looked at me and smiled, "Why the hell are we talking about this?"

"I don't know," I said. "All I know is that it is a real serious topic for a second date."

"I don't look at it like that."

"I know you don't consider what we're doing a date."

"I think if you go out a second time, it is closer to a date than the first date, but you're still not there yet. You need five dates to really know someone's bullshit."

"I think you're right, Robert," I said. I had never heard a man talk like this, except in the movies.

Robert looked at me and gave me a knowing grin. He had such a handsome face.

"I want to know more about you," Robert said. "Tell me three facts about you that you don't think you have shared with a single person in over a year."

"This is an interesting way to get to know someone," I said. I thought about Donovan when he asked me about my passions. Both these guys were one of a kind.

"Why not make it fun, and sometimes you find some really cool stuff about people?"

"Okay, let me think. I like questions like this that make me think in-depth about myself. I'm very self-centered that way," I joked. I thought about it and I said, "My first fact that I hadn't shared with anyone is how much I loved my mother. I loved my mother deeply. We were old souls when we were together."

"Why haven't you shared that with people?" Robert asked.

"Because she is in a special place in my heart and it's hard to share that part of me."

"I feel honored you shared it with me," Robert said. "She seems like a real woman."

"Yeah, she was. She loved me with all her heart. I loved her right back. She was the most amazing woman. I had some serious female role models in my life, I was extremely lucky."

"They must have been because you're pretty spectacular." Robert smiled at me and I knew he meant every word. I just did. I felt his honesty and it warmed me.

I looked at Robert and he was trying hard. Doing all the little things, saying most of the right things. Maybe a little too honest, but he laid it all out there. Most men never opened it. You left the relationship knowing less and less about the guy because he hid himself more and more.

The waitress walked up with a tray that had two gigantic Monte Cristo sandwiches with fruit and a saucer full of strawberry jam. "That's how you eat a Monte Cristo. Try dipping your egg battered sandwich in jam."

"It's almost like having a French toast sandwich. I can feel the pounds already settling in my stomach. This is probably the most delicious-looking sandwich I have ever seen."

"And you haven't even tasted it yet," the waitress said. "I'll be back with more refills."

The waitress left and Robert took a bite of his sandwich. His eyes lit up the second the sandwich hit his taste buds. "My goodness, that is delicious."

"You truly feel the face of God smiling on you after you take your first bite."

"I'm not sure if it was that spiritual of an experience for me. It is really good. I have to be honest, it's hard to eat a sandwich that makes you feel so gluttonous while eating it."

"Okay, buzz kill," I said. "I'm done eating." I looked down at the sandwich and it really was gluttonous looking. "The fruit kind of offsets the batter-dipped sandwich that is meant to be dipped in jam when it already has powdered sugar on it."

Robert smiled at me and said, "I think you put too much pressure on this poor sandwich. It couldn't possibly live up to the hype you were dishing. I don't think I have ever eaten anything in my life that gave me the kind of experience you're promising with this sandwich. I'm just saying, you might want to pull back a little." Robert winked to assure me that he was keeping the conversation light.

I ate my own sandwich. It was really good. It was just like I remembered. I knew I wouldn't be able to finish it.

I looked at Robert. He was trying to eat his sandwich and it was falling apart all over him. I laughed out loud and said, "Let's get out of here and go for a walk before you have to leave."

"All right."

"Excuse me," Robert said to the waitress. "Could we have our check? We're going to take off."

"Was the sandwich okay?" the waitress asked.

"It was delicious," Robert said.

"I'll bring you guys out a couple of containers."

"That's okay," I said. "We're kind of in a hurry." I didn't mind, I was almost done with it.

Robert paid and left a tip and we went back outside and decided to walk in the front of the stores and go down Harbor. There are a lot of cute, quaint shops.

"It was a very good sandwich," Robert said.

"We can talk about something other than that sandwich?" I asked.

"Okay, you still have two things you have never told anyone for a year."

I thought about it and said, "I'll name one more and then you have to give me two?" I said to Robert as we walked. His hand slipped down and touched my hand. Then we began to hold hands. It was nice and I was going to have to think of another thing. I wanted to keep it light on the second one. "My dream car when I was younger was a white Corvette."

"Very sexy car," Robert said.

"I always thought so. Now, it's your turn."

"I tell you what. I'll do the same thing you did. I'll give you one serious one and one fun one."

"Or two fun ones," I said. I really didn't want this date get any heavier.

"Okay," Robert smiled. "I was arrested once when I was sixteen for going through a block and hitting every trash can I could with my truck."

"Did you have anger issues? At that age?"

"Not really. The two friends I was with all thought it was funny. It was funny until a guy cornered us in a cul-de-sac that looked pretty huge and we were stuck. The police weren't exactly nice about it. I had to do community service and pay for a couple of trash cans."

"You are a rebel," I said. "Ever been arrested as an adult?"

"No, and they sealed my records when I was eighteen. So, I have no record."

"That's good to know after I have been to your house to pick you up for a second date."

"What about you? Have you ever been arrested?"

I laughed. "I have a story similar to yours," I said. "Hey, this is becoming the third thing I'm telling you," I protested.

"You brought it up."

I looked at Robert and said, "Yes, I did. I worked at a retail job when I was sixteen and was stupid enough to take a twenty out of the cash register, knowing there was a camera on me. The loss prevention security guys had me arrested within an hour. It was scary. But I was also able to seal my records."

Robert and I both laughed out loud. "We were a couple of rebels. Trash can hitting and stealing twenty bucks."

"You now have two more things to tell me, mister."

"Okay," Robert said. He thought about it. "My brother is my best friend."

"He is? How many siblings did you say you have? I remember you mentioned it on our first phone call."

"I have one brother and three sisters."

"And your brother is your best friend."

"He and my assistant."

"I forgot you told me you had an assistant. Where does he live?"

"In a room in my house most of the time, but he travels around a lot."

"Sounds like a busy assistant."

"Oh, he doesn't travel because of me. He just likes to get away."

"Okay, your brother and your assistant are your best friends. You have to give me one more."

"I haven't loved a woman in the way I know I can in ten years."

I looked at Robert and I said, "You broke the rule. You went heavy."

"It was something I wanted you to know," Robert said.

Robert and I had consistently funny and endearing conversations. He really made no mistakes on this date and that was great for a second date. We went back to my car and he did the same thing where he opened my door to let me in. The driver side door. He gently took my keys and found the one he needed and opened the door for me. He was two for two in a big way. We'd see how long that would last. By date ten, he'd be asking to drive.

Date ten? What was I thinking?

Chapter Twenty-three

The date ended with me driving us back to Robert's house. I got out and walked with Robert to his door. It seemed like the right thing to do.

Robert hugged me goodbye, and leaned in and gave me a fantastic kiss. It was as if his lips had electricity. I went back in for a second, third, and fourth kiss and I only do that when I liked a guy a whole lot.

What the hell was I doing?

I'm not hurting anyone. One of the guys I liked had a spell on him and didn't even know what he was probably doing. The other guy seemed to like me a whole lot for me for who I was as a person. I liked who he was as a person, too. Robert was very charismatic, all the while maintaining a gentleness that seemed incredibly humble.

Robert hugged me and held me in his arms a little longer than one should if they were hugging a friend. This was definitely a romantic hug. I hugged him back strongly. His body was both hard and soft. But it felt right, being in his arms. He smelled incredible.

"What are you wearing?" I asked.

"Guilty by Calvin Klein."

"All I can say is yum."

We released our hug and Robert said, "Would you like to go to dinner on Tuesday night?"

"What's on Tuesday night?"

"Nothing. I just thought if you could put me on your schedule, you would be expecting me to come over to pick you up at the right time."

"I get it. Get a commitment on the second date so you don't have to wait around for an answer. And once again, I want to say I'm sorry for doing that to you."

"It was my decision to stay," Robert said. "And now, I'm glad I did."

"Where would you like to go?" I asked.

"Do you like Italian food?"

"I love Italian food," I said.

"Well, there is this really cute family restaurant over on Ball Street. It's called..."

"Mama Cosa's...I've been there, I love that place. You're talking about the place that has all the celebrities on the wall."

"Sure am."

"That sounds awesome. Pick me up at 6:30 on Tuesday night. If you still want to go."

"Of course I do. So, it's a date," Robert said.

"A third date?"

"Yes, I must say this second date has been a lot of fun."

"Just fun?" I asked.

"Okay, it has been exhilarating spending time with you," Robert said in a very genuine-sounding voice.

"Spending time with you has been romantically interesting."

"I'll take it," Robert said, laughing. "So, I'll pick you up in a little over seventy-two hours."

"Sounds very Special Agency."

"I'm a little anal when it comes to time. Like, I know I have exactly forty-seven minutes to get to LAX so I can check-in just in time. It's a time frame I give myself. It seems like I never have anything to do after I check in, but forty-seven minutes is my goal."

"Is that enough time?"

"Yeah, I already checked in online. I was being a bit dramatic. I have one hour and sixteen minutes until I board."

"That's a little bit scary," I said. "Can you turn that off?"

"Of course I can turn it off. I used to be a big flake and the only way I beat it was by becoming super anal about time. I only turn it on when something is really important to me."

"A plane trip is pretty important," I said.

"That wasn't what I was referring to."

"You are so sweet. I'm horrible with time. Thus, I was ten minutes late picking you up."

"You were twelve minutes late, but that's beside the point...I am totally kidding. I knew you were late, but not twelve minutes on the dot. It was more like eleven minutes and forty-two seconds."

"You need better time management."

"Easier said than done."

"Believe it or not, one of my jobs in college was to go to high schools and teach high school students how to budget and manage their time. I can give you a couple of tricks Tuesday night that I know will make a huge difference if you follow the plan right. It's how I finished college."

"Thanks. Well, you better go," I said, "I don't want to make you late for your flight. I don't think I could live with myself if that happened," I said half-kidding. I did a little wave goodbye and I turned around and walked to my car. "Hey," I said and turned around.

Robert looked at me.

"Have a safe flight," I said. "Also, be safe driving to the airport. Let's just say be safe."

"I will," Robert said. He looked pleased that I cared enough to say 'be safe.' three times.

Then I did something that surprised even me. It might be the first time I had ever done it. I blew Robert a kiss.

Robert didn't know how to take it. So, he did this goofy thing where he pretended to catch it. Then he blew a kiss at me.

"See you in seventy-two hours," I said.

"Now who has the OCD?" Robert yelled.

152

I looked back and gave Robert a big smile. He was a cool guy.

I opened the driver's door and I sat down and checked my mirror. My car still smelled like Robert's cologne. I liked that. I looked over at Robert's door and he was waiting for me to drive off. He was a true gentleman. I had a great date. He was now three for three. If we had a great date on a next date, Robert would be in very fine company. Only Johnny Redville, my senior year boyfriend, and Curtis Smart, my freshman year in college boyfriend, had ever made the list.

Unfortunately, Johnny only had three good dates in him. But Curtis got it up to six. He was an extremely seasoned dater. He always knew what to do. He always knew how to act. Most importantly, he knew exactly how physical to be without scaring me away. Yeah, he was probably the one that got away. But now, he was married to some woman from Chino Valley and the last time I heard, he was up to six kids.

We were worlds apart now. I was still watching season two of *Gossip Girl* and he was carpooling and changing diapers.

But when Curtis was at the end of his life, he was going to have six kids by his side and that was a beautiful thought. Not the dying part, but being such a great father that you have six adults who loved you so much that they would stop everything they were doing to be by your side. I knew he was a great father. He was a great human being. It was odd how I could both pity and envy him for the same thing in the same moment. That was me. Never defined. Never understood. But a heart just waiting to be loved.

Chapter Twenty-four

I went inside my house and I looked at my phone. There were no phone calls from Donovan. It bothered me a lot that he hadn't called. Our supposed date was in two hours.

Did he remember that we had a date?

He was the one who had asked me out. I hated when guys did this. I knew it sounded silly when I just went on a great lunch date with an entirely different man. It was the principle involved. I was getting mad.

I decided to get my mind off Donovan and look through my spell books. The good ones.

It was nearing 6:00 p.m. I just bit the bullet and called him. I was doing exactly what I had done to Robert. It did feel really shitty. I didn't care if I sounded desperate. I was going to call him.

He answered after three rings. "Hello," he said in a sexy voice. Not as sexy as Robert's, but I thought that was the only thing that Robert beat him at in the sexy department.

"How are you doing? It's Sahara."

"Hey, Sahara. How's it going?" Donovan had no clue.

"How's it going?" I said. "Did you forget we had a date tonight?"

"No, I didn't," Donovan said. "I actually just got off the phone from finalizing the plans."

"Really?" I asked.

"Yeah, really," he said and now he sounded a little insulted.

Great I'm going to have to apologize to this guy for not calling me. I'm not going to do it. Principles are principles.

"Where to?" I asked.

"Parker's Lighthouse in Long Beach. It's in a cool spot called Shoreline Village. Right next to the pier."

"I like that place," I said. "Fish food, right? My junior prom date took me there and then proceeded to talk to his buddy that we were double-dating with the whole night."

"So, you still good to go?" Donovan asked. "I kind of spent all day getting ready."

"Getting ready? How?" I asked.

"I got a trim and bought some clothes and I got this new cologne. It smells pretty awesome."

If it was on his body, I imagined it would smell quite lovely. "I'm sorry for thinking you forgot or decided you just weren't going to go."

Dammit. He got me to apologize.

Donovan paused and said, "I'm really sorry if you were expecting a phone call to confirm. Once we set it up, I set it in stone."

"You probably don't have too many dates cancel on you," I said.

"Yeah, I really don't know what that is like. You never answered my original question."

"Yes, we're good to go," I said. "When do you want me to pick you up?"

"How about six," Donovan said.

That was in less than an hour. Was this guy crazy?

"When are the reservations?" I asked.

"I think they said 9:30," Donovan said.

"You think?" I laughed. "There is a big difference between 7:30 and 9:30."

"I know it wasn't 7:30," Donovan said. "Maybe it was 9:30. Why don't you pick me up in about an hour and we'll head up that way? If it is 9:30, we can walk around the shops and enjoy our surroundings."

"That actually sounds really great. Okay, you live ten minutes away. Long Beach is about forty-five minutes from your house. It's 5:15 right now, so that gives me at least an hour to get ready."

"All right, I'll see you then," Donovan said.

You would think I was good as far as primping because I got fixed up this afternoon. No way, a dinner date along the shore required some serious extra attention.

Again, I used up every minute I had to get ready. I was wearing a cute little dress that was high on the knees and low on the cleavage. I liked this dress because it seemed to magnify my best features. My legs and my chest. At the same time, it sat on my less-flattering places rather nicely. It was an amazing dress. And it was black. I decided to go a little more Goth tonight than I normally did. My makeup was darker and my foundation was whiter. I looked like I had a little more edge to me. I wasn't sure at what level Donovan was attracted to me, but I thought I would at least have some fun with the spell before it wore off.

I got back in my Mazda and headed over to Donovan's house. It was pretty easy to remember where he lived because I grew up in this area and apparently he had, too. We had just had way different lives.

I had to be honest with myself. Why was I continuing to see Donovan, even though I knew his fondness for me wasn't legitimate? I knew the answer. I kept seeing him because no one that beautiful had ever said the kind of things he'd said to me. He sounded so genuine that I forgot he was under a spell. I just thought this sweet, gorgeous man was expressing who he was. He was rough around the edges. But I saw a diamond in the rough. He was as not well-rounded and well-versed as Robert, but he was just as honest and real.

I pulled up to his driveway. I decided to honk for his butt to come out. I wouldn't ever do the picking him up bit we did at the gym ever again.

I was just about to get reheated by that when Donovan walked outside. He was dressed in an outfit that made him look a tad like a pirate. He had on scarves and accessories that I had never seen a man wear. He pulled it off the way Johnny Depp had pulled it off in that movie. With a cavalier sense of style.

I unlocked the passenger door and pushed the door open. I could at least do that. Donovan stepped in and he smelled exactly like Robert.

"Is your cologne called Guilty?" I asked Donovan.

"I think it is. I went to this fancy place in West Hollywood earlier today and I took like this electronic test that was on the wall of the shop. It has you pick all your interests. When you're done, it tells you your perfect cologne match."

"You know for sure the cologne is called Guilty?" I asked.

"Yeah, I got a ton of it back at the house. What's the big deal about the cologne?" Donovan asked.

"Nothing, I just have a friend who wears the exact same cologne and it's just weird, that's all."

"It has been known for two men to wear the same cologne," Donovan said, laughing. Again, his humor was random, but he was trying to be funny and I thought that was cool.

I input the address to Parker's Lighthouse in my GPS on my phone. And then, we were off as I listened carefully for my GPS to get me to Long Beach. For some reason, that part of Long Beach had always confused me and gotten me turned around. So, using this GPS was going to be extra important.

We got to the freeway shortly and the GPS voice said that we had 14 miles until the next freeway and I thought it would be safe now to talk to Donovan. I had so many questions to ask him.

I spent the next twenty minutes having one of the freshest, most engaging conversations I had ever had. Not only did he answer any and every question I asked, he did so with vigor and then asked me the same questions back.

157

Some highlights of our conversation were that we both had our houses given to us by our parents. That was the extent we had anything else in common. He liked the kind of music I hated. He liked the kind of movies I disliked. Okay, he passed one item. He liked *Seinfeld.* Didn't love it. He said he liked it.

How could anyone with half a sense of humor not love that show?

So far, from what I can tell, Donovan does have half a sense of humor.

The most engaging thing he told me was he was a Big Brother to a kid from Whittier, the same city I'd worked in. He said he took him out for pizza and to baseball and basketball games. I thought that was amazing and I told him so.

"What about you?" Donovan asked.

"What about me," I said.

"Do you give back?"

Give back? That's an interesting way to put it.

"I do my fair share of giving to others," I said. "I'm a pretty damn good person."

"I believe you. I wasn't implying anything, I swear." Donovan reached out and held my hand. Just his mere touch shot tingles through my spine.

We were getting closer and closer to the restaurant. Donovan continued to hold my hand. My forehead was sweating. Donovan did something to me that was magnetic.

We made idle chit-chat until I got to the Shoreline Village parking lot. I parked my car rather close to the front. I got lucky. *Maybe spells are working already for me, even in parking spots.* Or just maybe it was a coincidence.

Chapter Twenty-five

We made our way through Shoreline Village to get to the restaurant. Donovan was no longer holding my hand, but he did walk rather close to me and treated me like I was the only woman he saw. I loved that.

"Want to check when the reservations were?" I asked.

"I already did. They are at 8:30," Donovan said.

"And you still made me rush to get here by 7:30?"

"I just thought it would be romantic to walk around and look at the boats and stuff while the moonlight in its fullest form is over the ocean."

"Donovan," I said. I took a deep breath. "Why are you here with me on a Saturday night when you could be dating every supermodel from here to kingdom come?"

"I like what I like," Donovan said, giving me an endearing smile and my heart completely skipped a beat.

"What exactly do you like?" I asked.

Donovan walked up to me and I thought I was going to die. He was so intensely hot. "I like your eyes. Your chin. The way your neck curves. That is very feminine. I like the person that you are. You seem like a really wonderful human being."

I was almost mesmerized by his words. I was putty in his hands. But I couldn't let him know that. "Looks can be deceiving," I joked.

"You have that other thing," Donovan said.

"What other thing is that?" I asked.

"You are just so inherently good that it makes your entire aura so beautiful."

Wow. That about the most amazing thing I had ever heard.

"Thank you," I said. Under a spell or not, he made me feel really special.

I began to feel emotional and guilty. I was emotional because I had no idea what was this guy's true personality. I felt guilty because Robert really liked me and I was out here playing games with the super handsome Donovan.

Donovan looked at me and said, "What's the matter?"

"Why do you think something is the matter?" I said to Donovan.

We were standing in front of a chocolate shop—a store where they only sold big chunks of incredible chocolate in bags.

"Do you want to go inside and get a treat before dinner?" I said to Donovan in my kind of sexy, flirty voice. It was less sexy and flirty, and more commanding. But I usually got what I wanted.

"I don't eat chocolate. It's bad for my complexion," Donovan said. "It's one of the few foods that gives me endless zits. Zits would be a career killer for me. I don't mind if you get a piece of chocolate."

So, we went inside the shop and I wasn't too much of a piggy. I got a modest size piece of dark chocolate. We left the shop and we made our way to the docks. We talked the whole time. I enjoyed every bite of my chocolate delight. I had one last piece and I asked Donovan to take the last bit.

"If I get a zit," he said, "I'll have my agent talk to you."

"You'll be fine. It's delicious." I fed Donovan my last piece of chocolate. I was hoping for this real, sexy moment feeding a gorgeous man chocolate. I didn't get that at all. I shoved the chocolate too fast in his mouth and he cough half of it out on the ground. Very sexy.

"That was harder to get down than a triple shot of Southern Comfort."

"I kind of jammed it in your face. Sorry about that."

We were nearing the docks, and Donovan reached out and grabbed my hand.

He is so weird. He just holds my hands at weird moments.

Then I thought about what the two places had in common. It was when no one else was watching that he held my hand. I needed to not think about that and I could have been completely wrong.

"Have you ever been in love?" I asked Donovan. This should be an interesting answer.

Donovan looked at me and just smiled. His smile was very sweet.

He had been in love.

"When were you in love?" I asked.

"I was twenty-three and she was twenty. I had just started to lift weights because I was tired of being picked on and called 'pretty boy.'"

"People did that when you were twenty-three?" I asked.

"Bullies are bullies. I was picked on most my life. I have always been told what a pretty man I was."

"Well, you are, Donovan. You can't stop that. You should embrace that," I said.

"It has been a lot easier the last couple of years since I've gotten pretty big."

"Your kind of big shouldn't be called big."

"What should it be called?" Donovan asked.

"How about *ripped*? Now, weren't you telling me about your first love?"

Donovan looked at me and smiled, almost as if he'd tried to steer the conversation away from the one we were having.

"Do you really want to hear this story?" Donovan asked.

"Yes," I said. "I'm the reason the cat is dead."

"What cat?" Donovan asked.

"You know the phrase... 'curiosity killed the cat'?"

"Yeah, I think I heard that once."

"Once?" I couldn't believe he thought he had only heard that phrase once in his life. "Please start your story," I said. "I'm dying to hear about your first love."

Donovan stopped and sat on a white bench. I walked over and sat next to him.

Donovan was looking straight ahead at one of the boats in the dock.

"I remember seeing her on the street," he said in a very soft, low voice. "She seemed lost and I did something that would be way creepy nowadays. But back then, it was something you did for people. I stopped and asked her if I could help her. I got out of my car, and I helped her sort out her directions. We exchanged phone numbers."

"What happened next?" I asked.

"She moved to Rome."

"Rome?"

"Yes, Rome...Italy."

"Why did she go there?"

"She was Italian. That was where all of her family lived."

"Was she on vacation?" I asked.

"That was the sucky part. We eventually figured out that we had lived just two miles apart all of our lives. But now, thousands of miles separate us."

"So have you and me," I said. I had no idea why I thought I needed to tell him that when he was trying to open up to me. "What did she look like?" I asked.

"She had long, beautiful, reddish-brown hair, just about your length. I have always been a sucker for redheads."

"You loved her?"

"We would write letters. Remember those? We wrote the most spectacular, beautiful letters. I mean we were up there with the romance letters of the Civil War."

I laughed. This guy was very cute. "What was it about her that made you feel the way you did?"

"She had such a deep soul. I loved her with all that I had," Donovan said.

"What happened?"

"She stayed in Rome and met a guy. They got married and had a couple of kids. She seems very happy."

"What about you?"

"Heartbroken."

"Even still?"

"A part of me is," Donovan said. "I think there will always be this part of me that is a bit broken because she is no longer in my life. I'm not stuck by any means. I'm wide open for someone to love me the way I know I can love." Donovan gave me a look like, 'Holy shit! What did I just say?' He looked deeply into my eyes and just nodded and said, "Yeah."

I almost fainted.

"Inside me is a deep soul, too," Donovan said. "And I have an insane amount of love to give."

Wow. An *insane* amount? What an answer. If this was a game show, he would have won the first prize.

"What about you?" he asked.

"Have I been in love?" I thought about the answer and I had one for him. "I thought I was in love a couple times in my life and I even told one man I loved him. But I realized I have never loved in the way I used to dream about when I was a younger."

"Look at Miss Open Book," Donovan said in a rather unsmooth way. "I like it. I've never been more attracted to you than I am at this moment."

"Are you serious?"

"Why do you question so much? Let my yeses be yeses and my nos be nos."

"That's from the Bible," I said, realizing that Robert had said the very same thing to me. *Hey, what's going on with that?*

"Yeah, it is. My mom taught me that when I was younger before she died."

"Were you two very close?" I asked.

Donovan looked at me and gave me the cutest, simplest smile. "I have loved no other the way I loved my mother."

"She sounds amazing," I said. "What about your dad?"

"My dad?" Donovan laughed. "When I was growing up, his name for me was Sissy Boy. Just because of my good looks."

"That's awful," I said, almost dumbfounded with Donovan's openness.

"He used to tell me I looked like a girl when I was a kid. He never did anything weird, but he was hurtful with his words. I never made him proud. Ever."

"He died when you were ten," I said. "You made him proud; he just had a hard time showing you."

"Was your father like that?" Donovan asked.

"My father went into a metamorphosis during my lifetime when he was still with us. When I was a little girl, like ages six to ten, I remember my dad being extremely strict and very overprotective. But after my tenth birthday, he started chilling out more and more, all the way till the day he died. I swear, if you heard some of the things he was saying right before he died, you would have thought he lived his entire life as a hippie."

"That was because his true self was a hippy," Donovan said.

"Why are you certain?" I asked.

"Aren't you? The man finally can be all the things he wants to be and he chooses to be completely liberal."

"He was leaning toward Libertarian points of view. Especially toward the end there." I looked at Donovan and smiled. "I have to say, I'm impressed with your social insight."

"You're amazed that I'm not completely stupid for a model?"

"I don't think you're at all stupid. That's a horrible thing to say about yourself."

Donovan looked at me and said, "I'm sorry. I just have been told those words for a very long time by a lot of different people."

"I'm so sorry to hear that." I was getting emotional.

What was I doing? I cared for this man. My defense of him was the most obvious sign. I didn't like him calling himself stupid.

"I think both of our fathers weren't fathers of the year," I said. "Mine had good intentions."

"I think mine did, too," Donovan said. "He died before I ever really got to know him."

I felt bad for Donovan. I felt sorry that he didn't get to share adulthood with his parents. I thought that being an adult and having your parents still alive was a very special relationship one could have.

"I'm sorry that you had a tough childhood," I told Donovan.

"I so want to pig out right now, it's insane. Let's head over to the restaurant."

Chapter Twenty-six

Donovan and I walked back to the restaurant. "I won't be eating that much," I said as we walked over.

"Why is that?" Donovan asked.

"Because I might want to sleep with you later and I don't want to be gassy."

What the hell? Did I just say that out loud?

I looked over at Donovan and tried gauge his reaction to what I said. I still couldn't believe I'd said that to him.

"I don't get gassy on a full stomach, I get stronger and I have more endurance." Donovan gave me a wink. What the hell was I doing? I just basically invited this man to have sex with me tonight!

"I am so sorry for my candor. I don't want you to get the wrong idea."

"It makes perfect sense to me," Donovan said in a practical way. "When a man and woman make love, the woman receives most of the thrusting. So, she has a higher likelihood of getting gassy. This is our second date. There's a chance we will close the deal at the end of the night and you're just being careful with your meal choice. I like that, actually." Donovan then gave me a giant, cheesy smile.

166

"I don't like that I said it," I said. "And if you can strike that from the record, Your Honor, I would highly appreciate it."

"Look, Sahara, we are all animals," Donovan said as he stopped me about fifty feet away from the restaurant. "We have hungers, attractions, and passions. Don't be ashamed of wanting more sexually. We all do on some level. The best sex I ever had was when I was in the deepest love." Donovan shook his head at me and said, "I don't think I have ever been this open with another human being."

I took that opportunity to be even more inquisitive about his past. "So, you did see the girl from Italy after the first day you met?" I asked.

"We saw each other five times before she got married."

"Really?" I said.

Again, that made me sad because I felt I was as open as I usually was. Especially when I was interested in someone, it just showed me how I couldn't trust anything Donovan had said to me. It might be just a way to get me into bed.

I looked at Donovan in his interesting pirate-type outfit that looked like something Errol Flynn wore, back in the day. He had on a real blousy shirt with baggy pirate pants. Donovan reminded me a little of Gaston from *Beauty and the Beast*. A much better looking, taller Gaston.

I had listened to Donovan open up and share a memory of his father that was painful. He also told me how much he loved his mother, which I found priceless.

Donovan looked at me and smiled. "Because most people assume I'm not too smart. It helps me out in the modeling world because you get babied everywhere you go when people think you are incapable of making simple decisions. So, most people during my professional day see a caricature that I created. It's one that I imagine a model to be. Is the caricature me?" Donovan asked himself out loud. "Some of it is. But it's mainly me trying to overpower the parts of me that make me the most...scared."

Donovan was speaking so beautifully. Maybe it was because we were feeling an amazing ocean breeze; one that was sweeping in where we were walking, and giving us a gentle romantic nudge.

167

I leaned forward and initiated a kiss with Donovan. It startled him at first, but he was a slick guy. He was able to get into the kiss very fast.

Once again, it was a sweet, gentle, kiss that made me feel all tingly inside. This kiss was a good five seconds longer than the other times we had kissed. It was...to put it as corny as I could...heavenly.

Dammit, Paris, I thought. *Your spell is working way too well.*

I was fighting my desire to fall for this guy and this wasn't fair because I'd rather keep talking to him and hearing how he felt about family, life, and other things than to just have one meaningless sexual encounter with him. *I have a feeling the second I sleep with him, that is when the spell wears off.*

Who would want that? It was bad enough if you sensed regret on a guy after making love, but to know the moment it was coming was a horrible thought.

I pulled my phone out of my purse and looked at the time. "We should walk over to the restaurant," I said. "They will probably seat us. Our reservation is in 15 minutes."

"Okay," Donovan said. Then Donovan did something he had never done before. He held my arm and talked with me as we walked. He wasn't ashamed of me and I could only imagine what people thought of a male supermodel holding hands with a lady in her thirties dressed way too Goth for her age.

What I noticed was that no one cared or paid attention. This wasn't high school anymore. We were all adults now. These were people going out and having nice Saturday night. Seriously, who had time to judge?

We went inside the restaurant and I waited for Donovan to check in with the hostess. Instead, he just sat in the waiting section. I don't know if he even expected me to do it, or he was a little ditsier than I wanted to admit.

I walked back to where he was sitting. "Do you want to let them know that we're here and that our reservation is about ten minutes away?" I asked Donovan.

"Didn't you just do it?" Donovan asked.

"No, I didn't do that. You are the one who made the reservations."

"Is that how it works? The person who makes the actual phone call has to be the same person that checks in? I think as long as you know the name...you're good."

"What are you saying?" I asked. "You don't want to get your butt up and check the reservation?"

Donovan looked at me and said, "I really don't. I would much rather sit back and allow others to do things for me. But, I see how much this irritates you, so I will be the man in this situation and confirm my own reservation."

The love spell that Donovan was under was obviously making him act and say weird things. I didn't know how many of these pseudo-dates I could handle.

Donovan got up off his butt and waited in line to talk to the hostess. He was third in line and he got to the front reasonably fast. He smiled and laughed with the hostess within seconds of talking to her. Then he proceeded to talk rather intimately with her. At least, it looked that way from a distance.

Before I knew it, he turned around and waved me over, saying we had a table.

Okay, that was too easy. I wonder what he said to her.

I'm not much of the wondering type. As soon as the hostess seated us at a table by a window that faced the ocean, I wanted to know what Donovan had said to her.

"What did you say to the hostess?" I asked Donovan. I wasn't messing around.

Donovan started to say something and then he just mumbled and blurted out nonsense that sounded very similar to the squeal that Robert had done the other night. This was really weird. Both of these guys wore the same cologne and had the same quirks? I thought I was going crazy.

"I'm sorry," Donovan said. "I have no idea what any of that was about."

"Maybe you got something caught in your throat," I said, trying to make sense why he would make such a horrid sound.

169

"Yeah, it was something like that." Donovan had a funny look on his face and then asked me one more time, "What was the question again?"

"I asked you what you said to the hostess. She seemed very eager to give us one of the nicest window tables in this two-story restaurant."

Donovan was about to make some weird noises when he said something really fast and I didn't get every word, but I knew it wasn't flattering to me.

"Talk to me slowly," I said to Donovan.

Donovan looked at me and as if he wasn't giving himself permission to tell me. He was doing so against his will. Donovan took a deep breath and said, "I told her I was on a friend date with my best friend's older sister and if she seated us quickly, I could take you home after dinner, and come back to get her and we could go for a ride on my motorcycle."

"Take me home?" I said. "Didn't I drive you here? Or, were you planning on leaving me here and taking my car to a dealership to buy a motorcycle? Unless you already have a bike at your house, then I can just take you home." I was livid.

"No," Donovan said. "I don't own a motorcycle. I'm actually a little scared to ride one."

"But you're driving up the coast later with Blondie the hostess," I said, a bit patronizing.

"Do you understand," Donovan said, his expression very serious, "that I said what I did so she would seat us quicker? She told me they were running one hour behind on their reservations tonight. One of the cooks didn't show up."

"Why did you tell her such an elaborate lie just so we could get a table? Is any of what you told the waitress true?" I asked, knowing this answer could sting a little.

"None of it," Donovan said firmly. "I only said what I said so we could get a good table. I had no intentions of sticking around here and going up the coast on a motorcycle I don't even own with a woman ten years younger than me."

"Really?" I asked. "Now I feel sorry for her. You lied to her to get us a table. It wasn't just a small lie. You made her believe in hope. She saw you and fell for you on sight. It wouldn't have taken much from you to have gotten us a table. You didn't have to break a girl's heart to do so."

"You're right," Donovan said. "Should I tell her the truth?"

I looked at Donovan and said, "It will hurt either way. You're better off not putting yourself through that. I just feel sorry for her." I couldn't believe it was the same girl I was just previously hating.

"I don't know why I did that," Donovan said. "Talking bullshit felt good. Not because I liked her, but because it was light and fun. We have been having some doozies of conversations. I was just getting us the best seat I could."

Was he full of shit? He was just as full of shit to the poor hostess. Why should I believe anything he says when he freely admits he lies to others to get what he wants?

What he was saying about trusting me so fast was pulling at my heart strings a little. Just being around him was making me crazy. I needed to talk to Paris. I needed for her to break the spell and if that meant Donovan went bye-bye, then I would be okay with that. But not knowing what is up or down with a guy begins to make a person nuts.

Chapter Twenty-seven

I decided to switch gears and just have fun. The rest of the night went pleasantly. Donovan was a perfect gentleman the whole time. We quit talking so intensely and changed the mood to that of young folks having fun on a date. I liked that. We were still being incredibly open with one another.

I was ecstatic when Donovan took out his credit card when the bill came. He had no idea how much that meant to me. Not because I'm a gold digger by any means. It was that Donovan wasn't a gold digger. As if I had any gold to offer him? Still, I needed to know if this guy had some genuine gentlemanly qualities. That was what was most important to me.

We talked and walked all night. We didn't shop. We didn't need to. Just walking by his side and feeling his hand in mine was a nice place to be. I didn't think I was going to get the chance to be here much longer. My emotions couldn't handle it, and it was slowly breaking me up inside.

Eventually, the date came to an end. I took Donovan back home to his house and I still hadn't asked him yet why he didn't have a car. Maybe there was a part of me that didn't mind picking up this gorgeous guy and hauling him around town.

I was pulling my car into his driveway.

This is where it's going to be weird. If he just steps outside and doesn't say anything, what does he expect me to do?

I parked my Mazda all the way up on the driveway. Donovan looked at me and didn't open his door. "You want to know something?"

"Yeah," I said.

"I think you're a real cool chick."

"A cool chick?" I said nodding.

"Okay...forget the chick part. I think you're a gentle soul that reminds me of a couple of different people in my life."

"Who are they?" I asked.

Donovan gave me a look as if to say why did you ask me that? Then he took a deep breath and squealed a tad. Again, with the squealing. I never had a guy squeal, ever on a date, for any reason whatsoever. While Donovan and Robert are having a squeal-off.

"You remind me of my mother. Not in a weird maternal way, but in her spark, in her eyes. She gave me comfort, much as you do. She was a bit fragile just as you are."

"Who is the other?"

"The only other person that ever reminded me of my mother."

Then it dawned on me he was saying I reminded him of his first love.

"The woman from Italy?" I asked.

Donovan smiled. He nodded his head slightly to confirm my question.

Was he full of crap?

"Donovan!" I just came out and said, loudly. "Are you being truthful with me?"

"I don't think I have ever lied to you about anything."

"You don't think?" I asked. "Do you lie that often?"

"I'm not really a liar, I omit details if I think it benefits myself or the person I'm talking to. For the most part, I always try to be as honest as I can."

"Okay, let me ask a direct question, so there isn't a way to omit any part of the answer."

"Okay, go ahead," Donovan said.

"The first time you kissed me was there any spark in the kiss from your end?"

"You questioned the authenticity of our first kiss?" Donovan asked.

"I don't want to."

"Sahara, our first kiss came from a real place. Just as all the rest of our kisses have." Donovan looked at me as if he was being as real and honest as one humanly could be without being a sociopath.

"I want to ask you a question it is probably unfair if me to even ask it, but I'm laying it out there because it's that important to me." I paused and looked at Donovan and said. "Are you promiscuous?"

Donovan stared at me and laughed a little under his breath. I wasn't sure what that response meant my curiosity didn't last long when Donovan said.

"I don't do that. I have never done that. I have been offered a lot of money to become a male escort multiple times and I turn it down every time."

Donovan looked at me as if he was a saint for not sleeping with women for money.

"Why would you turn it down?" I asked. "I mean...I know why I would turn it down. I was wondering, what were your reasons?"

"I believe each time two people make love, even in a one-night stand or an agreement, as you were...that person is permanently imprinted on your soul. There is a closeness that happens between two people when intercourse happens. To participate in it frivolously is just irresponsible."

I took a step back and tried to process what Donovan had just said to me. Damn, I wanted to be imprinted on his soul. This guy was saying all the right words and pushing all the right buttons and we were still sitting in the front seat of my Mazda.

"Would you like to come in?"

"Yes," I said. "I mean no. I want to, but I know I can't. Not yet. I hope you understand."

What was that?

"Can you at least get out, so I can give you a proper hug goodbye?" Donovan said in a cute way.

"Of course," I said. I opened my door and got out and just walked over to Donovan. I knew I wanted to kiss him, feel, him, taste him, and love him.

Donovan and I embraced at the front of my car. I left my high beams on, so my car was blasting us with major headlight action. It was epic, like a goodbye scene from an old movie.

Donovan looked me in the eyes and said, "I had about as much fun as I've ever had on a date."

"You're just saying that."

"No, I'm not. You are really fun to hang out with. Are you sure you don't want to go inside?" Donovan pressed his body up against me. My back was now pressed up against the hood. I could feel him getting stronger as he pressed. It was good to know that he was sexually attracted to me.

Unfortunately, I was going to have to leave him to take a cold shower. I just couldn't allow myself to be with one man and have strong feelings for another. That was why I couldn't sleep with either Robert or Donovan. I held my ground and Donovan backed up when he sensed my hesitation.

Very inquisitive.

"Donovan, I need to go. I had a lovely time and thank you for paying for dinner."

"Of course. I'm the man," Donovan said.

"Yeah, Donovan, you're the man," I said, smiling.

"Donovan," I asked simply. "Why don't you own a car?"

Donovan froze for one quick moment, but long enough that I saw. It was freaky. It reminded me how weird that guy at the all-night market acted when he was under one of Paris's spells. Paris's spell was absolutely screwing with my head on a level that was slowly making me feel like I was going insane.

I repeated my question. "Why don't you own a car?"

Donovan stared into my eyes and a tear began to drip as he stared without blinking. "I don't own a car for a reason that I have never told another soul."

I looked at Donovan and I had no idea if he would continue speaking. I was hoping he would. I was intrigued, to say the least. This was going to be deep and tragic. I felt a crazy story coming on.

"My dad was Rodney Haynes," Donovan said.

"Why does that name sound really familiar?"

"He was one of top ten auto racing stars of all time."

"How come you have a different last name?"

"Because my dad was a racecar driver when they were still trying to sell the sport to America and he changed his name so it sounded easier to say and more American. It just rolled off people's tongues a lot easier, kind of like Fred Astaire instead of Frederick Austerlitz. Or Michael Caine instead of Maurice Micklewhite."

I smiled and waited for more.

Donovan paused and I knew he was just trying to get ready to tell me the hard parts.

"The weekend before he died, I was ten years old, like I said. For some strong reason, I knew my father shouldn't leave and race that weekend. He had a fever, and he needed to be checked into a hospital, not going to a racing competition. I had never asked my dad for anything. I was always too afraid to. But not on that day. That day, I asked my dad not to go race. I was worried. He looked so pale and sick. I pleaded with him to the point that I was on my knees, holding onto his leg, so he wouldn't leave through that door. I knew it was going to be the last time I would see him."

"How did you know that?"

"Something told me. I had always felt it was a power of some sort. You can call it God. But I was being prepared for what I was going to witness on my black and white TV set that I had in my room as a kid. That was where I watched my dad's races, as he didn't want to be worried about me sitting in front, in the stands. It was dangerous."

My eyebrows raised a bit. I believed everything I was hearing and I knew Donovan was going to a dark place that I don't think he had ever revisited since this had happened almost twenty years ago.

I practically held my breath, waiting for him to speak.

Donovan lips began to quiver. The tears kept coming and I felt selfish.

Or was I being selfish? He seemed to voluntarily want to tell me his deepest, darkest secret. *But is he under a love spell or not?* I knew in my heart of hearts that he was speaking the truth. I wanted to know everything there was to know about this man. And if it all turned out to be a fairytale, then so be it. Right now, he was making a believer out of me.

Donovan looked at me and simply said, "During the race, and going into the curve, my dad crashed into a wall. At first, they said he died on impact."

"Was the crash because he was sick?" I asked.

"Being sick didn't help, but racecar driving killed him. I saw the whole thing on TV alone in my room. Alone in my house. I saw the whole thing play out like a docudrama right in front my eyes. They wheeled my daddy out on a gurney right there on live TV. I didn't even know if he was alive. I wasn't sure if I was seeing his corpse on a gurney being dragged along the racetrack to get into an ambulance. Even as a child, it seemed over the top. Why did they have to wheel my dad along the race track in front of all of the people? Why didn't the ambulance drive closer?"

"I'm sorry for you," I said.

"Later, they said he actually died in the ambulance. If that was true, the little stunt the network pulled for a dramatic effect, that he had died on impact, was purely about the television ratings and to make a big show of it to the people in the stands. The traumatized people. Wheeling the gurney down the track just might have been the seconds and minutes he needed so he could have...lived. I don't want to drive a car. I don't want to own one. I'm kind of traumatized by the entire scene as it played out. I don't want history to repeat itself."

I took in a big breath and let it out. "Where was your mom?"

"She was down the street with the neighbors. The neighbors usually got together and grilled in the front yards and watched the race together, with a TV pulled outside and plugged into a long extension cord. My daddy was really good. He would win or be in the top just about every time he raced. It was a guaranteed show. He was like the folk hero of the neighborhood, before, and after, too."

"You really loved your father?" I said to Donovan.

"He was the only dad I had, and I knew he wasn't always right. But he did take me fishing and we played miniature golf once. He called me *princess* the whole time, to tease me, but at least we did something together." Donovan stopped talking and took a moment, then he said, "I clearly remember him once telling me that he loved me."

"When did he do that?" Again, I was feeling so selfish for asking, but I had to know.

Donovan smiled at me as if this was going to be a different kind of memory. Maybe a happy one.

"I was six years old and I got real sick. Strep throat."

Okay. Maybe not.

"I was going in and out of consciousness on the hospital bed. I heard my dad tell me very clearly that he loved me and he needed me to live so he could have his little buddy back. I opened my eyes and I looked at him and my father, for the very first time, gave me a loving smile. No teasing or calling me *princess* or *cowgirl* for being too handsome. He finally called me 'Donovan.' And he said he loved me. I had to practically be on my deathbed for him to call me by my real name."

"I don't know what to say. That's one of the most wonderful, yet heartbreaking stories I've ever heard."

Donovan paused and I got the same feeling that he wasn't done speaking about his father dying. He hadn't told me about his mother. I was thinking I'd wait for that story until he was ready to share that. I wasn't going to ask. Not right now.

"I found out every detail about his death from a TV set. As if I was watching someone else's life. I couldn't believe it was my dad. My life, too, because he was secretly my hero, you know?"

"Yes, I can see that. Did your mom finally come home and comfort you?"

"Yes," Donovan said. "Oh, my God. I can't do this..." He looked like he was in physical pain as he talked to me.

"I mean it. You don't have to say anything else. I'm not asking you to."

"I need to tell you. I'm not sure why, but I feel incredibly *compelled* to tell you."

"But you have never told anyone else?" I asked.

"No. I think it's time, though."

"Why now?" I asked. "Why now, with me?"

"I trust you. It's the way you look at me. It's as if you see me for the man I am on the inside. Not just for the man I am on the outside. I have never told anyone what I'm telling you."

I was so morbidly interested, I couldn't stop now. I also knew I didn't want this guy to get so broken that he couldn't function. I thought he needed to let this out. I didn't even want to know what he was trying not to say. All I knew was, he needed to tell someone. And I was the one who was here, so that someone was me.

"Donovan, as much as I want to know more because you have already told me so much, I think...maybe I'm supposed to hear it. I think it will help you. I meant every word," I said.

Donovan leaned his back up against his garage door. I could see him remembering what happened. He said, "I had found out the news around 4:00 in the afternoon that my father had died. As I said, my mom was watching the race down the street at her friend's house. Actually, they were my parents' best friends. She usually did that when there were Sunday races."

He seemed stuck on that.

"And then what?" I asked, trying to get him to tell me the rest.

"Once I heard on TV that my daddy had died, I just walked aimlessly outside. The whole neighborhood was out in the yards talking and just looking at me as if I was the ghost of my father. No one came up to me. The neighbors went to each other, but no one felt the obligation to come over to the ten year old who had just seen his dad die on TV."

I was absolutely mesmerized by what Donovan was saying. "Would you like to go to your living room?" I said. This guy was being way too honest for it to be weird.

"Why would we do that?" Donovan asked.

"So you could sit down and possibly get a Kleenex and a glass of water." Damn, I was sounding like a mom. I wanted to make it clear we were not going to sleep together. Even though I was going inside, I knew there wasn't much hope for me if I walked into Donovan's darkened house at one o'clock in the morning. I could almost hear the farewell trumpet of *From Here to Eternity* playing on the way in.

I went in anyway.

I sat at the end of his couch. Donovan went into his kitchen, poured himself a glass of water and grabbed a paper towel to wipe his eyes.

"Would you like something to drink?" Donovan asked from the kitchen. I knew he was trying to regain his composure.

"Like alcohol?" I asked.

"No, like water or iced tea," Donovan answered.

"Do you have alcohol?"

"Sahara, I've got half-consumed bottles of wine in the cabinet."

"No, thanks," I said. "I don't want the alcohol scraps of your one-night stands of the misspent days gone by." I gave Donavan a wink to let him know I wasn't being harsh. I was being funny, or at least, trying to be.

"You really think I have slept with gobs of women. I actually know my exact number of women I've been with. Do you know your exact number of men you've slept with?" Donovan asked me.

I started counting my love affairs of days gone by in my head really fast. When, I realized I was already at twenty before my college senior trip to Cabo and that had been eight years ago. I had stopped counting and decided that twenty-three was a good number.

"How many men have you slept with, Sahara?"

I looked at Donovan and in my mind, I was thinking twenty-three, twenty-three, twenty-three, and I said, "Thirty-eight."

What the hell did I just admit out loud? Why would I give him my honest answer because Cabo was a long two weeks of free loving in the spring of 2005?

"Wow, that's a lot more than I thought," Donovan said.

"Thanks," I said. Now I felt like a loose Lucy. This conversation just might guarantee me getting out of here, sex-free. "Okay, pretty boy, what about you?"

"Please don't call me that," Donovan said.

I immediately felt awful because I remembered how hurtful he said his father was about his masculinity, especially calling him *princess*.

"Okay, how many?" I asked.

"Fifty-two."

"Fifty-two? And you act all high and mighty when I said thirty-eight? Fifty-two is a lot."

"The percentage of women I walk away from is nighty-five percent."

"That's insane. Does that mean you have had over a thousand women throw themselves to the point you knew you could have had sex?"

"I'm not proud of it. Well, maybe just a little. But I take pride in not sleeping with just anyone."

It was hard to believe that he didn't ask out three women a week, the way he had asked me out the first time at the gym. "How old are you again?" I asked.

"I'm twenty-nine."

"How old were you when you had sex for the first time?"

"Eighteen."

"Okay, that was eleven years ago, so that leaves about four or five girls a year. That's not that insane for a guy who looks the way you do. I think you would have said a number in the 300s."

"Seriously?" Donovan asked, disgusted.

I nodded because I was being completely honest.

"Wow, you thought I had a lot more and I thought you had a lot less."

"A lot less?" I pretended to sound insulted. I wasn't sure to be flattered or disgusted. "So, anyway," I said. "How did we get on this horrible subject?"

"I think you asked me a question."

"How come I answered first?" I asked.

"Because I am that good," Donovan said.

"It's getting late," I said, trying to free myself from the sexual clutches of Donovan, before I threw myself at him. "I think I better leave."

"We were talking about the day my dad died," Donovan said.

"I don't want to make you relive the pain. We don't have to talk about it anymore tonight," I said.

Donovan looked at me and gave me a strong stare with his beautiful brown eyes. "Okay," he said. "We don't have to talk about it."

"Okay," I said.

"Okay," he repeated back to me.

I walked out to my car and Donovan walked me out. He gave me a hug and a kiss on the forehead.

"Goodbye, Sahara."

"Goodbye, Donovan."

Chapter Twenty-eight

I got in my car and headed home.

What a night!

As I pulled into my driveway, I could see multiple lights on in my house, ones that I knew I didn't leave on. I could also hear my TV blaring so loudly that I could hear it in my garage. I was nighty-nine percent sure I wasn't robbed, only that my new BFF had made herself more at home while I was out.

I opened my front door, which was unlocked, by the way.

I expected to run into Paris, but I didn't. There was a strange brownish-red headed woman lying on my couch holding my remote control watching my TV.

"What the hell are you doing in my house?" I said, almost to the point of screaming.

"Hello, Sahara."

I started to feel dizzy as if the room was spinning around. When I got my senses back, I realized who the lady was.

It's Abigail! And she is wearing another hideous green dress.

This one was the color of dark grass.

"I haven't been able to remember you till this moment because you spoke to me?" I asked.

"Yes, you're real close to figuring out how to defeat the spell in your everyday life."

"How so?"

"With understanding comes knowledge. Your growth is astounding. You're making quite a buzz in both the witch and spirit communities."

"I would prefer to not be a subject in either community," I said.

"Do you remember what I asked you the last time I saw you?"

"Yes," I said. I knew Abigail had power and she was making herself at home in my living room. She had confidence through the roof. The only time I had seen a chink in her armor is when I brought up Paris.

Maybe I can use that to my advantage?

"Regardless if I remember who you are or not, why are you in my house?"

"I'm ready to see what your answer is."

"You want me to decide right now?" Then, I remembered her telling me if I didn't have an answer for her about whether she could train me in Black Magic, then she wouldn't be happy.

"If you need a decision at this moment, I'm going to say no."

"Why have you decided on that?"

"Because you're pressuring me. I have had like five minutes to think about it. You haven't given me much time with your spell that is on me."

"I'm sorry. Do you feel pressure?" Abigail said, in a menacing tone.

"Are you saying I either say 'yes' or you're going to kill me right here?"

"Kill you? No one wants to kill anyone. Giving pain to the living is much more fun."

"So, you're going to torture me."

"Have you made your final decision?"

I looked at Abigail and I was scared. She was the most threatening woman I had ever come across and she looked like she could be me.

I wasn't sure what to say. I knew what I wanted to say, but what would she do to me if I told her no? I took a couple of deep breaths and said, "Can we go outside to my backyard? I need some fresh air."

"I would think having two dates would have given you all the fresh air you would need on such a fine day," she said with an alluring wink.

"How do you know about my personal life?" I asked Abigail.

"Your personal life? There is so much magic going on in that love triangle. It doesn't take much to get word of it."

I was so freaked out that the witch world and the spirit world were watching my every move.

"Who the hell am I?" I said to Abigail.

"If you haven't figured that out by now, then I don't know what to tell you. But I will ask you one more time. What is your decision?"

I held my breath and said, "I will not be mentored by you. I choose Paris."

"You choose Paris?" Abigail began to get extremely angry. I was worried that my neighbors might hear her, being that we were standing in the middle of my backyard...again.

"When did you see her, Sahara?"

"The last time I saw her was this morning."

Abigail looked at me and said, "Wiser is she, wiser is he. You won't remember me until the next time we speak."

Chapter Twenty-nine

"Sahara. Wake up? Are you okay?"

I opened my eyes and stared at Paris from a weird angle. "When did you get here?"

"Just right now. I tried knocking like you wanted me to. I knocked and rang the doorbell at least ten times. I sensed something was wrong. So, I came in and I saw you on the couch nearly passed out. I wasn't sure if you were dead or not."

"I'm not dead. I'm extremely exhausted." I wasn't sure why I was so tired. Oh wait, I had gone on two dates today. No wonder I was so tired.

"I'm not sure when I fell asleep. The last thing I remember is walking through my door, thinking you were inside."

"Why did you think that?" Paris asked.

"Because the lights and TV were on," I said.

"I haven't been here till now. If the lights and TV were on, they were left on by someone else."

"Someone else?"

Paris looked at me and said, "Something has happened. Someone else is pursuing you. It might be Abigail."

"Abigail?" I said. "Abigail has made zero contact with me."

"Has she?" Paris asked.

I tried to think, but I couldn't think. My mind was a fog as if a cloud was blocking my memory. It was a fuzzy cloud that had colors. "Something *has* happened," I said. "I'm not sure what, but something is blocking my memory."

"It's a spell."

"I'm under a spell?"

"Oh, sweetie. There is so much magic that surrounds you."

"Someone else told me that," I said.

"Think, Sahara. Was that someone else Abigail?"

I tried to think and all I could see is a bit of red in my memory. "All I see is a bit of red."

"Abigail has red hair."

I concentrated with all I had within me. I focused on that memory. "I see two women. Both women look as if they could be me."

"That's because Abigail looks just like you," Paris said from right next to me on the couch.

"You never bothered to tell me that?" I said to Paris.

"There was no reason to. The less you knew about her, the better."

"Why? If she is the enemy? Shouldn't I know all there is to know about my opponent?"

"Abigail has been visiting you and you don't remember. Has this happened before? Where you wake up and you can't remember falling asleep?"

I looked at Paris, horrified. "Yes, it has happened a couple times before in the last week. I thought it was because I was exhausted."

"Abigail has been here. She has sat right where I am sitting. That's the evil. She is the evil."

"I'm scared, Paris. I don't remember anything. I just see a picture. It's a still shot like a photo in my mind."

"You need to rest. Maybe if you rest your mind that might help. Let's talk about something else."

"Okay, what do you want to talk about?"

"How about the little love triangle that you and I have created?"

"Paris, I need to know what kind of spell you put on Donovan. He is all over the map with me. I have no idea what is true and what is false."

"Really? Love does that to you?"

"Does what?" I asked.

"Not allow you to see what is right underneath your nose."

"I am totally confused, Paris. Quit talking in riddles." I was tired and I had seen and heard a lot of weird shit tonight.

"I can't tell you."

"Why not?"

"Because if I tell you without you guessing it, every good thing that has happened because of my spell will unravel."

"So, you're saying I have to figure out your spell if I want to stop it?"

"That is your test. I thought these spells would be fun for you and I had no idea they were going to get all twisted up like this."

"*They?*" I asked.

"Yeah, they," Paris replied.

"There has been more than one spell cast on Donovan?"

"Oh, there has been more than one. I had to do combos and everything to get this spell exactly right."

"And you can't just tell me what you've done?"

"I can. But then, I couldn't mentor you anymore. You need to be strong, Sahara. You can figure this out. I have faith in you."

"That will be when the spell is over? Once I figure it out?"

"Yes, but you need to understand there is more than one spell at work here. And you can break all spells that were cast by me whenever you want, the second you figure out what the spell is. You have to know it, not guess it. There is a big difference."

"So, it's over, once I understand what the spell is?" I asked.

"That has to happen and then you need to do a physical act followed by a few words."

"What's the physical act?" I asked. "What are the few words?"

Paris looked at me and said, "You need to stand with your arms crossed like a genie and say this phrase, 'Make right what is right.'"

"Make right what is right?" I repeated, but without crossing my arms like a genie.

"That's the phrase," Paris said.

"I don't know why everything has to be so difficult," I said.

"What you need to understand is, we're the ones making things difficult. Spells and witchery is the craft of constantly offsetting the balance of nature. The good witches are constantly trying to fix everyone else's mistakes."

"Whose mistakes?"

"Humans and dark witches."

"So, you are saying that making a guy fall for me against his will is your way of balancing nature?"

"I wish I could tell you more, but it would ruin everything I have taught you."

"Why?" I asked.

"You'll learn from your own mistakes. Trust me when I say to you that. But, with this particular spell I cast. If you don't figure it out. It will be active. I can't stop that from happening. There are seriously powerful spells at work and if my intuition and feeling are correct, Abigail has cast a memory spell on you."

"Seriously?"

"That's why you can't remember her. If you see two women that look like you, then you are describing Abigail as the other woman."

"This is just great," I said sarcastically.

"You need to be more observant at all times and try to see her before she sees you. She won't know you know anything and if I know Abigail, she loves the dramatics. I'm pretty sure she is showing herself to you well before she actually does speak to you."

"She would do that?"

"Oh, she is so manipulative and cunning. She takes joy moving in slow on her kill." Also, pay more attention on your dates and you will be able to figure out my spell. That is all I can tell you."

"I'm not going to be on these dates much longer," I said.

"Good," Paris said. "Because we want to fast track you to being a High Witch."

"Who is *we*?" I asked.

"Well, me and...magic."

I looked at Paris and this was the first time I didn't know who to trust. I wanted to trust Paris, but she was acting extremely weird and mysterious.

For now, I put my trust in her. If I was sensitive at all to the magic and spirit worlds, then I knew Paris was good. I know it from the innards of my soul.

I just didn't know why I was trying so hard to convince myself.

Chapter Thirty

I spent the next couple of days reading every love spell I could find in my stack of books. I wanted to break Paris's spell. Paris looked to be in pain because I hadn't figured it out yet.

I also went on the Internet to see what I could find. I had no idea what the spell could be. None of the love spells I ran across would make a man act the way Donovan had around me. And if there were more spells at work, I had to figure that out, too. I mean, if she'd put one on Robert, too, that made me want to throw up because I had believed everything Robert told me was genuinely from his heart. His real heart. Not some spell-manipulated heart.

Don't get me started how freaked out I was over Abigail possibly visiting me. I had tried my hardest, but I couldn't muster out a memory. I just saw the same blurry picture.

I needed to focus on Paris's spell. That was the only thing I could control. I would not let the Magic control me.

I needed to focus on Donovan. Donovan was the only person I knew for sure who had a spell on him. I needed to dissect how he acted toward me. At times, he spoke and acted really juvenile. Then, at others, he was a wide-open book, and had amazing life stories to share.

He was real honest, real sweet and gentlemanly. What got me more than anything was how genuine he was. I couldn't find a love spell anywhere that had that in the description.

I had a date with Robert on Tuesday—we went to a movie, which was a very low-key date—and after that, I decided I would go ten days and not see either guy. My date with Robert was really nice and I noticed he didn't say much on the date, but of course, we were in the theater. He was extremely quiet after the movie and reserved, too. He was extremely courteous. He gave me one of his doozies of a kiss at the end of the night. But he was really quiet. That concerned me.

I decided I would talk to either guy on the phone during my ten-day dating hiatus, but they would have to call me. I needed to see who was interested more. I needed to get my mind straight. I was living in a bubble and I needed to step outside it and gain some perspective.

I also wanted to see if I saw a redheaded woman that looked similar to me. Because if I had, it was Abigail stalking me. Each time I left for work, I was hyperaware of every person around me until I would get home.

During this time, Paris had come over just about every other day and we would go through the spell book. I had to be honest, the days she didn't stay over, I was extra anxious. And I barely slept those nights. But, I mainly wanted her there because I was afraid of whatever Abigail was doing to me. Paris taught me one more spell that could help me defend myself if I was attacked. The only warrior spells Paris knew were defense and defense with a counter attack. I had her teach me a defense with a counter attack spell.

The first one Paris taught me was a short and sweet spell. They were my favorite kind of spells.

"Move back, strike one, strike twice. Hold." It was written on a small piece of paper Paris handed me. She couldn't tell me the spell aloud because she was so powerful that it would work against me and smash me a couple times something fierce.

I looked at Paris and asked, "What's hold? You have never taught me that?"

"Hold," Paris said, "is put in there so you're not able to do multiple strikes against your opponent. It's there, so you if you lose your mind in a fight and just want to abuse your opponent, and you just want to strike your opponent over and over again...well you're not able to."

"Why is it there?" I said in defiance. It made me angry that if I was attacked, I would basically get my butt kicked after my spell worked once. Talk about a pacifist. Paris straight out wanted me to run.

I don't run. I have never run from anything in my life.

"I just want to say we should learn stronger warrior spells because it has officially gotten very serious for me."

"The spell I taught you is as strong of spell you can do before dipping into Black Magic."

"Seriously?"

"It'll work for you. It's worked for me every time."

I looked at Paris and knew there was so much about Abigail and her that she'd never told me.

"Paris, if you're not going to teach me a way to fight—basically, a strike and run away—then at least equip me with knowledge. What is Abigail's entire story?"

"I won't tell you everything. Someday, I might, but for now, all you need to know is this: One time, Abigail came for me using Black Magic and this spell knocked her back so hard that she nearly broke her neck against a tree that she flew into. We were at Hillcrest Park."

"Why were you there?" I asked.

"It's a good place to battle. I was lured there and Abigail wanted to hurt me badly."

"Why?"

Paris was extremely quiet.

"What is it, Paris? Please tell me."

"Now we are moving into the territory where I can't tell you everything. Having Hold in the spell basically makes it so you can use the spell once."

"How long until you can use it again?" I asked.

"Twenty-four hours. The two strikes they will receive will be more than enough for you to leave the confrontation."

"But if I can't leave the confrontation? What if I'm being attacked by multiple Black Magic witches? Why don't we learn stronger warrior spells?" I said, all the while knowing I had already practiced stronger warrior spells with my Black Magic book.

"I need to know, Paris. What happened between you and Abigail?"

Paris walked back into the living room and sat on my recliner. She was looking straight ahead at my TV that was turned off.

"Abigail is my younger sister," Paris finally said.

"What?" I gasped and nearly passed out. "How is any of that possible if what you previously told me was true? Mainly, according to you, you look nothing alike."

"Come with me into the bathroom."

Paris got up and I followed her into my hallway bathroom. She stopped in front of the mirror. I stood next to Paris and we were both looking at ourselves in the mirror. I looked at both of us and said, "Why am I in here with you?"

"Look at us, Sahara. We have the same nose. The same cheek structure. We could easily be sisters."

I looked at Paris and never realized how much we did look alike. It was a bit weird. Just our faces did. I had long flowing red hair. Paris's hair was cut in a pixie. Her platinum-blond hair was an obvious attempt to get rid of any red hair she might have showing. Also Paris was rail skinny with average boobs. I was chubbier and let's just say, I was two cup sizes bigger in that department.

"We do look alike. So, how much younger is Abigail than you?"

"One year and eleven months."

"How come you talked about her character? Wouldn't you know by the time you're an adult that your sister might have some character issues?"

"No," she said. "She has always been very secretive. I never knew what her deal was growing up. She was very shy."

"How do we get from that to her being the most notorious Black Magic witch? Those were your exact words the first time I met you."

"She came to me four years ago. Since high school, she had a job at a library and would just go to her room when she was done and play multiplayer online games like *Second Life*. I thought she was a social misfit because she never had a boyfriend. Never had a best friend that she saw in person. This was my little sister and my heart went out to her. So, I decided to teach her to be as strong as me. I thought that would break her out of her shell. Well, it did. Once she discovered what her true personality was...she abandoned my mentorship."

"Where did she go?"

"I don't know. She was a very strong witch already. More powerful than I was. She was even more sensitive to the spirit and magic worlds than me."

"What about me?" I asked.

"You are even greater than I." Paris smiled at me and nodded her head.

"How is that true? You're mentoring me?"

"You don't think pro athletes have coaches? I guarantee you, every pro athlete can play their sport better than their coach. I only train people who will be as strong as me or stronger. I have known for a few days that you were much stronger than I am. It is just a matter of time before you learn everything. What you need to understand is that magic is complex and we can defeat Black Magic by doing a variety of spells. The more spells you learn, the more you can do just about anything you want. I hope you use it for good. But I learned, if I can't stop my baby sister from being tempted with Black Magic, I probably wouldn't be able to stop anyone. So, that is why I look at two things now. Do I sense the person has a sensitivity to magic and the spirit world?"

"And?" I said, knowing what was coming next.

"And I learn about their character before I train them. You had no idea how much you were under my scrutiny when we first met."

"Thank you. I'm sorry about Abigail and you. Sisters. Wow."

"I had big dreams for Abigail and I thought we could have a similar life. One, where we both were helping others. We would live our lives as sisters and protect those who can't protect themselves. Instead..." Paris stopped herself from talking. She began to get extremely choked up.

"I understand now, Paris," I said. "I just want to know how she attacks. Does she use all magic? Or does she do some actual fighting?"

"You don't ever want to fight Abigail. She's ruthless. She was willing to kill her own sister. God knows what she has been doing to other people for the past three years."

"Okay," I said. I decided to allow this conversation to end. I learned more about Abigail than I thought I would.

Paris said we were done for the day.

Chapter Thirty-one

I decided to pick Paris's brain before she left for the weekend.

"When will I start learning more serious spells?" I asked.

"I have to be honest with you, Sahara. You are learning so fast and I think you're centered enough that magic is attracted to you as if you give off some kind of joy to do your will. I have never seen anything like this. Your aura is electric."

"I've been doing my aura spell each morning."

"You know, you can do it more than once a day. Some days, I have to do it every hour, on the hour."

"Look, you are saying so many wonderful things to me that no one has ever said about me or to me. I just need to know this answer: When can I learn bigger spells?"

"You don't need to ask me," Paris said. "Mother Earth has a weird way of showing you herself."

"Is that what happened to you?" I asked. "Is that when you became a Most High Witch?"

"The answer to that question is 'yes,'" Paris said. "But it was a journey into both the physical and spiritual realms. The closer you are to finding out your 'truths' around you in your daily life, the closer Mother Earth wants to wrap her arms around you and make you the highest any human-turned-witch could be."

"All of this is tied to spells?" I asked.

"No, Sahara. It isn't. All of this is tied to *life*. All of this is tied to how you handle the Magic that has been sent your way."

She was starting to talk in riddles again and I hated when she did this.

"How to handle the Magic? That is a little vague," I said.

"It's not. Just do what I told you to do before. Pay extra attention on all your dates and see what is happening. Once you're confident you know, claim it out loud and then do the physical part of the spell and everything will go back to normal from that moment on. So, all the good things that happened during the spell will still be there. Now, you are going to have to figure out how to solve it without magic. And that is when Mother Earth is looking at you the closest. What you do then will determine the rest of your destiny."

My mouth actually dropped open. "This sounds a bit apocalyptic and extremely dramatic. Holy shit, all right. I thought I was inviting some fun into my life, not raising the graves of dead saints."

"What is happening in your life is not that extreme in the big picture of the entire world. But as far as your life goes, it is. You're at a crossroads. That's all I can say, and from here on out, I can't help you any further in regard to the spells."

I gasped at the realization that now I was pretty much on my own in regard to developing my powers and understanding how to break spells and make them. "Okay," I said. "I've got to do what I've got to do."

"That's the spirit," Paris said in a very cheerleader type of way.

"Don't do that," I said.

"Too 'puny.' Got ya."

Paris left and I wouldn't see her all weekend.

The next day was Saturday and I got an itch to go back to the Black Magic shop. I could own being a Black Magic witch, but I would only use it against other Black Magic witches. Otherwise, all my spells would help others and myself.

I got into my car and I started to back up when suddenly, my car was lifted off the ground. All I could think was, *What is happening and what are the neighbors going to think?* Suddenly, my car dropped from what seemed to be about ten feet high to my hard driveway and I felt completely sore. I looked in my rearview mirror and saw a woman who looked like she could be my twin.

A fear sent a chill through my spine and out my chest. She refused to say anything. She just stared at me. My body was aching from the landing of the car. I got out of my car because I didn't trust what Abigail would do to me if I remained in my vehicle.

I stepped out of my car and my back hurt.

What do you want? Abigail looked at me and didn't say a word. I thought this was extremely unusual. Abigail led me inside my house and into my living room.

There she said, "Hello, Sahara."

Then a gush of wind swooped into my living room and my head began to feel faint. I opened my eyes and I could see Abigail and I could remember everything that had happened between us. The last time we were together, I had said no to her mentoring me. I thought she came here to punish me and I began to feel extremely scared.

"Why are you, here, Abigail?" A prickle of fear sizzled up the back of my neck.

"I'm here to see if you have reconsidered."

I looked at Abigail and I knew in my heart that Paris's side was the side for me. "No, I haven't."

"Why not?" Abigail asked. "You have seen the power of both sides. One is clearly more powerful than the other."

"It comes down to trust. I trust Paris more than I trust you."

"What is there to trust? I teach you the way. You go about your life and use the Magic for whatever you want. I'm not rallying troops. I'm just trying to prevent the other side from signing a hot prospect."

"I know you are. That is why I know you will never be truly sincere to me."

"Let me guess. My honorable sis...Paris...is as sincere as they come."

"Yes, she is. She is raw and beautiful."

"I'm done with this."

Suddenly, Abigail went to the other side of my living room. My natural reaction was to go to the opposite side of the room and square off with her, my back to the wall. We weren't exactly feeling the best buds' vibe.

"I am so disappointed that you're forcing things to come to this. I wish you would have chosen me. I wish you would have chosen my side."

I decided that it was in my best interest not to tell Abigail that I hadn't made a decision about Black Magic. I had just made a decision that I wanted to remain with Paris as my mentor.

Abigail stared at me as if she was looking through me. Then she raised both her hands and said, "Master of Peace, Master of Darkness. Fill me. I am your mistress."

Some kind of force was now in my living room and it had a blue glow that was pouring itself into Abigail's body. I had no idea what was happening. I couldn't run. I couldn't do anything. I just stood there and waited. I waited to defend myself against Abigail's attack. Suddenly, her arm went from being up in the air to pointing both her hands in my direction. Then a yellow light came out of her hands and they shot at me like lasers.

As the lasers hit my body, I felt the pain of a puncture and then the force rested inside my body and caused me to have more pain than I thought was humanly possible. My brain was rattling and I just stood there taking Abigail's abuse because I was unable to move.

Was she killing me?

Finally, while still taking Abigail's abuse, I gathered myself and I began to call out the first spell Paris had taught me.

"Strike one, strike twice. Hold." I repeated the spell again and nothing happened. So, I tried the other spell that Paris had taught me:

"I take back my power.

At this very moment,

This very Hour."

Abigail began to laugh in a mocking tone that led me to believe she didn't think too highly of the spells Paris had taught me.

Still, nothing happened. I said each spell one more time, but nothing happened. The pain was excruciating.

Finally, and realizing it was the exact spell she had used, I said one of the warrior Black Magic spells.

"Master of Peace, Master of Darkness. Fill me. I am your mistress."

Suddenly, my own glow filled me, but my glow was red. I had never felt more powerful. The spell was helping to defend me from the exact same spell she had invoked against me. I no longer felt any pain.

Abigail's eyes bulged with her effort to hurt or kill me.

"Lose control. Face your fate," I said my first attack spell. A green glow came out of me and nailed Abigail back as she desperately still tried to fill me with pain and sap my life. But it wasn't working. I felt no pain. I felt *vengeance.* Abigail was going to pay for coming into my house and attacking me in my own living room. I pointed my hands at her and she went to her knees. Tears were dripping from her eyes. I was hurting her something fierce. I could have kept going and killed her, but that was not my intent. I only used the Black Magic to defend myself.

I lowered my hands so they would no longer attack Abigail.

"Go!" I said, giving her an easy out.

"You are far more powerful than I thought." Abigail looked at me and said, "Wiser is she, wiser is he. You won't remember me until the next time we speak."

Chapter Thirty-two

I woke up and the last thing I remember was pulling up to my house. Great something must've happened. I got up and walked around my house checking every room, every close, behind every shower curtain to make sure I was alone.

Even though I was alone, I was still feeling very uneasy. I decided to go back to the living room, and sit in my recliner that faced the TV. I wasn't in the mood to watch television. I needed to start making some decisions. On the guy front, I decided the first guy I would see again would be Robert. I missed him more. I wasn't sure why because he was the last guy I saw. Maybe it was because he was so quiet. I think I wanted an answer.

Paris had told me to pay attention on both dates I went on with these guys. She must've meant to compare and contrast. See what one does and what the other one does. I guess I was examining all of their human behavior. Cool, I was going to look like Jane Goodall to these guys as I tried to examine them and their surroundings.

I called Robert on Sunday night. The phone only rang once. I was shocked that he answered so quickly.

"Hello," Robert said in a voice that ran about three octaves lower than his normal voice. Extremely deep. Extremely sexy.

"Hi, there. Good morning to you," I said in a voice where I was trying not to sound like myself. But no matter how hard I tried, my normal voice came out.

That was extremely weird.

"Well, it could only be Sahara," Robert said. "Because I'm not currently talking to any other female on a regular basis."

"Who are these women you speak of?" I asked and then said, "Hello, by the way."

"Hello," he said again. "They are hangers-on of dates that went bad, but I managed to get small friendships out of the deal. That kind of thing."

"Hangers-on?"

"They are dates that didn't go too badly but you're both pretty sure there is nothing more than friendship coming out of this and usually, you just stop talking."

"Gotcha," I said. Robert was a lot more seasoned of a dater than he was letting on. He even had invented terms for women who he had no sexual chemistry with, but kept as casual friends. That was some serious dating insight.

"You're a smart guy," I said.

"About some things." Robert laughed. I was really starting to like his laugh. "So, may I ask why I have the pleasure of hearing your voice at 8:30 in the morning on a Saturday?"

"I'm asking you out on a date," I said in my cute voice.

"Wow. That's real cool that you're asking me out."

"I'm like that," I said. "I'm weird."

"I think that is why I am so fond of you."

"Because I am weird."

"No, because you're genuine and honest. The good, the bad, and the ugly—it's all out there and I love all of it."

"Ugly?"

"In your case, the good, the bad, and the gorgeous." Robert made a sound over the phone as if he was relieved that was what came out of his mouth.

"What's the bad?" I asked.

Robert coughed and then made a squeal similar to the one Donovan had made the other night.

Oh my God, Robert is under a spell, too. Are you kidding me? Both these guys were under truth and love spells. I didn't know if anything either one of these guys had said to me had been genuine. When you thought you were in love, a truth spell would be positive things that would pour out of your mouth. This was what both men had been—amazing listeners and talkers.

I'm such a fool.

"Robert, you don't have to answer that question because I don't think I want to know."

"Okay," Robert said, relieved.

"Was there a specific reason why you called?" he asked.

"Robert, the reason why I called is, I would like to see you tomorrow night."

"You would?

"Yes, I would."

"Where is this date going to take place?" Robert asked. He was sounding more and more relieved as the conversation progressed. I think he might have thought this was going to be our last call. Maybe he thought I was breaking off whatever this was with him.

"To be honest, I hadn't thought about a specific place. I just knew I wanted to see you tonight."

Tonight? What the hell was I saying to him?

"I would, however, would like to pay because I'm asking you out," I said.

I had no idea why I said that.

Words were coming out of my mouth with very little thought beforehand.

"I can't let you do that," Robert said quickly. "I'm thrilled you asked me out. It would be an honor for me to pay."

"Chalk one up in the incredible guy category," I said.

Okay, now I'm just being corny.

"What's the bad category called?"

"I don't know yet. You haven't earned one of those chalk-ups yet."

"Oh, good." I could visualize Robert giving me a really sweet smile.

"Well, Robert if you're buying, then you choose what we do. This way, I don't have to make a choice. I put it all on you what we do on our date."

"Okay." Robert took a pause as if he replayed what I just said in his head and he didn't like it the second time either. "I would like to go to a Mexican food restaurant, but I'm afraid it might give me gas," Robert said. "What the heck did I just say?"

"Do you have one in mind?" I asked, holding in a laugh.

"Yes, it's Roberto's. You can say I like the name and it's cheaper than most places."

"Is money tight? I seriously can pay," I said. I really meant it.

"No, Roberto's is nice. It's a quaint place and I think you'll dig the vibe."

"Sounds like a date.

Our fourth date," I said. "You know you're now in really rare company. You are three for three on great dates."

"That's good to know. Now, I have pressure to make this date awesome. I would want to make it awesome, anyway."

"Nice save," I said.

"It's the truth," Robert said.

"I'll see you around what time?" I asked.

"Let's say six," Robert said.

What was it with these two guys wanting to go out at six?

My dinner dates had always been seven or eight p.m. dates. It might mean that both men wanted to spend extra time with me. If that was the case, that was really cool.

We got off the phone and I decided I would do some primping errands for our date later on and for life in general. I could get my nails redone and maybe paint them not such a dark purple. Maybe even go with red—that would be different.

I'll get my hair dyed a little and I'll get a little trim.

I wanted to look pretty. I liked Robert. I liked him a lot.

Chapter Thirty-three

I called into work on Monday. It was the first time I had done that in a while. I spent the day getting my nails and hair done. I had my usual stylist highlight with purple a strand in my hair. She added black streaks into my long reddish-brown hair. Then mixed in the purple to the top bangs and in the back. It looked pretty punk. I loved it. The colors worked incredibly together. It gave me a dark look which I liked. Not that I want to do Black Magic. I was just tired of being normal.

This edgy look had always given me confidence over the years. This was the first time I thought I looked like a witch. I used to think I was being dark, like a vampire or a zombie.

But never a witch?

That almost seemed too silly.

I'm realizing more and more each day that I have always been a witch, and I just haven't found my way yet. Because of Paris, I am finding my true self.

I had a strange awakening on this particular afternoon and it was causing me to be quite emotional. It wasn't every day that you realized what your calling had always been.

But I got through it by going shopping. Best therapy ever. I made my wardrobe look even witchier than it already was. I loved embracing this side of me. I was realizing I had always subconsciously shopped for clothes as if I was a witch.

When I got home, I had one hour before Robert was going to pick me up. I freshened up and watched a little TV while I waited. They were having a *Real World* marathon of the current season. This season, they put the house right smack in the middle of Baghdad.

Oh wait, my bad, it was Boise, Idaho.

Robert picked me up at one minute before six. The boy was punctual, I had to give him that. I looked through the peephole and he had a dozen roses for me. Or maybe it was two dozen. All I could see was a huge vase and a lot of roses through the peephole.

I opened the door slowly.

"Hi," Robert said. "I went to the floral shop and said, 'What is the biggest bouquet of flowers that would make me the most embarrassed?' I'm just kidding. I didn't say that. But here it is, I present to you, Mount Roses." Robert did a curtsy and handed me the giant vase full of roses.

"Come inside. You are very sweet. The roses are beautiful. You even put them in a kick-ass vase. You did quite well, Robert."

Why was I talking like this?

I walked into my kitchen and put the vase of roses on top of my kitchen table.

"They're beautiful. I've never gotten so many roses in my life."

"The truth is," Robert said. "It cost $49.99 for a dozen and just $59.99 for three dozen. I figured it was a pretty good deal to get two dozen roses more for $59.99." Robert looked at me horrified, as if he wished he didn't just tell me that. He was trying to talk, but he couldn't.

"Are you okay?" I asked.

Robert let out a huge sigh and said, "I don't know. I've been acting weird as of late and I'm not sure what it's all about.

Should we enter them as a float in the Rose Bowl Parade?" he quipped.

"Yes, we should. It's worthy of being called a float."

Robert smiled so sweetly at me. "Thanks."

Paris told me to pay attention on both dates. She also told me there were multiple spells. Did she possibly put a spell on me? I was saying things I didn't want to say, but everything I was saying was what I really thought, even though I wanted to lie or at least keep my mouth shut. I apparently had a spell on me that was forcing me to be honest. I had to play this out.

"Ask me my middle name, Robert."

My middle name is Anne and if I try to say Lisa, then I know my spell has to do with truth.

Robert looked at me like I was crazy. "You told me your middle name on our first phone call. I told you mine was Jake and you laughed."

"I did? I'm so sorry."

"It's okay, I got over it."

"Robert, I need for you to listen to me and I want you to do what I ask you to do."

"Okay," Robert said.

"Robert, ask me what my middle name is. Just do it." I wasn't playing around. I think I was on the verge of a nervous breakdown.

"I know it's Anne," Robert said. "But Sahara, what is your middle name?"

It was then that I squealed exactly the way Robert and Donovan had squealed the other night.

Holy crap. All of our spells are similar. Are they all the same?

But I needed to focus. I was answering his question and I was going to say Lisa if it killed me. I thought 'Lisa' ten times in my head, but when I tried to say my name out loud, I blurted, "Anne! My middle name is Anne."

Donovan and I had the same spell. He had a truth spell on top of his love spell.

Do I have a love spell?

I liked both guys a whole lot. But that was on person-to-person merit in regard to conversations and interactions we'd had. I wasn't ever told what to think, the way I'm being told to tell the truth.

I don't have a love spell. That's impossible.

But...one of Donovan's spells must be a truth spell and if that was the case, then he had been saying some remarkable, true things to me.

I looked at Robert and I didn't know what to do. So I just said to him, "It's a truth spell." Then, I crossed my hands and nodded my head like a freaking genie and said, "Make right what is right."

"What was that?" Robert asked, confused.

"I'm not sure," I said. Right then, I knew the spell was broken. I was able to lie. I knew exactly why I did what I did.

Holy moly. Everything happened just like Paris said. I need to talk to her immediately. I can't go on this date. Or maybe I can. I'm going to call her on my cell and go to my backyard so Robert can't hear me.

"I don't want to be rude," I said to Robert. "A friend of mine was having a rough day. I just want to check in with her before we go. Would you mind if I walk out to my backyard and have a short conversation?"

"Go for it."

I walked swiftly through my living room and opened my glass and screen door and stepped outside.

I walked over to the bench under the canopy. I called Paris. She answered on the first ring.

"I was just thinking about you," Paris said when she answered the phone.

"I have figured out half your spell," I said.

"Yeah? What have you figured out?"

"Well, the spell is broken up. I was able to knock out the truth spell that all three of us had. Now I know why I've been saying bizarre things and why both men would constantly say the first thing on their minds, because that was what I was doing."

Paris was quiet for about ten full seconds and then said, "Why do you think there any more to it?"

"Well, the love spell or spells. Please tell me you didn't put a love spell on Robert. I need to know that one of those guys really does like me."

"Sahara," Paris said, "come see me. I've been working on something all day and I would really love for you to come and see it."

"Where are you?"

"I'm at the coven camp."

"You want me to come all the way down there? I'm on a date with Robert. Well, it actually hasn't started yet. He is still at my house. We were about to leave."

"Look, Sahara, I'm not sure what you have to do. But if you come here, everything will make sense, I promise. Goodbye, Sahara."

We got off the phone.

I walked around my backyard, thinking about what I was going to do. This was insane. Everything that was supposed to be up was down. And what I thought was down was now up.

I walked into my house and told Robert something came up and I would come by later and talk to him. I knew I had to talk to both men tonight. I wasn't sure what I was going to say to either one of them.

Robert was a good guy and told me he understood and was looking forward to seeing me later tonight. He was such an incredible guy. He acted the exact same way, truth spell or not. *Who knows? Maybe if he still had the truth spell, he would have told me to F-off.*

I was seeing where common courtesy sometimes meant you need to lie to someone. A little bit, anyway.

Chapter Thirty-four

I decided to put myself together a tad before heading out to see Paris. I walked outside and smelled the fresh air I had no idea what was up ahead for me, I just knew that something epic was on the horizon. Epic how? That remains to be seen. I smiled at the dark night, and would have made a wish if a star had fallen. For now I was going to go on instincts and gut feelings, and yeah, a little bit of magic.

I walked into the garage and unlocked my Mazda with my key. Then I stepped into my car and I was off. I drove down the 91 to the 15 freeway south. I got off in Lake Elsinore and made my way to Ortega Highway.

It was a pretty scary ride at night. I went about fifteen miles below the speed limit. I wasn't flying off any mountain. Not without a broomstick. But that would probably be an advanced lesson from Paris.

In about twenty minutes, I got to the coven camp. I pulled into the driveway and I could see Paris waiting for me by the entrance to the chapel.

I got out of my car and I walked over to her.

"Hi, sweetheart," Paris said. "I have a surprise for you."

How any of this had to do with the spells, I didn't know.

Paris took my hand and guided me to a cabin that was about forty feet into the woods.

She went up the steps and I followed her.

"You ready?" Paris said. She was standing in front of the door. "We were assigned a cabin. I've been getting it ready for us all day. We are going to do some crazy magic in here."

Paris opened the door and I was instantly overwhelmed by the colors, the music, and the incense. She had designed the room in a way that totally fit my personality. It was clear we had two different sides of the room. My side had a lot of giant books in it.

"You can decorate your station any way you like. I just put some colors together that reminded me of you."

The color scheme had purple, black and red. The same three colors that were in my hair.

"Why are you showing me all this?"

"Because you're close, Sahara. Very close. I wanted to show you what we're fighting for."

"Fighting for?" I asked.

"I want to show you what you can have, and will be, once you come out ahead of this little love triangle that has developed between the two men in your life. Once you get a hold on that, I will be ready to train you to be a Most High Witch."

"Really?"

"Yes, Sahara. I've seen a lot in my day. You're a natural. This is your calling."

"Thank you for showing me this," I said.

Paris looked at me, and said, "I wish you would ask me questions and then I would be forced to tell you the answers."

"Forced to tell me? What the hell aren't you telling me?" I asked.

Paris looked at me and her eyes were so sincere. She said, "I have kept what I'm about to tell you from you only because I felt you should have judged this guy on his merit."

"Judge who?" I asked.

Paris looked at me and said, "Robert."

"What about Robert do you need to tell me?"

"Robert is a very inexperienced warlock."

I laughed because that sounded absurd. "He couldn't have kept that a secret," I said. "I think I really know this guy."

"Robert is a warlock," Paris said plainly. Now I knew she was being dead serious and just the thought of Robert being a warlock seemed maddening to me.

"Why now? Why are you telling me right now?"

"Because you're at a point where you need to choose. You know it and I know it. I wanted you to have all the information, so you can make the best decision possible."

"Are you kidding me, Paris? Now you tell me? Now, you tell me?"

"He is not dangerous. He is on our side. He's not one of our best, mainly because he hardly practices."

"Why not?"

"He's very Creator driven."

"What does that mean?" I asked.

"He believes in a Creator and therefore, he feels guilty about doing any kind of magic."

She knew an awful lot about Robert all of a sudden? There was a question I needed answered.

"Did you know Robert before I had a date with him at Knott's Berry Farm?" I asked Paris.

"When you asked me about it the first time we met, you weren't an official witch yet."

"So, in other words, you could straight-out lie to me." I was taken aback by her deception.

"I was protecting the situation for both of you. He has no idea you have become a witch either." Paris looked at me and she had love in her eyes, but I didn't know if I could trust her. She had lied to me.

"Oh, this is not a timely way to tell me things," I complained. I knew she did this for me because it came from a good place. But, I wasn't sure if I was on the right side anymore. "And if you're helping Robert, then why did you bring Donovan into the picture?"

Paris smiled and said, "I couldn't let Robert not have someone to compete with. It's our code. You always have a choice. It was for his own good that I brought Donovan into the situation. Also, it was for you. It was a chance for you to really see what happiness is. I'm not saying it's with Donovan. What I am saying is, you have two great men to choose from."

"And one of them is a warlock," I said. "Wait, is Donovan a warlock?"

"No, he is not. I know that for a fact. He is what we call 'oblivious.' That means he has no clue about anything magic and what the spirit world is doing."

"I think you're nuts," I said to Paris. "I think you and apparently Robert invited me into a world I am now wishing I had never been brought into."

"You know that is not true, Sahara. Look all around you. You know this is who you are. You know that deep down in your heart that you and magic were long-lost friends. You feel how intoxicating magic is."

"When did I become an official witch?" I asked. "You said earlier that I wasn't an official which yet. When did I become an official witch and when were you planning on telling me?"

"Your powers surpassed mine from the very beginning. I didn't want to scare you by putting too much on you."

"Are you telling me I have been a witch from the very beginning of all this?"

"Not until you did your first aura spell. From that moment on, I knew there was nothing you couldn't do. What happened to you only happened to one other person."

"Abigail?"

"Yes."

"Why didn't you tell me?" I repeated.

"I wanted you to try harder and I wanted to see how strong you could become and still remain on our side. You see, your heart is so good, Sahara, that I know that you will never choose the other side."

214

"Are you trying to manipulate me?" I asked Paris.

"I would never do that. Not to you. Not to what you and I have built as sisters in the craft."

"I have to go," I said. "I have to make two decisions tonight. Because, tomorrow I want to know exactly who I am and what I'm about."

"What are you saying, Sahara?"

"I have looked into Black Magic," I said. "Now, I'm wondering just because the phrase 'Black Magic' has the word 'black' in it, it might not be the wrong side. Black has always been beautiful to me. It's a comforting color. Maybe, Black Magic and me are lovers, not just long-lost friends?"

"Please don't say that, Sahara," Paris said. "Please look deeper than what is on the surface. Try to remember who you were when you were a little girl and just wanted to be happy. Try to remember her. She knows that my side is the good side and Black Magic is an unpredictable, awful side."

I felt Paris crying out to me, but I didn't know how authentic her intentions were. "I can see how people can abuse it, but I also see its power."

"Sahara, I need to take you into the chapel where *The Book of Shadows* is. You need to experience that power again. I still see an evil around you, and I now know why. Curiosity has gotten the best of you and you began to dabble in the black arts."

"Dabble? I take Black Magic seriously."

"You're not the only good witch this has happened to. It has happened to all of us who crave power. But endless power only subjects itself to abuse. This is why I have the chosen the Magic of Good."

"Are you good? Or is Abigail? I wouldn't know, because I don't remember a damn thing that has happened or that she has taught me for that matter."

"She doesn't want you to. She wouldn't teach you unless you were sold out one hundred percent, and I know that didn't happen."

"How do you know?" I asked.

"Sahara, you know at the heart of who you are, that you are an incredibly giving and caring person. Life has beaten you up a little bit, and you're a little bitter. I could see how the other side would seem attractive because you still have unresolved issues with life. That doesn't mean Black Magic is the answer. Please spend some time with *The Book of Shadows*." Paris looked at me and tears were dripping from her eyes. No one could have faked that.

"Okay, I said. "Let's go to the book."

Paris reached out her hand for me to take. I reached out and held Paris's hand like a sister. I knew Paris loved me. It might be the only genuine thing that has happened to me.

Chapter Thirty-five

Paris took me to a back entrance of the chapel and the two of us walked up to *The Book of Shadows*. I didn't know why I was a lot more emotional seeing the book this time. But I was. It was probably something to do with the conversation I'd just had with Paris. I was emotional and very drawn to the book.

"Okay," I said as calmly as I could. "What do you want me to do?" I asked Paris.

"I want you to close your eyes and really listen to what I'm about to tell you."

"Okay." I reluctantly closed my eyes.

Paris took her time and then she said, "I never put a love spell on Donovan and I especially didn't put one on Robert. They only had truth spells."

I nodded and kept my eyes closed.

"You figured it out. Mother Earth was showing you that you are ready.

"Sahara, you need to examine yourself and spending time with *The Book of Shadows* will help you see clearer."

"Or, it will put a spell on me and make me choose your side," I said to Paris as practically as I could. "I'm still reeling that Robert

217

has been a warlock this whole time. He has done zero things to indicate to me that he had that kind of power. Or any kind of power. I'm not sure if I'm on your side any longer."

"My side? Have you really separated yourself from what we're doing that you would call it 'my side'?"

"There are two sides to magic. I am not opposed to what you perceive as the darker side, the wrong side."

Paris couldn't take it. She fell to her knees and cried out, "Don't do this, Sahara. Please trust me. Look at yourself and ask yourself if you can trust me. Let that be your guide. Allow nothing else to influence you."

"All right," I said. "And another thing, why did you feel I needed a spell on me by you? Especially when you sensed I might already be in trouble with Abigail?"

"I told you very early on I was going to do it. I just waited for the right time to put the truth spell on you. I didn't give you one until you started the date with Donovan at the pier."

"You were there? Can't you see why I don't know if I can trust you? You're stalking me and putting spells on me. It's been manipulative, Paris."

"It wasn't a bad spell. I was somewhere close where I could cast a spell on you."

"How did it work?" I asked.

"You all had to be honest with one another, once I made it a triple. The two guys just happened to never talk to each other."

"Why would they?" I asked. "And we seriously need to talk about boundaries. It creeps me out that you're following me around and making things happen."

"I'm not following you around. I only have followed you when I felt you needed a little help."

"Well, stop helping me. Please don't ever put a spell on me again! Promise me!"

"I promise."

"Now, let's go back to what you were saying before." I felt completely manic and lightheaded. "You were saying there is no love spell. How come Donovan likes me?"

"Because he does. He seriously had a crush on you, even before you told me about him. Isn't that what you said?"

"Yes, that's what I said."

"That means he really did."

"So, you're saying everything both Donovan and Robert have said to me from the beginning has been the total truth?"

"Yes. I gave Robert the truth spell when you were at Knott's Berry Farm. I was intrigued by you from the beginning. I saw you and you looked just like Abigail. But that wasn't the only thing. I saw your aura and I knew you to be two things. You would be sensitive to magic, and you would use it for good."

"I don't like to be manipulated," I said. "I don't remember ever seeing Abigail," I said angrily. "So, you tell me. What if you're a master manipulator?"

"I wanted Robert to be honest with you. Have you bothered to read his books?"

"Actually, no," I said. "I've been too wrapped up in everything else. He says he writes paranormal romance."

"He writes some of the most romantic dialogue I have ever encountered. In his heart, he is a beautiful man."

"Why didn't *you* date him?" I asked.

"Because..."

"Of how he looks?" I asked. "He's a big man."

"He is also a passionate, loving man."

I nodded. "That is what I see. 'Looks' last as long as a one-night stand. Who a man is at his core is what he should be valued for."

"Sahara, that's why I knew he was at least a good match for you for a little while. Then, I saw how happy Donovan made you and I didn't know what to do. I introduced him to you and now, I was hoping you wouldn't pick him."

"Were you? As I recall, you have been rooting for Donovan this whole time."

"Is that what you thought?" Paris asked.

"Yeah, I do."

"Maybe that was my way to see if you are a better person than I am. And you know what? You are. You saw Robert for the man he is. Why not continue to see them both?" She continued.

"I can't do that. They both mean too much to me to screw with either of them like that. But who knows? I haven't even talked to the dishonest Donovan yet, but that isn't my only decision."

Paris looked at me and said, "Spend time with *The Book of Shadows*...please. It will guide you. Listen and try to hear what the Magic is telling you."

"Okay," I said. I was nervous approaching the book. Almost as if I had a big sin to confess to a priest. I walked in front of *The Book of Shadows*. I went to the book and touched it and once again, I felt its power.

I sighed and then something happened that took me by surprise. A rush of wind that seemed to be carrying a bit of pixie dust wrapped itself around the book and then flipped the book to a page and all I saw was a special spell.

The page read,

Special Spell
(This spell will release you from a spell by a witch weaker or the same as you.)
"You no longer have a hold on this child."
Release me now!"

I turned around and looked at Paris, who was watching me like a hawk. "Do I say the spell out loud?"

"Yes," Paris said. "Whatever the spell is, say it."

I wasn't sure if I was ready to see what Abigail had said and done to me.

"I'm not sure if I'm ready to say it," I said.

"That's the spell trying to take hold of you. Remember, you control the Magic. The Magic doesn't control you. Do you want to be released from Abigail's spell and therefore, you can make an accurate decision on who you are going to side with?"

220

"Yes," I said. "I want to be released. I want to have all the information I need."

"Say the spell, Sahara. Go outside, so it will be safer, but be careful, you might see something in your memory that you aren't ready to see."

I memorized the two lines and it wasn't that hard to do. I turned around and I walked to the front of the chapel and stepped outside into the cold night air.

I looked out into the night and down the mountain from the summit that I was on.

I shouted in a warrior yell, "You no longer have a hold on this child. Release me now!"

Suddenly, a gust of wind was so abundant that I was lifted off the ground by the Magic. I was just floating in the air. Then the memories started happening. I remembered the first time I had met Abigail at Timmy's Restaurant. Then I remembered her coming to my house.

I was lifted downward by the gust of wind so that my feet hit the ground. As I hit the ground, I got my footing, and then I remembered the third incident. There was a third time that Abigail came to me. This time, she came for me. She came after me. I gave her an answer. She asked if she could train me, but I had said, "No."

I began remembering everything she did to me. All of it. How she tried to sap my soul. I knew she wanted my energy. She wanted to be stronger than she already was.

I remembered that Paris's spells didn't work.

I had defeated Abigail by using Black Magic!

Now, I was more confused than ever.

I turned around and walked back into the chapel. Paris had watched the whole thing because I had left the double doors open.

"Did you see Abigail in your memories?" Paris asked.

"Yes, I did," I said.

"What happened?"

"She came to me three or four times. On the second visit, she asked to mentor me. She wanted to train me and I had said no."

"What happened the next time, Sahara?"

"She attacked me relentlessly and she almost broke me. I did every spell you had taught me in regard to defense and counterattacks. Paris, none of them worked for me."

"What happened?" Paris was almost too petrified to hear the outcome.

"I defeated her by using Black Magic."

"No, you didn't," Paris said.

"I'm not able to lie to you," I said.

"Sahara, I want you to listen to me and I want you to hear what I'm about to tell you. You need to keep an open mind and hear everything I say."

"Okay," I said. She had already told me that Abigail was her sister and that Robert was a warlock.

What does she have to say to me now?

"Look deep inside you, and feel the depths of your soul. Listen to your heart and it will tell you the answers you're looking for. To be given two gifts is quite the reward. One gift is whole, and the other is incomplete. Which do you choose?"

"That applies to both decisions I want to make tonight," I replied.

"I sure hope you have already made one of your decisions," Paris said.

"I have," I said. "Remind me to talk you about potions?"

I turned around and walked to the parking lot and got into my car and I left to return to Orange County.

Chapter Thirty-six

I decided to go straight to my house and just take in everything that had happened. I was alone, emotionally depleted, and scared.

I was sure of one thing, and one thing only; I didn't tell Paris what had been written in that book. It had been said that I could only break the spell if I became as strong or stronger a witch than Abigail.

It had been written. I read it and knew, but Paris did not.

I went to my bedroom, turned off the lights, and curled up in the fetal position on my bed. I cried aloud, and ached inside to have to choose. I knew I was either going to hurt one of the two men or break Paris's heart by not choosing her side.

What if I chose both of them?

Or would they both hurt me? The way my life had gone, that seemed like the inevitable conclusion. For sure there was going to be emotional pain at some point tonight because I had definitely made the decision to see them both at the same time.

My phone rang. I quit my whimpering and took a deep breath. It was Donovan.

Why would he call me so late, and on a Saturday?

Oh, my God. It's the dishonest Donovan. Must be for a booty call.

I answered the phone. "Hello."

"Hey, babe."

Hey babe?

Of course, truth spell no more! Donovan became a different person. That was so weird. I desperately needed to talk to him again, the Donovan I had fallen for; the one who uttered wonderful things to me with that voice; that look in those beautiful eyes of his I had seen before he left.

"What's going on, Donovan?" I asked, trying not to let on that I knew something was different.

"I was at my pad, and I was thinking about you," he said, in his usual silky-smooth voice. Dammit! He had me in a trance. I couldn't afford to keep going there.

"You were? What were you thinking about?"

"I was thinking what a cool chick you are. You get me." Then Donovan's voice changed to the voice I had grown to love. "I just wanted to hear your voice, that's all."

Wow. What a sweet thing to say. That sounded like the Donovan I had grown to know over the last three weeks.

"You are a sweetheart," I said as genuine as those words could sound. "So now that you hear my voice, what do you want to do next?"

"I want to see you," Donovan said, and my heart skipped a beat. "I want you to come over. I want you to spend the night. No strings. I just want to lay with you all night."

"I can't promise that," I said. "But what I will promise you is I will come over and spend some time talking with you tonight."

"It's late," Donovan said. "Get your sleeping bag and come over."

"No. You need to give me a couple hours."

"A couple of hours?" Donovan said. "In a couple of hours, it will be past midnight."

"And you don't want me to come over at that time?" I said to him. I didn't know how sexually attracted he was to me. I just knew

I had gotten him excited the other night. And he had hinted that he wanted to sleep with me. And he had the truth spell, so I could trust that he was into me. All of me. Now that the truth spell was broken, I was not so sure of his intent. What if what he remembered a girl he was interested in because of the truth spell and when he saw me, he was going to be grossed out?

Oh, this sucks.

"Of course, I want you to come over," Donovan said. "I'm excited to see you. It's been a while."

"I know it has," I said.

"Donovan?"

"Yeah?"

"Do you like me?"

Donovan laughed. "Do I like you? Yeah, I would say I do."

"Why did you ask the question before you answered? That is what people do when they are lying."

"I'm not lying, Sahara. I like you a whole lot. I said it as a question because everything I have done has shown you how much I like you. I questioned you only for having the question yourself. Not because I was dodging an answer."

Donovan sounded so cute. "I believe you," I said.

"Good."

"I'll see you in a bit," I said.

"All right. I'll have one of my smoothies waiting for you."

"That sounds delicious," I said.

Wait! Was he meaning that as a sexual euphemism and I just said 'that sounds delicious' to him. Uh-oh.

I said goodbye and I ended the call.

I went back to my bed and went back to the fetal position, but this time, I didn't cry. Instead, I was weighing the pros and cons of both men. I had been doing this for about an hour when my phone rang. I looked down and it was Robert. I answered it on the second ring.

"Hello," I said.

"Hi, Sahara," Robert said. "I'm not rushing you or anything." Robert got very quiet. After a long pause, he said, "I felt compelled to call you and tell you how I feel."

"You did?" I asked.

Okay, this is weird. All the spells are off.

"If you could just hear me out."

"Okay," I said.

Robert paused before he spoke. Then when he was ready, he said, "When we went to Knott's Berry Farm, I had a weird feeling I was going to meet someone extremely special. I don't know why. It was as if I felt your charisma, even before I saw you. What I'm saying is, I have wanted to feel this way toward someone for a long time. You're the first person who I have cared for in quite a while. I want you to know that."

"I'm going to ask you a question, but I want to do it in person. So, I'm going to cut you off right there. I will come by and still see you tonight. What I want to share with you, I want to share with you in person. I also want to ask you a question and I want to ask you it in person."

"Okay," Robert said, a little nervous. "I'll see you in a bit."

I got off the phone with Robert and went outside to the front of my house. I had no idea what to do. It was almost easier not to pick anything and just tell everyone to get out.

My life was dead before all of them came into it. I hadn't felt this alive ever.

It had been a while since I had a man pay attention to me, never mind two men. I hadn't had a close friend in years. I'd been so closed off and now I had two people vying for me. One person was going about in love. The other wanted me to choose her side or else.

I didn't know. I was truly afraid of Abigail. I had defeated her, but I remembered her being so strong. Her power was overwhelming. Part of me thought she left just because I used Black Magic against her and her mind...that was a victory, too.

I had to be honest. I had fallen in love with the idea of ending up with both men but I knew that wasn't a possibility. I wanted the type of love that I deserved in my heart of hearts. I had to at the very

226

least, pick one, but under no circumstances would I date both of them, the way both of these relationships were going.

That was what was hurting inside. I knew not only was I going to hurt one of them, I was going to feel my own pain...and possibly doubt my choice. I knew that once I chose one, I couldn't have the other one in my life. It wouldn't be fair to either one of them, and it wouldn't be fair to me.

I got up and went down my dark hallway and walked out my front door and made my way to the sidewalk. I walked out to my street and burst into a run. I ran as hard as my little semi out-of-shape body could run. I ran until it hurt. Once it hurt, I stopped. I was down the street from my house in front of Winchester Elementary School.

I stopped in front of the fence of the school and just cried out loud. If anyone was watching, Abigail, Paris...whoever. They would have thought I had lost my mind, but I had never felt this way. It was a combination of celebration and sadness. Both feelings made me want to cry.

I had to pick one of them. Both guys made me tingle. I felt that Robert had earned so much because I was so emotionally attracted to him. Let's just say, he was at a physical disadvantage going up against Donovan the supermodel who was also quite wonderful in his own way.

I cared for Robert and I opened my heart to the possibility of he and I being together. I felt his love for me early on. It was only three-and-a-half dates. But I knew early on that he was very, very much into me. Warlock or not, he was absolutely enchanted with me. Was it love? Perhaps. Not until recently had I thought I was capable of returning love.

Then there was Donovan. He was indeed eye candy, but he was at a distinct social disadvantage as women had come so easily to him that he hadn't really worked as much on his "people skills." Before he talked to me for the first time, I thought he probably couldn't run two sentences together. Instead, under the truth spell, he had been eloquent and even poetic at times. He was sweet and charming. He had a quiet passion that drove me nuts. I knew he needed to be unleashed.

But that's just my loins talking.

Damn, this decision was so hard.

I slowly walked back home and once I got to the house, I still hadn't made up my mind.

Maybe I had.

Chapter Thirty-seven

I drove around in circles for the next hour. I literally pulled in front of both guys' houses. I chickened out and got out of there. The men didn't live close to each other.

Currently, I was on the 91 Freeway just passing a casino in Compton.

I thought it was time to turn around. I had gone too far. I turned off the casino off-ramp and spent the next twenty minutes trying to find the on-ramp to come back in the other direction.

I thought of these two men. We were talking about three weeks. Half that time, I didn't even see either one of them. Was I making too much of this? Maybe neither guy wanted a serious relationship? The second I would think I was ready to pick one of them, I would miss the other as if I had already said goodbye. This was so emotionally draining. I wanted to listen to my heart, but I couldn't quite hear what it was saying.

Both men had shared a lot of themselves. But no matter how I played each scenario in my head, there was one man who I knew deep, deep, down in my heart was *the one* I most wanted to be with.

Once I had made my decision, I began to cry. I already missed the other guy so badly. I pulled off the freeway because I was crying

229

so much. I took Beach Boulevard and decided to just take the surface streets.

I decided I wanted to rip off the Band-Aid first. I knew I had to go to the house of the man who I was no longer going to date. I wasn't sure if it would get weird. I was so nervous.

I drove down his street and parked my car on his driveway. I didn't want to feel so familiar, but I didn't trust the street.

Dammit! Was I making the right decision?

I had to stick to one and that was it and the decision I made was the one that made the most sense to me at the present time. Should I be thinking of the present time or should I be thinking of my future? That remains to be seen. I took a deep breath, slowly got out of my car and knocked on his door...

Chapter Thirty-eight

I waited for him to answer the door. He opened it, I looked at him and said, "Robert, I can't take this anymore."

"Yeah, uh, me too," he said, excited. I wasn't sure what he thought what was going to happen, but I guessed I might have led him on by coming over past midnight.

"Can we go inside and talk on your couch?" I asked.

"Yeah, of course."

He opened the door and all the lights in his house were on. I kind of liked that. The mood felt safe.

Robert sat down at the end of his large white couch and I sat a good distance away from where he was sitting.

I looked over at him and he awkwardly waited for whatever I had to say, but he possessed a strength that was unmatched. Now I knew why, the ability to wield magic made him confident.

"Are you..." I asked, "are you a warlock?"

Robert remained silent and looked at me with a horrified look on his face. So I asked him again. "Are you a warlock?"

Robert looked me in the eye and said, "I was."

"You were one, but are no longer a warlock?"

"No. I haven't completely denounced it, but I haven't practiced any type of magic in quite some time. How do you know any of this? Only witches and other warlocks would know… wait a minute. Are you a…?"

"Yes and no," I said.

"What do you mean, 'yes and no'?"

"I became a witch while we were dating."

Robert looked at me, shocked. "Are you messing with me right now?" he asked.

"No, I am telling you the absolute truth, and actually, I've been trained by someone you know."

"Who?"

"Paris."

"Seriously? She trained you? You have no idea how freaked out I am that you gals know each other."

"You're freaked out? I'm freaked out. It makes no sense. I asked Paris for help in meeting the right guy. She chose you as much as I did. Now, I think she agreed because she knew you had something going on."

"I find her logic a little strange. Paris knows I no longer practice the arts."

"Robert, I know that you're very powerful, but chose to discontinue your practice because of faith in a Creator."

"Something like that," Robert said. "I guess Paris and you have been doing some pillow talk."

"Not pillow talk, but we have been having heart to hearts."

"She seriously thinks that I had potential as a boyfriend. Or as a warlock?"

"Not just potential, Robert. She told me you could be one of the very best."

"At which?" Robert smiled and then his face got extremely serious. "Why are you here, saying all of this to me?"

"Well," I said. "This wasn't the only thing I wanted to talk to you about."

"What's the other thing?" Robert asked.

I looked at Robert and knew I was about to hurt him.

"Robert, Paris put us both under a truth spell. That is why we've been so open with one another. That is how we got close so quickly."

"Oh, no. Seriously?"

"Yes," I said.

"I always knew something was up when we were together." He sighed heavily. "I have never shared the things in my life that I shared with you."

"And you know what, Robert? You're indeed a beautiful person."

"But..." Robert said, sensing bad news was coming.

"I need to come clean. During our time together, you know, over the past three weeks? I've dated another man, but just dating, okay? I don't want you to get the wrong idea."

"Wait. What? During the exact same three weeks?" Robert asked.

"I know it sounds really messed up, but it was such a random coincidence that I met two great guys at the same time."

Robert gave me a sharp look because he was understanding what I had told him. Then that same sharp look turned into a hopeful one.

He looked elated, probably thinking I'd chosen him.

And it was breaking my heart, like stepping on a puppy dog's face.

"I've decided to come clean—for both of you, and let the chips fall where they may. But I came here tonight to say, that um, we should no longer continue seeing each other."

"Are you serious?" Robert asked.

"Yes," I said. "I'm so sorry, Robert. I really am."

Robert stood up and paced slowly around his living room. I could tell he was trying to come up with the right words.

"If you made your decision and you chose the other guy, then what's done is done," Robert said, trying to put on a strong face, but his voice even cracked on the word 'guy'.

"Are you going to be okay?" Now, I was getting choked up. Here we were, two people whose hearts were breaking because we could no longer see each other and I really felt horrible. This was all my doing.

"Can I give you a hug?" I asked.

Robert nodded his head. I stood up and I hugged him real hard. It was hard. It was soft. It was intimate, too intimate for a man I was breaking up with. Was I making the right decision? I felt at home in Robert's arms.

I let go of our embrace, and so did he. I couldn't stay here any longer or this was going to kill me emotionally.

"One more thing," I said. "Paris introduced me to the other guy. I only think it's fair that you know that."

"So I would hate her."

"No," I said. "She wanted to put what we had to the test by lining up a choice for me."

"And I guess I failed your choice."

"No, Robert. You passed with flying colors. I can only choose one man. You both have touched me in a way I never thought possible. Please know how much you mean to me."

"Maybe we can still be friends," Robert said. "I like who you are." Robert got quiet and I could tell he was debating telling me something. Then he said, "I love who you are. I love you."

"I know. That is why it will be hard to be friends. We both have feelings for each other and it's not fair to anybody."

"Okay," Robert said. "Whatever you want." Robert put on a strong smile. I gave him credit because tears were dripping from my eyes. This was killing me. He needed to know how much this was killing me.

"Robert, I care about you so much. You have touched my life in a way I never thought possible, but so has someone else."

"I felt...love from you. It was real. Are you truly following your heart?" Robert asked.

I paused and took in Robert's question and I simply said. "I think so." My voice cracked and I knew I needed to go. "I'm going to go, Robert, okay?" I said.

"Of course. Drive home safe." He did everything he could not to cry, but I saw tears drip from his eyes. Tears were already pouring down from my eyes. I was sure my mascara was completely running down my cheeks like black tears.

I nodded and went to his door and walked out to my car, Robert came out and made sure I was safe, just like he did the first time. He was such a great guy.

The second I hit the main highway, I thought I would feel excited; instead my heart was aching because I felt I had left it back with Robert. Tears began to drip from my eyes from the loss I was already feeling. Now I had to pull over and I got off on Harbor in the city of Fullerton. I went left and pulled into a parking lot that was in front of a Tony Romo's rib joint. The restaurant seemed to be closing up shop with the employees going home. I parked my car and I waited. I waited for everyone to leave until I was the sole car in the parking lot. I thought about Robert. I thought about what a pure heart he is. A gentle soul with lots of charisma. The depths of the man seemed unparalleled. Then something happened to me. I began to cry out loud. It was a bellowing cry. I can't imagine now that I've gotten to know Robert and seeing how much we are alike. I can't imagine ending the connection that was started. Was I being selfish? And I hadn't even talked to Donovan yet.

I felt nervous. What if I told Donovan how I felt and he didn't accept it? Or what if his affection for me was wrapped up in his truth spell?

Oh, no! Did I make the right decision?

I was already second-guessing myself.

Every time I played it out in my head, it was a mutual tie. Then how come I chose Donovan; was it because he was more appealing to the eyes?

I thought I was completely following my heart by going to Donovan's tonight. Each time, I think about Robert being at his house alone and broken. The thought was all I could handle without bursting out in tears.

Chapter Thirty-nine

After a long while sitting at Tony Romo's, I felt I had the strength to do this.

I was going all in. Wow. Magic or not, I was going to find out what Donovan felt for me. I started my Mazda and headed over to Donovan's house. I pulled all the way in his driveway because I was the only car in his driveway.

I parked and turned on my mirror and checked my makeup. And fixed the smears with some tissues and spit.

Here goes everything.

I walked up to his house and I felt a knot in my stomach. I walked up to his door and I knocked three times.

In a few seconds, Donovan answered the door with his shirt off and he was only wearing sweats. He had been sleeping. I had one guy waiting by his door for me to come over with every light on and the other one was sleeping, his hair askew and only the blue flicker of the TV from the other room.

"Were you sleeping?" I asked nicely.

"Just after I made us smoothies, I totally dozed off watching this documentary on pandas. It's amazing how mean and angry those animals truly are."

All I could do was laugh. I was having a nervous breakdown tonight and this guy was watching panda documentaries.

I decided to relax and to just take it as it came.

Donovan invited me into his living room and turned on the lights. There were two full smoothies on his coffee table. That immediately made me smile.

Donovan sat on his couch. He was so tan that he must go tanning twice a day.

How much of this guy is real?

"I needed to tell you something." I looked at Donovan and he was beau...handsome. He was *handsome*. The most handsome man I had ever seen. He had a heart to match and I needed to know if his heart was true because I just did one gigantic leap of faith—one I hoped I wouldn't regret.

"Donovan," I said. "I'm a simple woman. Now, meeting you, I realize we are much alike. I may not be as good looking as you."

"I think you're gorgeous," Donovan said, cutting me off.

"Do you? Donovan? Are you really into me?"

"Why do you keep asking me that?"

I was quiet and I could hear a lot of silence go by. Finally, truth spell or not, I said to Donovan, "Because I'm afraid."

"Why are you afraid?"

"I care about you so much and I need to tell you a couple of things that might make you run for the hills."

"Well, at least give me one of them," Donovan said. "I can't read your mind."

"If I give you one, I will have to give you the other," I said.

"Then tell me both," Donovan said.

"The first thing I'm going to tell you might make you mad or you just might laugh me out of here."

"Do you think I'm such a horrible person that I would do that?"

"No," I said, tearing up. "It's just my defense mechanism. Donovan, during this time we've been dating, I was also seeing another guy."

Donovan nodded patiently like this was a typical thing he heard. Then he said something that surprised me. "Who is he?"

"He's a good soul. A hell of a guy."

Donovan looked at me and he seemed surprised that I was giving the other guy such a rave review.

"So what is your decision?"

"In regard to choosing the other guy or did I choose this?"

"Yeah."

I said very softly in almost a whisper. "I choose this." As vulnerable as I could be, I asked, "So what do you choose?"

Donovan walked over to me and looked me in the eyes and said in a monotone voice, "I choose this. I choose *us.*"

"Really," I said. I looked at Donovan and I knew I wasn't sure if I was following my heart. Then I paused and got up and walked to Donovan's front door.

"Where are you going?" Donovan asked.

"Outside, I need some fresh air so I can think."

Donovan and I walked out to his front yard and stood by the big tree in front of the house. We stood on either side of the tree opposite each other. Maybe I was trying to avoid him or maybe I was just gathering my thoughts.

"I love hard," I said to Donovan.

"Okay," Donovan said, dismissing the intent behind my words.

"Are you sure you can handle it? Are you strong enough to be my man?"

Donovan looked at me and seemed surprised that I had the confidence to call the shots. I still wasn't sure I was making the right decision. I should be a lot happier right now. My head was spinning no. It wasn't because of a spell. It was spinning because I was human. This was a decision that I believed would alter my destiny.

I needed to leave Donovan's house.

"Donovan, it's real late and I'm going to have to take off."

"Is everything okay?"

"Yes, I'll give you a call tomorrow."

I stood up and walked out the front door. I walked to my car and Donovan walked inside his house and didn't wait until I left. I stared at my dashboard, and shook my head. I was tired and needed to make the right decision.

I started my car and drove aimlessly for an hour.

I finally decided to go somewhere safe. I pulled up the driveway and parked my car.

I got out of my car and walked to the door and I knocked. I knocked a total of seven times. The door opened and I said, "I don't think we were done talking."

Robert invited me inside and I never went home that night.

The End

Sahara returns in:

A Witch's Magic

Heart of a Witch #2

About the Author:

H.T. Night is the #1 bestselling author of *Vampire Love Story,
The Werewolf Whisperer, Forever and Always, Vampires vs.
Werewolves, Werewolf Love Story, Getting Yours, The Rise of
Kyro, Romeo & Juliet: A Vampire and Werewolf Love Story* and
Everlasting Love: Poems. Please visit him at
www.htnight.com.

WITCH TO CHOOSE